LUCID WORLD

DENISE LAMMI

Lucid World
© Denise Lammi 2017

ISBN: 978-1-7750808-2-4

Cover Design by Diane Feught

Denise M. Lammi Inc.
Vancouver, BC, Canada

www.lucidworldnovel.com

LUCID WORLD

PROLOGUE

SHADOWS

There are moments that imprint upon us. Moments when we realize nothing will ever be the same again. For Kasta, such a moment began with his mother's insistent words. "Wake up. Get dressed."

Kasta, a slender, olive-skinned boy of nine, sat up in bed. He looked out the open window to a star-filled sky. "Wh-what? Why?"

She sat on the bed and put her arm around his shoulders. "I need you to come with me. We have to leave now."

"Where are we going?"

She replied, "On a journey. Come now."

At the foot of the bed, a cat stretched and joined mother and son. Kasta picked her up and held her close.

"She can come with us," Kasta's mother said.

"Can Djer come?"

"No. His family has the khaos. You know this, Kasta."

Kasta knew Djer's home life was miserable—so much fighting and unhappiness—but Djer wasn't that way.

Kasta cried.

Seeing Kasta's distress at having to leave his friend, his mother tried to cheer him. "We're going to a huge, magnificent cave!"

"Are we ever coming back?"

"No, Kassy, we're not."

"I need to see him. I can't go without saying goodbye!"

"Papa's waiting. We don't have time."

Kasta stood. There was no point in arguing. This journey was important. He may have been young, but he understood that. Before he could focus his eyes to search for his clothing, his mother slid a tunic over his head, positioning the armholes and sliding it down his body. She handed him a small leather bag packed with a few essentials. "Carry this and follow me outside. And we must be quiet, no talking or crying."

Stoically, the boy obeyed. He followed his mother outside, and his cat followed behind. In the distance, a cluster of over a hundred people stood in a shadow that cloaked them from the irradiating moonlight. Their outlines revealed bundles in their arms and on their backs. Kasta hurried to catch up with his mother as she joined his father at the head of the line. He took one last look at the only home he'd ever known. Djer's house was in darkness.

Joining the others, he comforted himself with the thought that he would see Djer again. Somehow, some day, he would find a way.

The cluster of figures, Kasta among them, moved soundlessly and purposefully, as if beckoned, toward a waning moon suspended above hills outlined in the distance, disappearing into the starry night.

CHAPTER I

DREAMS AND SCENES

Four thousand years later, the same star-filled moonlit sky shone through a window and illuminated the shape of a blanketed bundle, lying on a bed. The form moved ever so slightly as the figure within breathed in and out. A fifteen-year-old girl was sleeping in a deep dream state.

At the foot of the bed, a few items of clothing hung haphazardly on the bedframe. Shoes littered the floor beside the bed. Posters of people and places covered the walls. One read, "If you can read this, you're in my room: Get Out!" Bright-coloured scarves and 'blingy' necklaces hung on the edges of a mirror, above a small table. Lip gloss, nail polish, and hair brushes covered the table. A knapsack and a laptop computer — bearing the name 'Morgan' in colourful letters — rested on papers piled on a desk in the corner. A coat was strewn on the back of a chair. A wide open door revealed the inside of a closet. Its contents appeared to have erupted onto the floor.

As was often the case for the sleeping girl, dream scenes and characters came and went; changing like acts in a play. Tonight, the dream play was an original production with scenes and characters unknown to the dreamer.

Morgan walked through a lush green forest. Smooth, soft moss covered the ground. She looked down and saw her feet were bare. She noticed a small white object on the mossy ground and crouched down to inspect. It was a tooth, her tooth. She realized other teeth were loose, and she feared they might also fall out. Feeling panic and urgency, she placed the found tooth in her pocket. She walked at a faster pace. A brick office building, visible in the distance, seemed to be a likely place to find a dentist. She headed towards it. Snow fell, covering the ground. But Morgan's bare feet did not feel any cold.

Morgan arrived at the building but could not find a door, yet she saw people enter and leave. But every time she moved to where she had seen people come or go, she found only a brick wall.

A short round man with white hair and a full white moustache, wearing a vested suit, left the building. She ran after him and called out, "Please help me. I can't find the door."

The man answered without stopping, "You're just not trying hard enough."

Morgan went back to the building and saw a door with a sign that read *Dentist*. She walked to it and turned the handle. The door opened into a large lobby. Patterns of orange fish covered the lobby walls and floor. The fish were moving! The floor was a glass-covered pond, and the walls were a continuous aquarium. Both were filled with orange carp.

Behind a reception desk in the centre of the lobby sat a woman with a long neck, bulging eyes and an asymmetrical face. Morgan approached her and asked about a dentist. The woman said, "You should have come sooner. The dentist has gone for the day."

Morgan countered with complaints about her difficulty finding the door. The receptionist's bulging eyes assessed Morgan. She sneezed before she asked, "Are you saying you thought the door for others was the door for you?"

Morgan stammered excuses and blurted, "Oh great! Why didn't someone tell me I had to find my own door?"

No reply. They stared at one another. The receptionist's lips did not move but Morgan could hear a voice. It sounded like her name being called.

Morgan spun around but could see no one other than the receptionist whose lips were tight and pursed. The room faded, and she became dizzy and disoriented. She couldn't focus. Waves of nausea passed through her and she tasted vomit at the back of her throat. She tried to call out but couldn't speak.

She could hear noise — of what she didn't know. The sounds were soft, comprised of humming, tapping and clicking. The nausea subsided and so did the humming. Her eyes slowly focused. At first the lighting felt too bright and unpleasant. Then it softened, and she looked around. The room had changed.

The fish behind glass were gone. The walls and floor were not like any she had seen before. They resembled stone in a cave but were not rough, dirty or moist. Rather, the stone was burnished.

Confused, she looked around for something familiar to help her understand where she was.

Low shelves sculpted into the stone walls, lined the periphery of the room and held various objects: a crystal pitcher filled with water, set beside crystal drinking glasses, ferns potted in rust-coloured clay pots, and cushions covered with fabrics dyed emerald, saffron, amethyst, and magenta.

On the cushions, at least a dozen cats were dozing or stretching. Yes, cats: big-eared short-haired cats ranging in colours of chocolate-brown, blue-grey, cinnamon-red and golden-fawn. They appeared only moderately interested in Morgan's presence.

In the centre of the room, a large slab of polished golden yellow stone was suspended by cables from the ceiling. It appeared to serve as a table. Metal chairs, fitted with the same lively cushions as on the shelves, were arranged around it. An azure blue carpet covered most of the floor; and areas not covered revealed a floor of polished sandy-grey stone.

Drawn to the cats, Morgan tried to move towards them, but she felt unsteady and stopped. She comprehended she was seeing the room from an unusual perspective. Not from the perspective of seeing directly. Rather, from a point of view unlike anything she could relate to. She tried to speak. The words that came out were muddled and incoherent. She tried again.

"Hello?"

"Hello, Morgan."

Morgan looked in the direction of the voice.

Standing near the table was a brown-skinned young man of about eighteen. Medium-length jet-black hair fell in loose curls to the centre of his forehead, towards the bridge of his aquiline nose. His eyes were dark brown and below his eyes the skin looked blackish — not like dark circles — rather, close to his lower eyelids. Blue jeans and a loose purple T-shirt covered his broad chest and shoulders. He wore slipper-like footwear.

"H-how do you know my name? Wh-who are you?"

"I'm Amasis. You're in Lucid World. This is my home."

"What am I doing here? What do you want?"

Amasis moved closer to her.

"Don't you dare touch me!" she threatened.

Amasis backed away and said, "Don't worry. It'll be all right."

"I feel so dizzy!"

"Sorry about that. You aren't physically here. We're transferring information to you — and from you. The dizziness will pass. Focus on my eyes, it'll be easier."

His dark eyes were kind and reassuring, yet unnerving. Morgan looked away. He had looked at her so directly and caringly. This was too strange. Morgan needed to change the subject — now.

"So why did you say World?"

"We're still on Planet Earth, but our home is separate. We aren't part of the earth's countries and their people."

"How come …?"

"Thousands of years ago, your world and my world were one, until people became infected with an emotional disorder."

"I'm feeling sick. Let me go home."

"The sick feeling will pass. Let me explain. Just listen."

"What are you talking about? What do you mean infection?"

"We call it Khaos."

"You mean like really disorganized and messy? Like what my mom says about my bedroom?"

Amasis laughed. He had a nice laugh, like music.

"You could think of it that way, Morgan. I'll say a lot more about khaos later. All you need to know for now is that we hope you'll help us stop it."

The room faded, and she felt dizzy again. Morgan could hear her name being called in the distance. It was her mom, and she sounded angry.

CHAPTER 2

MORNING

W hat? Was it a dream? It was so real. Morgan sat up in bed. Her mother, Meredith, stood at the foot of the bed with her arms crossed. "Morgan! Now how many times are you going to make me call you? Breakfast is getting cold. It's Valentine's Day, and I made heart-shaped pancakes. We're waiting for you. Get out of bed NOW!"

"Sorry — didn't hear you. I'm coming. I'm coming."

Dazed, Morgan climbed out of bed and followed Meredith to the kitchen. Morgan's father Daniel, and her two brothers, Dylan and Ryan, were waiting at the table. Meredith stood at the table with her arms crossed, eyeing a stack of pancakes that had suspiciously shrunk while she had gone to fetch Morgan.

Before Morgan could take a seat, Meredith instructed, "Go and wash up before you sit down. You look like you're still half-asleep. I think you need to go to bed earlier." Meredith took a seat at the table and said, "Let's start without her or we'll all be late."

Morgan obeyed and headed to the bathroom. She felt her mother's watchful eye. The reference to bedtime was not a casual comment. It was deliberate and calculated. Morgan often had difficulty falling asleep; and considered it ridiculous and insulting to not be allowed to stay up later. She provided her parents with documented proof that the internal time clocks of teens were synchronized later than the internal time clocks of children. Even though a later bedtime was preordained by nature, her parents, mostly her mother, Morgan suspected, would not agree to it. But they did concede to a later bedtime on nights when there was no school the next day, so at least she gained some ground.

Meredith watched her sandy-haired daughter saunter away and thought, 'She looks like an adult; but she's not.' She shook her head.

Daniel, having just finished telling the first part of a Valentine's Day riddle, caught Meredith's head-shake and assumed she was taking part in the fun by showing she didn't know the answer. He repeated, "Well, what did the caveman give his wife for Valentine's Day?"

Daniel turned his attention back to Dylan and Ryan, who were blurting out wrong answers, and playfully said, "Hey come on. It's obvious. Ughs and kisses... hahaha."

From the bathroom, Morgan could hear them laughing. She looked at herself in the mirror. Was it only a dream or had she actually been with someone from another world? Her thoughts would have to wait. She hurried back to the kitchen to avoid further admonishment — and to get pancakes.

Seated at the table, Meredith passed her a plate of pancakes and said, "Don't blame me if they're cold."

Meredith's miffed mood stifled the table conversation and gave Morgan a chance to contemplate her (real or imagined?) conversation with Amasis. His words were, 'we hope you will help us stop it'. Stop what? The disorder he talked about? How?

To change the mood around the table, Daniel made small talk. It was a familiar family pattern. Morgan looked at her brother Dylan and caught his eye. She rolled her eyes upwards and towards their mother to say, "Really? Heart-shaped pancakes and then she gets mad...?"

Dylan answered with a slight nod to say, "I know, right?"

Back in her room after breakfast, Morgan looked around. She felt as if she was seeing it for the first time. Everything seemed surreal. Was she dreaming now? She remembered the dream about looking for a door. It reminded her of the scene from Alice in Wonderland when Alice found a little door that a golden key unlocked. The door-dream was nothing compared to what happened next. Lucid World… was that also a dream? Did it come from something she once read in a book or saw in a movie? Or was it a dream manifestation of something in her subconscious mind? A civilization separated from the world and a disease of the emotions? But her experience in Lucid World was too real to be a dream… or was it? Amasis had dark intense eyes. She'd never seen eyes like that before. Yet something about them was familiar. What? Then she remembered.

THE FENCE

Last Sunday, Morgan and her best friend, Cara, 'borrowed' Cara's father's truck to drive around town. They were hoping to meet up with some older boys who would likely be driving around, as they often did on a Sunday afternoon. Cara 'liked' one of them and Morgan suggested Cara might get his attention if she was driving, too. Cara and Morgan weren't old enough to have a driver's license and they took the truck without permission.

Cara turned the key and started it. The engine sounded noisy. Morgan wondered if the truck needed a new muffler or it just sounded loud because of her guilty conscience. She hadn't been serious when she made the suggestion, but Cara thought it was a good idea and now they were doing it.

Cara used the rear-view mirror to apply lip gloss. Next she pulled a few strands of her short brown hair out of her charcoal-grey knit cap, to frame her face. She adjusted the mirror, shoulder-checked like a pro, and backed out of the driveway.

They were on their way! They drove a short way down the street before Cara gained more confidence in her driving ability and accelerated the truck. Her display of confidence was ill-timed and caused the propelling vehicle to go into a spin on a patch of snow and ice. The truck pirouetted a few times in what seemed to be slow motion, and then, the inevitable *CRASH*.

Wide-eyed, the girls looked at one another. Their free-wheeling expressions of a few seconds earlier turned as severe and frozen as the road that had transported them right into a neighbour's fence!

Cara spoke first. "Um, I guess we'd better get out and look?"

Morgan rolled down the window on her side and leaned out to take a look. As she did, she saw a short woman with unruly fire-engine red hair, wearing a housecoat and slippers, sliding over ice and snow as she ran toward them. She came from the house next to the fence — the fence that was now fused to the truck.

"You sure smashed the hell out of my fence!"

As the hollering woman approached the truck, Cara turned off the engine and stepped out. Unlike Morgan, Cara was tall and had long legs, so she didn't have to hop to get in and out of the truck.

Morgan stayed in the truck, rigidly fixed to the passenger seat, and tried to look small. She barely breathed as she watched and listened.

The woman seemed more surprised than angry. Cara apologized profusely and promised that her father would fix the fence. The woman nodded and agreed. Her demeanor became calm, but now her calm manner was juxtaposed by her dramatic appearance: blazing red hair, milky white skin and eyes magnified by coke-bottle thick glasses. This combination of features cast a strange figure. Morgan marvelled at the strangeness; yet the woman was not unknown to her. She had lived in the neighbourhood for as long as Morgan could remember. Her name was Mrs. Byrd.

Later that day, back at their respective homes and on the phone, Morgan and Cara compared notes.

Cara reported, "I'm only grounded for a week. I told them I was going shopping for food to cook them a surprise anniversary dinner."

"Hahaha, that's hilarious. I can't believe they fell for it. Did they ask if you were with anyone?" Morgan moved her left hand back and forth as she blew on freshly painted fingernails.

"Yeah, sorry. I had to tell them in case Mrs. Byrd says something."

Morgan quit moving her fingers and blowing. "Makes sense. Still, I'm not going to tell my parents. My mom doesn't need another reason to give a lecture every time I want to do something."

"Oh. But what if they find out?"

"I don't think they will. Our parents don't hang around together and Mrs. Byrd is practically blind. No one else saw us hit the fence."

"Um, I'm not so sure about that," said Cara.

"Not sure about what?"

"That no one else saw us. When I got out of the truck to talk to Mrs. Byrd, I saw a strange guy watching us."

"How'd he look strange?"

"For one thing, he had really dark eyes, almost like he was wearing eye makeup. But I don't think he was. Also, he was holding a shiny funny-looking case."

"Really? What was he doing?"

"Just standing there, watching us. After I talked to Mrs. Byrd, he was gone. I haven't seen him around since. He must be from Lethbridge."

CHAPTER 3

AMASIS AND AVATAR

"Gooood-niiight," Morgan said as she popped her head into the family room where her parents were curled up on the sofa and watching a movie.

"Hey, Small Fry," Daniel called as he sat up straight. Morgan returned and stood in the doorway. "Everything okay…?"

"It's all good. Just didn't sleep well last night."

Daniel said, "Well, sleep tight, Small Fry. See you in the morning," and he settled back into his former place on the sofa.

Meredith, in a slouched position, eyed Morgan with suspicion; but said only, "We'll turn the volume down."

Wearing her newest pajamas, Morgan crawled into bed and stretched out on her back. Would it happen again? This felt weird. What was she doing? She laid out straight, like a magician's assistant about to be sawed in half. If it was like last night, it would happen while she was sleeping. As she got into a comfortable position, she realized she really was exhausted. Probably from the deep thinking she had been doing all day. Or it could be from the night before?

Morgan's thoughts muddled, and she was asleep. When her body's sleep cycle moved into a deeper phase, her conscious mind awakened and she realized, 'It's happening!'

At first, she saw nothing. It was like being in a room devoid of light. Then, as if a light switch turned on, she could see colours and shapes. Unlike the night before, the lighting wasn't harsh.

Tonight, it took a while for her to adjust to the transmission interchange, but this time it was with less nausea.

Amasis stood facing her, only a few feet away, holding a small device attached to a cord around his neck. He looked much like the night before, except his T-shirt was orange. She focused on his eyes. Was he wearing eye-makeup below his lower lashes? No. It was natural.

"Hello Morgan. I apologize for the abrupt manner our last visit ended," he said while dropping the neck-device into his shirt neckline. "To use vernacular you are familiar with, we encountered technical difficulties and weren't able to contact you until it was almost time for you to rise from sleep."

"So it wasn't a dream. I'm here, I think." Morgan turned from side to side and looked around; it was the same room. "Last night you said it was transmission technology. It feels like I'm really here, though."

"In your mind, you see Lucid World. Here, we see a hologram of you. This 3D image is a conduit for your voice, facial expressions and body language. It simulates how your body would sound and move if you were awake."

Morgan lifted her arms and then her feet to examine them. Amasis suggested she stand still while her brain adjusted to her non-corporeal body, to avoid dizziness. Remembering the unpleasant sensations from the night before, she stopped moving and stayed still.

"The likeness is superb," said Amasis. "I think you'll be impressed."

Morgan looked down at her torso and legs. "What am I wearing? Am I dressed like you?"

Amasis shrugged his shoulders and smiled lopsidedly. "I forgot to give the holographic image parameters for your clothing, so it defaulted to my clothing tastes."

Morgan wanted to look in a mirror. Amasis said he would arrange it for her next visit.

"So it's like I'm an avatar, like the ones people use in virtual games."

"Yes. Except that Lucid World is real and you control your avatar the same way you control your body."

Morgan looked at her fingers and moved them. She raised one foot and looked at it, then did the same with the other foot. She turned her head to look over her shoulder and did the same with the other shoulder. She looked up into the air and down again at her feet.

"So what's this about? And what are you talking about when you say you want my help?"

"Khaos is pandemic. Our founders were uninfected by the contagion; they believed it was just a matter of time before they, too, became infected. They extricated themselves from exposure and took refuge in a large mountain cavern. Generations later, we still live here."

"So we're inside of a mountain! And khaos infected the world! Do I have it?"

"I think so. Most people from Nosos World have it."

"Nosos World? Oh, that's what you call the rest of the world? But none of it explains why I'm here and why you think I can help."

"You aren't here. You're home in your bed."

Amasis positioned two chairs for them to sit upon while they talked. Morgan's avatar couldn't feel any difference in effort between standing and sitting, but the sitting posture made her feel more at ease.

"Am I hooked-up to electrodes or something?" she asked. "Oh my God!" She jumped up from her seat. "Did you plant a chip in my brain?"

Amasis laughed. "No, nothing like that. Each person's brain has an identifiable signal. We recorded an imprint of your brain signal. Using that signal, and equipment we installed near your home, we can communicate with you."

"WHAT! You're reading my thoughts??!"

Morgan backed away.

"No. We hear only what you would say if you were awake."

"Am I lying in my bed talking out loud?"

"While your brain is awake, your body is asleep and won't make any sounds or movements uncharacteristic for a sleeping person."

After Morgan calmed down from the notion her thoughts were being probed, she sat and listened while Amasis explained how Lucid World's technology was so advanced.

Lucid World's ancestors came from an advanced civilization which possessed vast knowledge. For example, they had the expertise to build the pyramids; sadly, khaos had already started and people were enslaved to provide labour. In Lucid World, information from earlier times was passed down by succeeding generations, while in Nosos World, this was not the case.

Besides its own research and development, Lucid World used and improved upon Nosos World's innovations. Whenever it was appropriate, they shared knowledge by influencing someone in Nosos World to conceive an idea or make a discovery.

"What's an example of something Lucid World shared with my world?"

Amasis leaned back in his chair and touched his hand to his chin, "Let me think of a good one to tell you." As he looked around the room, a bright cushion caught his eye.

He said, "How about the lint roller[1] used to remove small fibres from fabric?"

"Do you mean a roll of sticky paper on a handle?"

"Right. Elder Tabubu invented it. Her cats shed fur. She insisted on sharing the idea with Nosos World." Amasis chuckled, leaned towards Morgan and said in a conspiratorial tone, "Though, we usually only intervene in Nosos World's progress for humanitarian reasons."

"Cats. I saw cats last night."

"Elder Tabubu's chambers are next to this building. Her cats often visit and make themselves comfortable."

"We had a cat, but I was allergic to it so we had to give it away."

"Allergies won't be a problem for your avatar. You can watch and enjoy the cats with impunity."

"With who?"

Amasis laughed. "It's not who, it's what. I meant you can enjoy the cats with no risk of an allergic reaction."

"If I'm just a hologram, how'll they even know I exist?" Morgan asked.

"They'll hear you. Cats like the sound of friendly human voices."

Morgan looked toward where she'd seen them. The cats weren't there. Amasis said it was their feeding time, and they hovered around their food dishes. This made Morgan wonder what time it was, and where Lucid World was relative to the rest of the world. Amasis said he couldn't 'divulge' the location because it had to remain secret.

"Amasis, sometimes when you talk, you speak like I do. Other times, you talk like a professor using fancy words, like 'impunity'. Is that how people talk in Lucid World, casual and formal at the same time?"

Amasis agreed. He knew many languages but he didn't interact with people who use popular expressions in casual speech. Before contacting Morgan, he and two others who she'll be interacting with had studied the manner of speaking in her community. They had prepared to better converse with and understand her.

"To use words familiar to you," Amasis said while retrieving the device from inside his shirt, "sometimes I slip and revert to my normal way of speaking."

He looked at the device and stood. "Khyan has arrived; he wants to meet you."

Morgan's avatar had peripheral vision. A bright turquoise colour caught her eye, so she turned to look. It was the T-shirt of a young man, who appeared to be in his early to mid-twenties, with dark olive skin and intense blue-green eyes. His dark auburn hair was kinky and tied back in a ponytail.

Lean and tall, Khyan joined them and stood beside Amasis. Fascinated by their contrasting appearance, Morgan stared at them separately and together. Amasis was short: Khyan was tall. Amasis had dark eyes: Khyan had aqua eyes. Amasis was muscular: Khyan was willowy.

Morgan attempted to stand but her movements were clumsy so she sat back down.

"Hello Morgan, I'm Khyan. Please remain seated. I'll get a chair and we'll all sit."

KHYAN AND THE FORCE

Khyan seemed to have an agenda. First he assured her that transmissions could be ended whenever she wanted, at will. Next he asked if they could continue so he could tell her why they contacted her.

Relieved to learn she had a choice, Morgan agreed.

They wanted her help with a project: to reverse khaos. Their interactions would occur while her body was sleeping. While her conscious mind interacted with them, she wouldn't get the full benefits of a restful sleep. So their interactions would be limited to one hour per night. Most nights, she would be with Amasis or Iris. She would meet Iris tomorrow. They would teach and help her reverse her own khaos emotions. During her waking hours, she was to practice what she learned.

"Khaos, a disease affecting emotions? I don't think I understand. What does the disease do to emotions?" Morgan asked.

"It causes destructive feelings such as hate, jealousy, insecurity and greed," Khyan said.

Avatar-Morgan's nose wrinkled and her eyebrows pulled together. "Are you saying you don't have those feelings in Lucid World? You're perfect?"

"We're not perfect." Amasis's dark eyes lit up as he laughed. He looked at Khyan as if to say, I'll let you take this one.

Khyan returned the look with a slight nod. "Like you, we try to live our lives in comfort and happiness. But we do so without khaos emotions. Unwarranted or misdirected fear is the underlying cause for most khaos emotions. These emotions induce irrational behaviour which produces unfavourable circumstances.

"You will better understand and assimilate this in real experience, but I must prepare you: khaos is within you and all around you. Also, you may come up against a powerful sabotaging force. This force cannot thwart you, but it can create obstacles and diversions that keep you from your goal."

"What kind of force? Is it the devil or an evil sorcerer?"

Khyan grinned and said, "You have a vivid imagination."

He became serious again. "This force isn't an entity. Yet it's real and may try to stop you."

Morgan looked at Amasis. His expression was the same as Khyan's. Concerned.

Morgan's eyes widened, "How'll I know when it does it or tries it, or it happens?"

"You probably won't," Khyan said.

Morgan said to Khyan, "I'm confused, and kind of afraid." She looked to Amasis.

Khyan said, "Don't be afraid. Just think of it as a mystery. When you understand and recognize khaos, you'll know what the force is."

"Soooo, I have to get cured from khaos, fight an enemy force and solve a mystery?"

Khyan laughed and put one hand behind his neck. "Soooo," he emulated while freeing a strand of ponytail hair caught in a cord around his neck, "will you work with us?" The cord looked the same as the one Amasis wore, with the device pendant.

"I'm actually not sure how or why."

"We'll guide you. During your waking hours you'll be challenged with..." Khyan paused, touched his chin and said, "life."

"How'll I know when I'm actually cured from khaos and don't need to come here anymore?"

"I don't know."

"Great. Another mystery."

It was time to end their meeting. After they said goodbye, Amasis took the device out of his neckline. Morgan's avatar image faded and disappeared from Lucid World. In Nosos World, Morgan's body went into a state of sleep.

Amasis looked at Khyan and said, "When we first contacted her, we encountered avatar set-up difficulties. Otherwise, this introduction seems to have gone smoother than the other introductions."

"I agree, but why? We did nothing different with Morgan than we did with the others. Do you think we're just getting better at it?"

"I think the primary difference was Morgan, herself. She may be more adaptable to change."

Amasis and Khyan shared and compared thoughts on some of the other introductions before they parted.

As Khyan walked home, he reflected on what it must have been like for their Nosos World visitors to be contacted by strangers. He had asked Amasis to make first contact because he was the most gregarious and charismatic, despite his stocky muscular appearance and deep set black eyes.

How would Iris be when she interacted with the Nosos youth? Iris was complicated. She was intellectual and seemed to prefer her studies to most activities. She had strong opinions concerning the khaos condition and how to stop it. Her views, however, were diametrical to his own. That's why he chose her, to help him keep his perspective. He did not want his judgment clouded by early results and successes. He needed her to believe so he could believe.

All the Nosos youth seemed surprised to learn they were in a mountain cavern. He had never given much thought to the concept. It was the only place he had ever lived.

The mountain cavern hosted a small city of structures built of the rocks, clay and sand from surface of the mountain. The buildings adopted the colour of these materials: a warm gold. Today they took on an added glowing peachy hue, as the sun shone through the translucent ceiling dome.

Khyan looked up. It was magnificent. The sky dome accentuated what would be seen if one were to stand outside on the mountaintop. Today, the dome revealed a rich azure blue sky dressed with cirrus clouds. Breathtaking! Tonight if the skies were clear, the dome would be in deep shades of cobalt and indigo juxtaposed with brilliant shimmering stars.

He was pleased he and his team had found a way for the Nosos World youth to move around and interact in Lucid World, all the while staying within Elder Tabubu's mandated parameters.

He passed the bakery. The smell of fresh-baked bread caressed his nostrils and teased his stomach. He was hungry. He quickened his step and recalled his first meeting with Elder Tabubu.

LUCID WORLD—TWO MONTHS EARLIER

Khyan paced. He was in the quarters of Elder Tabubu, awaiting her arrival. He looked around the room for some clue why he'd been summoned. The room revealed the comforts and favoured belongings of Elder Tabubu. Colourful cushions and tapestries adorned the room. Placed on shelves carved into the walls were souvenirs of trips to Nosos: sea shells, driftwood, teacups, wood carvings and snow globes.

Tabubu entered. It was difficult to tell the age of Tabubu. She was perhaps somewhere between 60 and 80 years. Her face held lines revealing she had laughed and lived passionately. Her body frame was small, and she was about five feet tall. Her hair was white-grey with a hint of gold. Her movements were quick and graceful as she pulled her chair towards Khyan so they could sit facing one another. Tabubu leaned forward and rested her forearms on her lap.

"Tell me about the Nosos youth plan you submitted to the Council of Elders."

"Like many others, I don't believe khaos is viral, bacterial or genetic. Rather, it's repeating patterns of neural brain connections of khaos thoughts causing khaos emotions and more khaos thoughts. Khaos causes khaos. Embryos and fetuses experience khaos emotions of their mothers while in the womb and emulate the neural processes and emotions. If we could end the cycle, we could end khaos."

Khyan stopped, to respectfully give Elder Tabubu an opportunity to speak. She nodded for him to continue.

"Our efforts to reach rational intellectual Nosos adults, to create an awareness, have been unsuccessful. Most Nosos adults are too deeply absorbed in the 'khaos way'. Khaos is what they are accustomed to and what others expect of them."

Kyhan straightened his posture, "My plan targets Nosos youth to teach them to recognize and change these patterns."

Tabubu leaned back in her chair and put her fingertips together over her chest, "I read your submission. It says Nosos youth will be most responsive if interactions are with young people close to their own age. Why?"

"Nosos teens are more prone to be influenced by other teens, rather than adults."

Tabubu took a deep breath and let her hands fall in her lap. The plan contained many uncontrollable variables and risks. Also, there was the matter of interacting with Nosos World adolescents without parental consent. But time was running out.

The icecap which hid their mountain cavern home was receding at an unprecedented speed. Nosos World was now monitoring movements in the skies and remote regions to surveil other countries and political factions. It would be nearly impossible to re-establish in a new location without detection.

With conviction, Tabubu said, "Khyan, please put your plan into operation."

"Thank you, Elder Tabubu!" Khyan leapt from his seat as though he was about to charge out of the room.

"Khyan, our business is not concluded," Tabubu laughed. "Have you ever left our world and entered Nosos World?"

"Once. My father took me outside with him to make repairs to the icecap enhancement projection field. Pictures don't capture the openness and depth. It is amazing and beautiful."

Tabubu stood with one hand on her hip, and with the index finger of her other hand on her lower lip, said, "Why do you believe your plan will be most effective if the Nosos youth may visit our world? Why not communicate with them via communication technology available in Nosos?"

"If they can experience a world uninfected with khaos, they will better envision what I hope will become our common goal."

Tabubu said, "The visits to Lucid World will be permitted, provided you ensure everyone is kept safe from khaos."

CHAPTER 4

IRIS

A petite teenage girl, with a pale complexion and short taupe-brown hair, stood beside a life-sized sculpture of a goat-like creature: the female tur. The room held several large sculptures of animals: leopards, hawks, bears. The girl's loose fitting floral-print dress was a warm and cheery contrast to the smooth pale-grey stone figures surrounding her.

Khyan chose this room for today's meeting. Why? It seemed an unusual choice. But then, so was she. She and Khyan were acquaintances; not colleagues or friends and her interactions with him until now had been limited. They sometimes attended the same yoga sessions. She once heard him speak at a forum dedicated to the reversal of khaos. At this forum, Khyan and she subscribed to different theories regarding possible causes and solutions to khaos. And yet Khyan had asked her to join his small team for the Nosos youth project.

At first she thought Amasis was also an unusual choice. Amasis and Khyan weren't friends either. Besides the age difference, Amasis was more outgoing and less academic than Khyan. It was now apparent why Khyan chose him. When Amasis made first-contact with the initiates, his amiable personality helped assuage their fears.

Now it was her turn to orient the visitors. She used a voice command to instruct the computer to begin the next transmission.

Within seconds, Morgan's image appeared. She was wearing clothing considered fashionable and appropriate for a Nosos teenager.

The girl, standing beside the tur, regarded Morgan's clothing and nodded in satisfaction. She didn't speak. She wanted to give Morgan a chance to adjust to the interchange.

"Hi! You must be Iris."

"Hi. Yes, I am. And I see your disoriented sensations seem to be subsiding quickly. How do you feel, otherwise?"

Morgan noticed an interesting quality in Iris. When she spoke, her face brightened, and she became animated and expressive. She transformed from ordinary to charismatic.

Morgan twisted the upper part of her body from side to side. "I'm actually great with seeing, hearing, and talking, but not sure about moving. My avatar body sort of does what I want. But I don't know how it actually works."

"Your 3D holographic projection or as you referred to it, avatar, does more than just transmit verbal responses back to us. It also reacts to your brain the same way your body does when you're awake. Do you know how your brain makes your real arms and legs move?"

Morgan raised and lowered an arm in the air. "Actually, I never thought about it. It just happens."

"Your brain controls your body's muscles. When you think of moving your body, the motor cortex area of your brain sends a message to your muscles. The same brain commands that control your muscles control your avatar."

Morgan did a 360 degree turn. "What is this place?"

"It's an art gallery."

"Interesting. Hey, so why does Lucid World want to find a cure for khaos? And help my world, I mean, Nosos World?"

Iris explained. Lucid World's earliest ancestors were consumed with trying to cure khaos so they could return to their homes and reunite with friends and family who had been infected. As time went by, and generations passed, Lucid World became their home. Those left behind, and those who remembered them, grew old and passed away. Descendants continued the search for a cure to free Nosos World from khaos because they wanted to leave isolation and experience the entire planet. Now, another reason has developed: khaos is destroying that planet. Nuclear bombs and pollution threaten both worlds.

"I hope you find a cure for khaos, and soon. Khyan said that's the reason I'm here, to get cured from khaos. Why me, though? What about everyone else?"

"We've tried many things. Since khaos emotions are contagious, Khyan believes lucid emotions could spread the same way. So far, lucid emotions could not overcome khaos emotions because khaos is so ingrained in people. He conjectures that someone who challenges khaos at an early enough age, while surrounded by lucid emotions, will overcome khaos."

"So, if khaos is contagious, aren't you worried about catching it from me?"

Iris touched the side of the tur and said, "Unlike this figure, which I can touch, no part of your physical being is here." Iris reached over to Morgan's arm and her hand passed through. "You see? You aren't really here."

"Do that again. This time, keep your hand there. I want to see if I'm 'see-through'."

Iris laughed. "You're not see-through now, but wait."

Iris instructed the computer to reduce the density of Morgan's image by 50%. She then placed her hand on Morgan's upper arm and slowly passed her hand through. It appeared as if Iris's hand was inside Morgan's arm.

"Okay, this time make me even more see-through. I want to look like a ghost who haunts an old mansion."

Iris instructed the computer to make Morgan's image even less dense.

Morgan held her arms up and moved them in a floating motion. "Woo-ooo. Am I scary?"

Iris laughed and said, "Not to me. Maybe something's missing." She told the computer to play suspenseful music.

"Nope," said Iris, "Still not scary." They both laughed.

"But, if Khyan is right maybe you're still exposed by talking with me."

"Our interaction time is limited. Also, Khyan has set up a curriculum and protocols for us to follow. With this structure to our sessions, khaos will not imprint on me."

"How can my changing from khaos to lucid actually cure khaos on the planet?"

"If you, and others like you, succeed, the approach could be used globally and may reduce or eliminate it."

"Do you think his plan will actually work?"

"I think it can help and may reduce khaos over time, but," Iris stopped and her expression became sullen. "I think it will take too long and won't have enough impact."

Iris elaborated. She believed in a more scientific approach. Such as isolating what had changed in the human brain and started khaos. There had been a time when people didn't have khaos. Something changed. It could be viral or bacterial or something along those lines. But so far nothing of the sort has been found. Maybe a gene is triggered. More research is needed.

"How'd I get chosen to help with Khyan's plan?"

Iris's thoughts turned to the candidate selection meeting:

Khyan: *"Are we in agreement on the selection of candidates for the mission?"*

Iris: *"Mission? It sounds like a covert operation, like a movie. I didn't know you had such a flair for drama, Khyan."*

Khyan: *(chuckles) "It's covert, and it's an operation. If we're successful, perhaps it will be a movie." (Chuckles again.)*

Amasis: *"To carry on with the movie theme, there's one more role we should cast: Morgan, from the town, Coyote Flats, in Canada."*

Khyan: *"That area has minimal electro-magnetic field transmission interference and the time zone works well for us to schedule meeting times. However, I thought you reported that when you visited Coyote Flats you observed Morgan getting into some type of trouble."*

Amasis: *"She and a friend took a parent's vehicle, without permission."*

Khyan: *"That behaviour suggests she may be too far gone in khaos to reverse it."*

Amasis: *"I don't think so. She has a mischievous quality to her and she does break some of the rules set down for her by teachers and parents. She has a great propensity for compassion and does not seem to have qualities of meanness or cruelty."*

Iris: *"If our intentions are to teach them to question and change behaviours, who better than someone who questions and challenges rules?"*

Khyan: *"Then it's decided. We'll include Morgan from Coyote Flats."*

"Iris, can you still see me?" asked Morgan.

"Oh yes, sorry. It was based on an algorithm designed to select candidates with certain attributes."

"Am I the only one, or are there others?"

"There are others, six of you, and you're all from different places. I don't think you'll get to meet the others."

"Coyote Flats is actually really small and there's nothing special about it. Why'd you even think of having someone from there?"

"You're all from rural areas."

"Why not anyone who lives in a city?"

Like Amasis and Khyan, Iris wore a small oval shaped device around her neck. She looked at it and told Morgan they could continue the subject another time.

"Do you feel comfortable enough with your avatar body to move around if we take it slow?"

Morgan nodded.

"Follow me. I have something to show you."

They walked around and past the statues. Iris told Morgan not to walk 'through' them with her avatar body, which Iris suspected she might be prone to do, because the stone would act as a barrier and communication with Morgan's real body would be disrupted.

When they got to a wall, Iris instructed the computer to reflect their images. The stone wall turned into a mirror and Morgan saw her avatar.

"Wow! That looks just like me. Except," Morgan moved closer and looked at her face, "better! I don't have any pimples."

Morgan touched her hair but she couldn't feel it. She and her hair were holograms. She moved her head to swing her sandy-coloured shoulder-length hair from side to side. It moved like her real hair, but when she looked closely, she couldn't see individual hair strands. "Well, I'll never have 'split ends' in Lucid World."

Morgan assessed her clothing. "Nice," she twirled for the mirror, "You have better taste than Amasis."

They laughed.

Iris led her to the corner of the room where a flight of stairs was carved into the stone. They ascended the steps slowly. At first, Morgan struggled to synchronize her avatar's eyes and legs as she navigated the steps. By the time they got to the top, she mastered it.

Morgan's avatar followed Iris and stepped through a door at the top of the stairs and out onto a balcony overlooking structures and people and more!

Iris explained. "We are on one of the highest balconies in Lucid World. From this vantage point, you have a good view of the whole cavern."

Through her avatar's eyes, Morgan gazed at Lucid World and tried to absorb all she could see. Sunlight streamed down from what looked like a sky filled with bright clouds. The sunlight was not as intense and bright as sunlight in Nosos World. It was diffused and had a multi-colour rainbow-like quality to it.

The structures looked like the clay adobes of old Mexico. But they were more stylish, and many had large opaque glass windows and balconies. Most were three or four stories high. Structures were attached to one another or there was minimal space between them. There were open areas that appeared to be recreational parks and gardens, dotted with patches of green and bright colours. In these places, people were walking or sitting. Some were accompanied by dogs. Small children were playing. Birds flew freely through the air.

In one direction Morgan could see a continuous stone wall. 'It must be an outer wall of the cavern,' Morgan thought, as she remembered that Lucid World was inside a mountain.

There were pathways throughout. Instead of cars, there were small vehicles like tractor-trucks, all with large tires and an open box at the back.

Morgan heard footsteps from behind, turned and saw Amasis.

"Today the sun is shining through the ceiling dome. Join me on the balcony while I have something to eat."

Iris excused herself, promising to see Morgan again soon.

"I see you're becoming accustomed to your holographic body. Are you able to walk up to the table and sit on your own or would you like me to intervene and transport your holograph?"

"Actually, I think I can manage," said Morgan. "Let me practice a bit."

Morgan thought, 'Jump,' but nothing happened. Looking at

Morgan's avatar's strained facial expression, Amasis asked, "What are you trying to do?"

"I'm trying to jump."

"Do it the same way you make your physical body jump. Don't command your body to jump. Don't over-think it. Just jump."

Morgan's avatar jumped. Then, it twisted and moved in ways indicating some discomfort.

Alarmed, Amasis asked, "Are you all right? Are you feeling pain?"

"I'm dancing!"

"Oops sorry. Hahaha. Let's move to the table."

CHAPTER 5

GARGUEY AND BEARS

Amasis escorted Avatar-Morgan to a seat at a table. Once she was positioned in the chair, Amasis got up and disappeared inside a nearby doorway. When he reappeared, he was carrying a plate of food. He couldn't offer any to Morgan because the transmission technology wasn't intelligent enough for her avatar to eat food and relay the taste to Morgan's taste buds.

Amasis ate with a utensil resembling a fork. Most food items looked familiar: beans, lettuce, tomatoes and broccoli. There was one in particular she didn't recognize. It resembled slimy worms.

"Whaaat's thaaat?" Morgan said slowly while pointing at the mixture.

"It's garguey."

Morgan's avatar made a strange face with eyebrows turned inward, eyes narrowed and nose wrinkled. "Eww!" she said.

Amasis thought, 'Clearly she has mastered her avatar motor skills.' He almost laughed out loud. Instead he suppressed his laugh and asked, "What does eww mean?"

"It means it's disgusting, and it probably tastes disgusting."

Again Amasis almost laughed out loud. He had a pretty good idea of what was going on inside Morgan's head, but pretended not to.

"Why do you think it tastes disgusting?"

"I just know."

"How? To dislike a food you haven't tasted is illogical, and probably a manifestation of khaos."

Morgan conceded this point to Amasis and thought, 'Even so, it's still disgusting.' She also thought his face looked odd while they were discussing garguey. His lips were pursed tight. Maybe he didn't like garguey either and it was a 'Lucid World thing' to say he did.

Amasis resumed eating. Changing the subject, Morgan asked, "Aren't people in Lucid World ever afraid? Khyan said fear is khaos. But if a big grizzly bear was chasing you, wouldn't you be scared?"

"I'd be terrified," he said between mouthfuls.

"Then isn't that khaos?"

Amasis put his utensil down. "Not if I'm afraid while the bear is chasing me, but let's say I outrun the bear!" Morgan's avatar and Amasis both laughed. Amasis continued, "It would be khaos if I was still afraid after the bear was long gone."

"So shouldn't you worry about things like bears when you're outside in places they actually live, whether you see them or not?"

"Take precautions, yes. Worry, no. Logical precautions aren't khaos."

Amasis began eating again.

"So, khaos isn't actually just fear, it's illogical fear. So I should think like a Vulcan on Star Trek without feelings, right?"

"No. If you think with logic alone, you can't experience positive emotions, which are the best part of living."

"It would help if I had a text book or something to explain which emotions and thoughts are khaos."

Amasis had finished and moved his plate aside. "Morgan, when you seek an answer to understand khaos, it is anywhere you look. Open any book on any page. You'll find your answer."

"Huh — how?"

"When it comes to khaos, a part of your brain, which evolved long ago, knows the answers. Be alert to clues from your subconscious. They may come from anywhere and everywhere: through a dream, a rock formation, a comment made by a stranger. This is why people often see 'a sign' to guide them. The sign is a conduit to discover what they already know."

"All right, I'll try that," Morgan said sceptically, "but I'll never try the garguey."

Chapter 6

Welcome to Coyote Flats

She walked alone. She didn't limp or sway. Yet she was betrayed by her step, revealing her high heeled shoes weren't enjoying the walk and might rebel against her feet. Her tight dress rode up her thighs in a rebellion of its own.

While her trashy shoes yielded to the direction they were propelled, her revealing dress fought against her frequent tugs at its hem. Unlike her insurgent attire, her brassy blonde hair, large earrings, and generous round breasts all bounced freely.

She passed two women walking the opposite direction. Both wore expensive-looking jogging outfits and had full-on hair and make-up, including lipstick. One woman leaned into the other and whispered. Both looked back and snickered.

"Where do you suppose Franny's off to so early this morning?" one of them asked. Before the other could answer, she added, "Without a coat, in this weather?"

"She's probably just getting home," answered the other, with raised eyebrows giving extra meaning to her words. Then she added, "You know, the walk of shame."

The two women passed the bakery. The smell of freshly baked cinnamon buns filled their nostrils. Both made 'Mmmm' noises, pointed their noses upward, and flared their nostrils.

Standing in line at the bakery were Daniel and Meredith Kith. Daniel was looking out the window. "Hey there's double trouble."

"Now what are you looking at?" asked Meredith.

"It's not a 'what'. It's a 'who'. Don't know their first names, but last names are Meany and Bittar."

"Oh, I know who you mean," Meredith looked out to see them, but they were gone, "Enid and Winifred, the church patrol. They came to our door with a petition to ban 'certain' books from the school library."

"Yup, that's them. Crazy old bats."

"What were they doing?"

"They're outfitted for walking, but they don't strike me as the type to be out exercising and enjoying the sunshine."

Meredith motioned to the display case under the counter. "Neither are we. Which cake?"

"Uh, the kids like all kinds of cake, don't they?"

"Dylan and Ryan do. Morgan's fussier."

"Well then, what does Morgan like?"

"I never know. It changes all the time." Meredith sighed. "Have you noticed she's been acting more self-absorbed than usual?"

Daniel wasn't looking at the cakes. He was looking at a poster on the wall.

"Uh, I dunno. She's a teenager. Hey look, there's a contest for a new 'Welcome to Coyote Flats' sign. How's about a sign with a sugar beet and a coyote running away from a book with a big X through the word sex? Hahaha."

Meredith giggled and whispered, "Shhh, keep your voice down. We're up next. Which one?"

"Let's go with your favourite — chocolate."

"Oh my," laughed Meredith as she shook her head, "and your favourite too."

Daniel left Meredith standing in line and wandered over to the poster:

COYOTE FLATS 'WELCOME SIGN' CONTEST

Our Welcome Sign is a friendly hello to our visitors. Take part in designing a new sign by entering a submission representing this wonderful town. It should reflect our community as a special place, distinct from anywhere else.

Daniel didn't read the rest of the poster. Designing a sign was more fun to think about, or joke about, than to actually do. 'What does the old sign look like?' he wondered. It must be unremarkable because he couldn't picture it. What represented Coyote Flats? Was it really special or distinct from anywhere else?

The town existed for two commercial enterprises: agriculture and manufacturing sugar. His thoughts turned to his employer, Wilco Sugar. Everyone in town referred to Wilco Sugar as simply "The Sugar Factory". He had written a description of the factory manufacturing process for the company website. It involved condensing a lengthy scientific process into a short description.

Sugar Beets and the Production of Sugar
Sugar beet is one of the two main sugar crops used to make table sugar; sugar cane is the other. Sugar beet can be grown in a variety of temperate climates; sugar cane is restricted to warmer climates.
After sugar beets are harvested, they are transported to a factory for processing. There, they are washed, sliced and soaked in hot water. The resulting juice, rich in sugar, is heated and mixed with a lime solution which reacts with impurities in the juice. Carbon dioxide is added and reacts with the lime to form solid calcium carbonate. This separates from the sugar solution and carries with it the impurities, which are filtered out. The juice is then evaporated, forming a thick concentration. This mixture is fed into a centrifugal machine and high-speed rotation separates the crystals from the syrup. The result — sugar crystals!

Daniel glanced over to the line-up to check Meredith's progress. She had advanced to the front and was talking to the person behind the counter while pointing at a chocolate cake. A phone rang in the background and Meredith was abandoned while it was answered. Meredith looked in his direction. She made eye contact, crossed her arms and rolled her eyes. One of her pet peeves was store staff allowing others to interrupt while they were serving someone who has waited their turn. He threw her a grin, 'I know.'

Daniel wandered over to a display cabinet containing examples of themed cakes. They looked sweet and expensive. He considered their sugar content and the controversy about the nutritional value of sugar and related health concerns. In a recent meeting with executives of Wilco Sugar, he asked: what was the company doing to help people make informed and better food choices; and was the company considering diversifying into healthier foods?

Their stand was that oversimplification of science had confused opinions for substantiated evidence. To address the confusion, Wilco funded a non-profit association to represent the industry on nutritional affairs, providing science-based nutrition information to the public.

Daniel shook his head at their audacity. Their response to consumer and government concern about the health risks of sugar was to manipulate information and public opinion.

His thoughts turned back to the sign contest and the town name. According to the archives, before the town was even settled, trappers and early ranchers referred to the area as Coyote Flats. There was an abundance of coyotes on the surrounding grass-covered lowland, a natural habitat for coyotes and other small animals to thrive. Settlers' memoirs said the vocal ability of the coyote left a lasting impression on anyone who heard it, whether living there or just passing through. Daniel shivered as he imagined the lonely sound of yips and howls across the plains under star-filled skies.

What about the people? What represented them?

People who lived in the town and nearby farm families were a diverse group. The businesses on the town's two main commercial streets, Centre Avenue and Station Avenue, reflected their diversity. Family-owned businesses included an Italian restaurant, a Chinese restaurant, Japanese specialty foods, and Daniel's present location, the Dutch bakery. A farm implement dealership stood beside a women's designer fashion store. There were two veterinarians: one for small animals and one for livestock. There was a liquor store and a Mormon bookstore. There was a seniors' centre and a baby clothing store.

Some of the townspeople were slightly poor. Some were slightly wealthy. Daniel thought the phrase 'big fish in a small pond' explained the rich of Coyote Flats. Even though the gaps between rich, poor and middle were not as great as elsewhere, the gaps still existed.

The fish in the Coyote Flats pond didn't seem to care all that much about a person's cultural and economic characteristics, but they noticed a person's conduct. Community members often criticized the behaviour of others, regardless of whether it was positive or negative. Most often, feedback was not communicated to the offender. Rather it was dispatched when the relevant person was absent. Daniel thought of instances. If a child did well in school it was said, "Oh, they think they're so smart." If a child did poorly in school or was too rebellious it was said, "Oh, look at the parents to see where the problem is." If someone got married: "It will never last." If someone left for the city: "How ungrateful! How'll his poor father manage the farm without him?"

What was said about his family? Best not to think about it. Besides, it doesn't matter, does it?

Daniel realized he had not been thinking about his town in a positive light. The people of Coyote Flats were not without their merits and positive attributes. Most were caring, many were judging. Why was that? Was it a small town thing? Are members of small groups always seeking affirmation of their choices, and so perceive dissimilar choices to be an affront? Daniel stalled at this notion, to consider it more deeply. He sensed that feelings of insecurity may be the underlying reason for this behaviour; but behaviour is habitual and habits are hard to break.

Had Daniel known his musings were regarding a khaos condition, he may have concluded, "If life is complicated, then life with khaos is complicated all the more and life in Coyote Flats is especially complicated."

Daniel's musings ended when Meredith arrived at his side carrying a white square cardboard box.

CHAPTER 7

EVACUEES– THEN AND NOW

During Morgan's chat with Amasis while he ate his garguey dinner, she asked questions about the world before his ancestors separated from it.

Unlike Nosos World, Lucid World retained complete and accurate archival information about ancient times. When Lucid World separated from Nosos World over four thousand years ago, civilization at the time was far more advanced than generally thought. Much of the knowledge, technology and tools of the time were lost to Nosos World due to the spread of khaos. Lucid World's ancestors came from the geographic area near places now known as Egypt, Syria and Turkey. Morgan wondered why her Lucid World friends didn't dress in ancient clothing styles. Amasis explained. The clothing of ancestors would have been based on climate, materials and tools of their time. Lucid World was in a mountain cavern and had progressed.

Morgan was privy to knowledge of historical events and details which Nosos World historians could only speculate about. It was incredible: Lucid World was unknown to the rest of the world. She spent hours searching on the computer for any mention of such a civilization. She found nothing. She read everything she could find on early history, looking for clues to events leading up to their departure. Her Lucid World mentors had described their history, but she wanted to find information that could corroborate this. The only information she could find was published conjecture by some historians that slave labour had been used to build the pyramids in Egypt. However, she also found published conjecture by other historians that slave labour had not been used.

What about the word 'Nosos', used to describe her world? She'd never heard the word before. Perhaps it might be mentioned somewhere in historical archives. She learned that nosos is a word from the ancient Greek which means disease. So while the name fit to describe khaos, it didn't lead her to any new information.

Morgan then used a different approach. She searched for legends of lost civilizations and soon discovered a legend of an ancient kingdom hidden somewhere in Asia, called Shambhala. Ancient texts described Shambhala as a place of peace, tranquility and happiness. Historical archeologists postulated the legend may have stemmed from writings of a man named Djer, and his wife, dated back to 2100 BC.

Djer's boyhood friend, Kasta, allegedly vanished with his family, and several others from his village, in the still of the night. Djer spent his adult life searching for answers regarding Kasta's disappearance. Based on Djer's recollection of events leading up to the night of his friend's departure, he presumed those who disappeared had fled to a place devoid of cruelty. In the language of the time, and subsequent etymology, the phrase used by Djer morphed into the word Shambhala in the Sanskrit language. Unable to find any trace of Shambhala, Djer speculated it was a realm teetering on the edge of physical and spiritual reality, a place only pure and enlightened persons could enter.

Djer's wife was the sister of the then ruling king. In his advanced years, Djer confided to her that Kasta had visited him. Djer revealed only vague details of the supposed meeting and a snippet of their conversation. Kasta apologized for leaving without saying goodbye and said he hoped his friend had a good life. Djer's wife wrote she feared her husband's lifelong obsession caused him to lose his mind. To placate Djer and to quell his obsession with Shambhala, she asked her brother, the king, to commission an obelisk bearing a lengthy inscription written by Djer.

It was written in an early form of the Sumerian language. By assimilating translations and information known about Djer, historical archeologists conjectured the inscription conveyed the following message:

> Before the building of the great pyramids, we were a peaceful and prosperous people.
>
> We accepted our history, lived in the present and planned for the future as nature and circumstances necessitated.
>
> We were happy, curious and adventurous. We had good sense and avoided danger. We accepted loss and recognized death as essential for life.
>
> We strove for harmony, not perfection. Mishaps were lessons of life and fodder for wisdom.
>
> As time passed, we changed. Initially, change came slowly, but quickened with time. It was akin to water through a hole in a dam made of stones — at first trickling and then suddenly crashing through the structure, leaving only rubble in its path.
>
> Fear replaced good sense and trust. Thoughts turned away from the present and towards past disappointments and future anxieties. Love of life and of adventure was lost. Destructive emotions replaced love. Mishaps evoked shame, judgement and blame.
>
> Those who knew of the transformation, and recognized the malaise was contagious, tried to stop it. Their efforts were futile, for it was already too late. Too many were infected and although they could not see change in themselves, they accused others.
>
> The few who were yet uninfected left us. They did not abandon us. They held tight to the hope to stop the contagion. They now live in the land of Shambhala.
>
> Pray all who read this know they too can live in Shambhala if they open their hearts and their minds to love and happiness and reject unfounded fear.

Morgan continued to search, but could find no more about Djer, Kasta or the obelisk. The revelation fascinated her. Could Lucid World be the land of Shambhala, or Shangri-La as it is referred to in more recent times?

The next night, Morgan was transported into a beautiful

grotto. White stalagmites and stalactites resembled columns in a cathedral. There was a clear pool which emitted coloured lights of emerald, turquoise, and sapphire, and filled the space with colour.

In the breathtaking grotto, she and Amasis sat on a stone bench and she shared the findings of her research.

Amasis said, "I know of the legend of Shambhala, and of the ideas and stories attached to it as both a place and a philosophy. It never occurred to me that the place might be Lucid World. One of the first Lucid World inhabitants was named Kasta. The name Djer sounds familiar."

Amasis touched the oval device around his neck and said, "English language. Lineage for first settlers named Kasta. Respond for all in proximity."

A clear masculine voice filled the grotto. "There is one first settler named Kasta. Lineage displayed."

A list of names, printed in large black letters on an off-white background appeared in the air in front of them.

Amasis scanned the list and said, "Kasta's first born child was a male named Djer. Kasta may have named him after a friend."

"Djer said Kasta visited him. Do you think Kasta was there? Could he have visited Djer the same way I visit you?"

Amasis touched the oval device, and the list disappeared. "Lucid World didn't have avatar transmission technology back then. If Djer saw Kasta, and he didn't imagine it, it means Kasta was physically there. It's possible Kasta had a reason to visit Djer, a reason which he believed outweighed the risk."

Morgan recounted the obelisk inscription. Amasis again reached for his neck device and asked Morgan to describe the search parameters.

The same webpage Morgan found on her computer at home appeared.

Amasis read the information and then made it vanish. "Kasta must have told Djer about Lucid World. But he didn't tell him where it was. Djer understood the reason Kasta and others left and sought Lucid World. The last line of the inscription, saying that anyone can live in Shambhala if they are open to love and happiness and reject unfounded fear, reveals he also understood love and happiness is not found in a place. It is found within oneself.

To think otherwise is khaos."

"Why would that be khaos? What's so illogical about wanting to be somewhere nice?"

"It's not illogical to want to be in a nice place, but it is illogical to believe happiness may only be found in such a place. Let me tell you a story about Boethius, who was born in ancient Rome."

ILLUSIONS

Boethius was a rich and respected public figure and had a loving family. His charmed life took a great turn when he was sentenced to death by torture.

He defended a fellow Official from accusations of treason. As a result, he was charged with treason himself, and sent to prison.

Mistreated and awaiting death, he reflected upon true happiness. He reasoned that his former good life, compared to his current wretched life, proved that fortune is a changeable illusion and cannot provide real happiness. Happiness is not found externally; happiness is found internally. A person's attitude causes them to feel happy or sad.

After Amasis finished the story, Morgan asked, "How do you know about this? Was someone from Lucid World there?"

"No, Boethius wrote a book."

"Did he escape?"

"Historical records tell us he was executed."

Morgan looked disappointed. Amasis said, "Let's walk around for a while. I know you can't feel it, but this seat is uncomfortable."

While walking and admiring the natural beauty of the grotto, Amasis answered her questions about how Lucid World stayed hidden.

"From the air, the icecap looks bigger than it is. It's an illusion, created by projection equipment, to conceal light and air passages, and to compensate for the receding icecap. If the icecap gets too small, we won't be able to keep up the illusion."

"So that makes sense for planes flying over the icecap. What if someone was actually walking on the mountain?"

"We'll see them coming. If they get too close, we'll create a nearby avalanche or windstorm."

"So why worry about the icecap shrinking if you can just keep showing fake images?"

"Snow and ice is easy to fake for planes and satellites. Rocks and trees would be harder to fake. Also, if the snow and ice is gone, people will come to explore and we won't be able to avalanche or wind-storm them all away every time."

"Has anybody ever actually found Lucid World?"

"Not at this Lucid World location. Another Lucid World location that once existed was discovered, and the discovery led to its destruction."

They took a seat on a flat ledge covered with grassy-moss, beside the crystal blue-green pool.

"It happened a long time ago. I'll tell you what I know."

LUCID WORLD'S EARLY HISTORY

When Lucid World's ancestors separated from the rest of the world, they followed legends of a mountain cave so large it could contain an entire village. By using ancient maps, they were able to find it.

Their new home presented many challenges, especially around getting food. In the early days they trapped animals and relied on natural vegetation on the mountain and valley below. But later, these sources proved to be insufficient and unreliable. Fortunately, on a neighbouring mountain, there was a highly combustible mineral capable of producing great amounts of heat. They constructed large hot air balloons fueled by this combustible mineral. They could then travel vast distances to plant and harvest food in fertile places with suitable climates.

On one of their food gathering expeditions, they discovered a lush and uninhabited island. The island was surrounded with coral reefs and jagged rocks, and was perched on top of high severe cliffs. It seemed unlikely anyone from Nosos World would happen upon this isolated island. Half of the population of Lucid World, numbering almost five hundred, moved to the island.

The island colony cultivated enough food to feed both Lucid World locations. This living and food production system thrived for centuries. One day a severe storm blew a Nosos ship off-course and it crashed into the rocks below the cliffs of the island. The island inhabitants performed rescue operations and saved several of the crew and passengers of the wrecked ship. They also salvaged the ship for repair, and to get the marooned people on their way as soon as possible. However, this took many months. When the time came, and the ship was ready to sail, several of the castaways refused to leave the utopian island.

The island Elders did not want to banish or isolate those who stayed. They considered it an opportunity to study the khaos infection. This extended exposure to khaos caused many Island Lucid World inhabitants to contract khaos, and before long everyone on the island was suffering from it.

Island Lucid World formed its own government and rebelled against Mountain Lucid World. The islanders had many complaints and demands. They did not want to do all the work to produce all the food, to which they were only entitled to half. They wanted to build a port so they could travel away from the island by ship. They wanted to mine gold and precious gem deposits on the island, and to trade these commodities with other civilizations. They wanted wealth. They wanted slaves to do the work. They wanted, they wanted, they wanted.

Mountain Lucid World reluctantly, and sadly, severed ties with Island Lucid World. They took the hot air balloons and reserves of fuel on a one-way trip to Mountain Lucid World.

During the years when food was transported from Island Lucid World to Mountain Lucid World, significant improvements were made to the design of the hot air balloon. The improved design enabled them to travel faster and further. Since growing seasons varied, Lucid World planted and gathered food in both the northern and southern hemispheres. Despite of their efforts to avoid detection by Nosos World civilizations, there were mishaps. None were as strange as what happened in southern Peru.

A food gathering team in South America were on their way back to Lucid World. One of the air balloons in their convoy lost altitude and had to make an emergency landing. The emergency landing happened in an arid area seemingly uninhabitable and unpopulated.

The necessary repairs were extensive. Parts and tools had to be brought from Lucid World. The damaged air balloon was temporarily abandoned until an equipped crew could return to repair and recover it. To mark the location for a repair crew to identify the site from the air, they cleared away rocks and soil from the ground, creating a geoglyph. The marking was 100 meters across and resembled a wounded bird. The 'artists' could have used a simple geometric shape. Instead they were creative and expressive.

Air balloons and a repair crew returned a few months later. To their surprise, there wasn't a single geoglyph marking the spot. There were hundreds! Birds, spiders, hands, trees, celestial constellations.

On landing, they discovered the area was not uninhabited. A tribe of people lived in a nearby hill area. From their hill top home they witnessed the balloons landing and could see the 'wounded bird' marking the spot of the damaged balloon. Believing the air balloons to be gods, they made their own markings to entice the gods to return.

Unable to convince the hillside people they were not gods, the repair crew hastily repaired the fallen air balloon and departed. After that, different flight paths were used for future food expeditions. But the damage was done, and as we now know, the indigenous people created even larger geoglyphs to entice their 'gods' to return. This phenomenon has been the subject of much speculation and has become a major tourist attraction in Peru. The area and the geoglyph patterns have become known as the 'Nazca Lines'.

Amasis took off his slipper-like shoes, rolled up his jeans and waded into the pool.

"What about the island? Island Lucid World – what happened to it? What's it called now?" Morgan asked.

Amasis walked until the water level was almost even with his rolled up pant legs. He stopped and turned around to face Morgan. "Something terrible happened."

After the separation, when Lucid World air balloons ventured out for food, they were careful to avoid the island. From one of their flight paths, the island was visible in the far distance. When two different convoys passed near the island and reported they could not see the island, a team was sent to investigate. They discovered the island had disappeared.

"What? An island can't actually just disappear, can it?"

"There was a volcano on the island. It was thought to be extinct. It may have been just dormant and became active."

An eruption could have destroyed the island. Another possible explanation was a severe earthquake caused the island to be swallowed by the sea. Either way, the island and everyone who lived on it vanished without a trace.

Morgan watched the light dance on ripples Amasis created by moving a toe over the surface of the water. She said, "But you said its discovery led to its destruction."

"If the island wasn't separated from Mountain Lucid World, hot air balloons could have been used to evacuate the island."

"Did the island have an actual name?"

"Yes. Atlantis."

"Oh, everyone's heard of Atlantis.

"The Greek philosopher, Plato, named it Atlantis. The rescued ship passengers, who returned home, must have told stories of a beautiful island with a utopian society. They started the legend of the lost civilization of Atlantis."

"Are there any other stories … like what happened in Peru?"

"They're more like ramifications than stories."

Amasis shared another instance. The phenomena of 'crop circles', crops flattened in circle patterns during the night, were caused by Lucid World food gathering machines. The machines were transported into the fields with hot air balloons. That's how they got in and out without leaving tracks.

"Wow! And everyone thinks aliens and UFOs are doing it."

"That's why we quit."

"But I thought crop circles were still being found."

"The ones you hear about now are hoaxes."

"Do you still use air balloons?"

Amasis answered, no. When countries and companies launched satellites, they had to stop using air balloons. They now produce food locally in an artificially lit greenhouse in a neighbouring mountain.

Their current mode of transportation into Nosos World is by helicopter. Transmissions from Lucid World secretly brought a defunct satellite back to life. Still orbiting Earth, this satellite tracks their helicopters in flight. It triggers a sensor to produce a signal that cloaks the aircraft from detection as an object. So while the helicopter is still visible to the human eye, it's invisible to laser beams, radar, pulse waves, and such. The Lucid World satellite appears dormant because it uses wave frequencies undetectable by Nosos World.

Amasis came out of the water and stood in front of Morgan who was still seated. "Our time is up."

"Wow, already? I've actually learned so much tonight!"

Amasis shook his head and admonished in a caring tone, "But not the things you are here to learn."

CHAPTER 8

PERSONALITIES

Most often, Morgan never knew who'd be there to greet her in Lucid World or where they'd meet. They couldn't tell her in advance because they didn't know in advance. They had team meetings before their guests' avatars arrived and divided resources accordingly.

Morgan was surprised to realize that Khyan, Amasis, and Iris had very different personalities. Even though Khyan and Amasis were different ages, and Iris was a girl, Morgan had assumed they would behave more similarly to one another due to their common trait of not having khaos emotions.

Khyan was enthusiastic, analytical and practical. The project had been his idea, and he oversaw all aspects of it eagerly and sensibly. Morgan found he was nurturing and intuitive. Even though she saw him least often, he seemed able to anticipate her feelings and needs.

Amasis was easygoing and time flew by when they were together. He always had some activity or special location planned to help her relax and to make their sessions fun. When he gave Morgan answers to questions, or ideas to think about, his explanations were easy to understand and often entertaining. He was the most flexible if they deviated from planned lessons, and they often talked about things Morgan was interested in.

Iris often seemed deep in thought. Likely she was. When she spoke, as Morgan had noticed when they first met, her appearance changed and she 'lit up'. While she took on a vivacious quality, her voice was full of calm, peace and wisdom. Iris was passionate about science, and her preferred area of study was geophysics. She was focused on receding icecaps and glaciers, and new technology to better camouflage Lucid World. When she put her serious studies aside, she was very creative.

Morgan thought Iris's talents were wasted on a bunch of ice and rocks. Yet Iris seemed to love such things and was passionate whenever she talked about her studies.

Morgan wanted to have more in common with Iris than just khaos studies, so she did some reading on geophysics. Morgan soon realized it would take a long time to become well enough informed to have a meaningful conversation on the subject. She approached it from a different angle.

"Iris, I was reading about what the earth is made of, plate tectonic forces, faults and stuff. Can I ask you a question about that?"

"Sure!"

"What did the first tectonic plate say to the second tectonic plate?"

Iris's former expression of keenness turned into one of confusion. Then she grinned and said, "I don't know, do you?"

With a stern avatar face, Morgan said, "There's too much friction between us."

"Haha, that's good."

"So then, what did the second tectonic plate say?" asked Morgan.

Without waiting for an answer, Morgan delivered her punchline, "It's not my fault."

They both roared with laughter.

Iris was mindful about using their time together in the most productive way possible; so she used the geophysics joke as an opportunity to teach Morgan about the khaos that can hide in humour.

A joke is a form of communication and a potential conduit for khaos-driven emotions and behaviours such as anger and superiority. A joke can also be a conduit for positive intentions, to help people relax in uncomfortable situations.

What about the joke Morgan just told? If laughter and bonding are desirable behaviours, how do you know when humour is khaos driven?

"It depends on the underlying emotions and motivations," said Iris.

A HEATER BUTTON JACKET

"Now Arlene, I'm saying I have no idea what a heater-button-jacket is. I'll ask Ryan about it."

Meredith put down the phone. She turned around, put her hands on her hips and asked, "Ryan, what's a heater-button-jacket?"

Ten-year-old Ryan sat at the kitchen table across from Morgan. They were both working on homework.

Ryan looked down to avert her accusing eyes, crossed his arms and slid down in his seat mumbling, "It's just something Jimmy and I were talking about."

"Talking about? Do you have a heater-button-jacket?"

"Well, nah, no. I told Jimmy it would be a good invention."

"Hmmm, I think you did more than that. Jimmy's mother just told me, you told Jimmy that you have a heater-button-jacket. According to her, not only do you have one, you were wearing it today and showed him how it works."

"Well, he always wants to have what someone else has, so I thought I'd play a trick on him."

"Now Ryan, what is a heater-button-jacket and what trick did you play on Jimmy?"

Ryan replied while raising himself out of the chair. "I'll show you."

He sauntered sheepishly toward his bedroom. When he returned, he was holding the new jacket Meredith bought for him on the weekend. He put it on. It was a casual style and had shiny smooth snap buttons on the front pockets.

Ryan stood, in an open stance, and demonstrated. "This is a heater-button-jacket. If I feel cold, I push this button to warm the jacket up." He touched the snap button on his right pocket. "If I feel hot, I push this button to cool the jacket off." He touched the snap button on his left pocket. "You see. It's a heater-button-jacket."

Morgan laughed, but stopped when she thought about what she learned from Iris concerning khaos and humour.

Meredith, too, laughed but stopped. She looked at Morgan and then back at Ryan. She said, "Ryan Kith, we taught you better than that."

"It was just a joke, Mom," defended Ryan.

"Now Ryan, playing jokes at the expense of someone else is mean."

Ryan shrugged his shoulders. "Everyone does it."

"That doesn't make it right. Just think how you'd feel if someone played a trick like that on you."

Ryan grinned, "I'd think it was funny."

Meredith crossed her arms and titled her head in an expression to show 'I'm not amused'. She said, "Now, I want you to phone Jimmy and apologize. After you're done, pass the phone to me."

Meredith sighed, "I need to tell his mom there's no such thing as a heater-button-jacket," and shook her head. A slight grin appeared as she thought to herself, 'She wanted to know where she could buy one for Jimmy. Oh my.'

CHAPTER 9

THE VISIT

Meredith had a tentative expression on her face as she walked out the back door to find Daniel. She found him puttering in the garden shed as he often did on Sundays.

He looked up from a paint can he was prying open and said, "Uh, you look like you just ate a lemon."

"If I haven't, I probably will. Winifred just called. She and Enid asked to come over for coffee. There's something they want to talk to me about."

Daniel mimicked her 'sour lemon' expression and said, "Well, that can't be good." He stood up. "Need me to have your back? I can get cleaned up before they get here." Looking down at the paint can he added, "Uh, though I wanted to paint the fence today."

Meredith let him off the hook, saying she'd meet with them alone. She went inside to put on a fresh pot of coffee.

Before long, the front doorbell rang. Taking a deep breath, Meredith opened the door.

There stood Enid and Winifred. Enid wore a navy sweater-jacket over a navy dress, with a short pearl necklace. Her perfectly arranged short platinum curls revealed matching pearl earrings, part of the set. Heavy wrinkle lines pointed towards her thin tight lips.

Winifred wore a tan skirt suit and a beige overcoat. Her shoulder-length blunt-cut hair was steel grey at the roots with browner hues closer to the ends. Other than crow's-feet lines at her eyes, her skin was flawless. Meredith couldn't help but wonder how much younger Winifred would look without grey in her hair.

As Meredith welcomed them into the living room, Winifred said, "We're sorry to intrude on your obviously busy schedule, but we need to speak with you about an important matter. We didn't see you at church, so here we are."

Meredith ignored the church remark. Once they were settled on the living room sofa, Meredith called Morgan. She introduced her, and asked her to bring in the coffee and cake.

From the kitchen, Morgan heard the two women explain the reason for their visit. Winifred and Enid were co-chairs of the church committee sponsoring a refugee family. It was up to them to oversee settling a family in Coyote Flats.

They said they had come across an obstacle Meredith might help them with. They needed to find housing for a family of seven. There weren't any homes available to rent with a suitable number of bedrooms and they hadn't raised enough money to build a new house. Even if they had, there wasn't time because the refugee families were arriving soon.

"So can you help us?" Enid asked.

"I'm sorry, I don't understand. Help how?" asked Meredith.

"Help find housing, of course," replied Enid.

Morgan came into the living room holding a tray with hot coffee. Meredith jumped up to help her.

As soon as her mother's back was turned, Morgan noticed Enid roll her eyes to the ceiling as she made eye contact with Winifred. Winifred returned the look with a slow head-shake that seemed to denote agreement with Enid and disbelief at their hostess.

They didn't seem to care that Morgan could see their non-verbal insults to her mother. It struck Morgan that it was like watching mean high school girls.

As Morgan went back to the kitchen, she heard Winifred say, "Well, don't you work as an accountant at the hospital? Aren't you the one who found a house for the new doctor and his ridiculously large family? My sister-in-law's a doctor at the hospital and that's what she told me."

"Ahh," Meredith stuttered. She seemed shaken by the tone of Winifred's curt remark, but she recovered, and said, "Yes, I helped. That was right around the time that the new subdivision was built."

Enid cut her off. "Well, that's not an option for us. We asked and there's nothing available."

"Does it have to be right in Coyote Flats?" asked Meredith.

Apparently it did. To fulfill the conditions for the sponsorship, the family needed to be able to access various services. If no member of the refugee family had a valid driver's license, which they initially wouldn't, it would be impossible for the committee to fulfill their sponsorship obligations.

Enid raised her arms in the air in a gesture of exasperation. "Well, that's it, Winnie. The church has to withdraw its sponsorship application. Meredith was our last hope. She doesn't have any special housing connections."

"I may not have any special connections," said Meredith, "but since we've been talking I've come up with a few ideas."

It was the strangest thing. Enid and Winifred said they came for her help yet they shot down every idea. Either they had already tried some version of it, or it had too many obstacles, or according to them, someone on the committee would hate it.

Meredith said, "Now, I don't think being negative will solve anything. You should keep a positive attitude. Have you tried?"

Morgan didn't hear anymore. She finished in the kitchen and went outside to check the progress of the fence painting.

Daniel, Dylan and Ryan were stationed at separate fence sections. Dylan and Ryan were laughing and glancing over at one another's progress. Daniel called out to them, "Boys, I know you're having fun with your fastest painter competition. Just be sure the job is done properly."

Seeing Morgan, Daniel said, "Hey, grab a brush and give us a hand. Put one of these old shirts on top of your clothes." He motioned to the box of painting supplies.

Morgan chose a section of fence which ran along the far end of the driveway. As she got into the rhythm of brush-brush-dip-brush-brush-dip, her mind wandered to the conversation she'd just heard and, in particular, her mother's suggestion to keep a positive attitude.

She realized she'd been applying the paint too thick, and some of it ran to the other side of the fence. She went around to the neighbour's side of the fence and hoped they weren't watching as she fixed her sloppy work. She set about the task as quickly as possible.

The fence was about four feet high and Morgan was invisible to the driveway side of the fence as she bent over to complete the task. She heard footsteps and voices. She looked through the fence planks to see Mrs. Bittar and Mrs. Meany leaving. Their car was parked next to the fence and Morgan heard one of them say, "Who does she think she is? How dare she insinuate we're not trying hard enough?"

Morgan stood still and listened carefully. She heard Mrs. Bittar say, "My sister-in-law says Meredith's always been a know-it-all. You know I didn't even want to ask for her help, but it was the only way to get the committee off our backs. At least now we can tell them that even the person who found housing for the new doctor's family didn't have any answers."

"Well, Winnie, maybe now they'll drop this whole refugee idea and we can get the elevator to the choir loft. My knees aren't getting any younger, you know."

"All of that positive attitude stuff. How does she think things work? Houses don't just magically appear because a person's happy."

"Why, of course they do. Just go to the store and buy some 'happy dust' to sprinkle around." They laughed, got in the car and drove away.

POSITIVE THINKING

That night, in Lucid World, Morgan told Amasis about the visit from Winifred Bittar and Enid Meany and the refugee housing conversation. Amasis was sitting at a potter's wheel, shaping a lump of clay. He had placed a chair facing across from him for Morgan's avatar to perch upon.

He told Morgan that he agreed with Meredith's positive attitude advice. Thoughts go into the subconscious as ideas. The subconscious then looks for opportunities to manifest the ideas as events in the real world.

Morgan nodded. "I've heard about this; if you want something, all you have to do is think about it."

Amasis grimaced. "You're referring to 'the law of attraction'. The principle is 'like attracts like'. Positive attracts positive; negative attracts negative. Unfortunately, it overlooks the importance of effort."

"I'm confused. So does positive thinking work or not?"

"Thoughts can help us to notice opportunities; and thoughts can cause us to notice problems."

Morgan asked again, "So does positive thinking work or not?"

He laughed. "Yes, it works. But positive thinking alone can't achieve a desired outcome. Action is required, too."

Amasis placed a finger close to the clay bowl he was forming, but didn't touch it. "If I want to alter the shape of this, just thinking it won't make it happen. Now if I place my finger right on the clay as it spins … watch what happens."

"Wow, the whole shape changes."

"So, as you can see, just thinking about changing the shape doesn't make it change. What positive thinking does do is this: it gets me thinking about ideas of how to change the shape. That is the prelude to my action of touching the clay, and creating the change you saw."

"So is it khaos to not use positive thinking?"

"Positive thinking can be just as illogical and problematic as negative thinking. For example, if someone believes everything will be fine when a disaster is occurring and doesn't react to control the situation, things get worse. Sometimes people need to be concerned so they can take appropriate action."

"I thought worry was a khaos emotion?"

"It is. Coming up with practical realistic solutions to a problem is not a state of worry. Worry thoughts are unproductive; problem-solving gone awry."

CHAPTER 10

THE PARTY

Morgan fidgeted with her necklace. She was in the back seat of a car, beside Cara. Cara's father was driving. He was taking them to an un-chaperoned party but he didn't know that. The girls concocted a story that their classmate, Katey, was having a birthday party sleep-over and her parents would be there. Morgan was glad her parents went shopping that afternoon, so Cara's dad ended up driving them. Had her mother driven them, she would have asked non-stop questions and may have learned the truth about the party.

To the girls' credit, they had come up with a plausible and perhaps impenetrable story. The party was at Katey's house and was a birthday party, but not for Katey.

Jeff, Katey's older brother, was turning eighteen. Their parents were out of town. Since they were new in town it was unlikely that Morgan's parents or Cara's parents would ever talk with Katey's parents about the birthday party.

Morgan told Khyan she was staying at a friend's and they would probably stay up late talking, so she'd be unable to communicate with Lucid World that night.

All obstacles had been taken care of. It was Saturday night. All the popular kids would be there and Morgan didn't need to go home at her normal curfew time. It would be the best party ever! Well, maybe not the best party ever, but definitely the best party Morgan had ever gone to.

As they drove up to the house, Cara's father said there seemed to be a lot of cars parked in the driveway and on the street. Morgan felt a surge of panic. She looked at Cara. Cara leaned forward in her seat so her mouth was closer to her father's ear, as if that was necessary for a driver to hear a passenger in the back seat, and calmly replied, "Oh, Katey's family has prayer meetings at their place on Saturday afternoons. Some of them must have stayed to have birthday cake."

Cara's father grunted, nodded his head and said, "Some people really like to celebrate birthdays. I don't know what all the fuss is about. Everyone has to be born on a particular day, don't they? Oh well, I guess birthdays keep the card companies in business." He chuckled at his joke and then changed his voice and mannerism to say, "Make sure you girls remember to mind your manners and to say please and thank you. I'll be out front at ten tomorrow morning. Don't keep me waiting. I have golf at eleven."

Cara and Morgan stood at the curb holding their knapsacks, waving goodbye to the rear window of the car driving away. As soon as it went around the corner, they burst out laughing.

"Really? A religious meeting! How'd you come up with that?"

"Oh, when I told my parents about the sleep-over, they were, um, really asking a lot of stuff about Katey's family. I said they moved here from Lethbridge and were really religious. So obviously my dad doesn't know anything about them."

Cara reached into her pocket and retrieved her lip gloss. "Did you see how happy he was when he pictured us sitting around eating cake and singing kumbaya songs?" She applied her lip gloss and held it out towards Morgan, "You want some?"

As they approached the house, they heard music and voices. The sounds beyond the door caused Morgan to feel a pang of guilt for lying to Khyan. It was curious, she thought. She didn't feel guilt for lying to her parents. As far as her parents were concerned, she only felt worry about getting caught lying. She supposed the difference was her parents were old and always said 'no' to anything fun or different. It was probably more complicated and there were other things to consider, but it would have to wait because the door swung open to greet them and Jeff stood there holding a tray of green jello in small containers.

"Hello lovely ladies. Hola, hola. Please, I mean por favor. Accept my welcome gift of margarita shooters. Lime jello with tequila."

Jeff was tall, and he hunched down so the tray was elbow level for Morgan. His speech was slightly slurred, and he seemed to have trouble holding the tray straight. Morgan wondered what time he and the others had started.

Morgan had never had hard alcohol or spirits. Her parents sometimes poured her a small glass of wine with dinner on special occasions; and she'd had beer which she and Cara snuck from Cara's dad's fridge in his garage. She didn't know if tequila would be the same or different, but thought, 'How bad could it be? It's just flavoured jello.'

Trying to look confident and worldly, Morgan reached for a tiny plastic cup containing the shiny green gelatin and said, "Gracias." Cara, too, took one and the girls 'clinked' plastic cups as if they were drinking champagne out of expensive crystal.

Cara wished Jeff a 'happy birthday' and they talked. Morgan stood quietly off to the side. Jeff was attractive and older. She was nervous. She thought about what Amasis would say if she asked him how she could control nervousness and feel relaxed. 'Morgan, ask yourself why are you nervous? If it's because you want to be liked, consider why that's important to you. You don't need the affirmation of others to bring you happiness. You want people to know the real you and not some made up person.'

'All right,' thought Morgan, 'here goes.' She felt a surge of confidence.

Her confidence may have come from the imagined conversation, or the tequila. She interrupted, "So Jeff, margarita shooters are actually like potato chips. You can't have just one."

Morgan was surprised at her own voice. 'Was that rude or funny?' she wondered.

It must have been funny because Cara and Jeff both laughed.

While holding the tray out for Cara and Morgan to take another, Jeff chortled and said, "We could make potato chip shooters. Vodka mixed in with sour cream and spices and then a dollop on a ripple potato chip."

The conversation didn't go any further because Katey came to the front door where the three were standing and said, "Come on you two. Let's move into the real party. Jeff, some people just arrived at the back door. Go be a proper host."

Cara and Morgan obediently followed the attractive blond. Katey was less than a year older than Morgan and Cara. However, she looked, acted and dressed much older. Katey was popular with boys and it was rumoured that she had sex with several. Morgan didn't care about the gossip concerning Katey. Katey was 'in' with the popular kids and was always friendly to Cara and her.

The three girls walked through the living room to the kitchen. At the table, a boy stood behind an assortment of bottles and coloured liquids. Katey said, "This is the official party bartender. He'll fix you up with drinks."

The 'official bartender' was a bit chubby. He wore sloppy clothes, had a bad complexion and beamed at the mention of his title. Morgan hadn't seen him at school. As if she'd read the question in Morgan's mind, Katey answered, "He's my cousin Matt, visiting from Lethbridge."

Morgan recognized beer, wine and scotch whiskey in the bottle-scape on the table but the rest was foreign to her. Morgan was just about to say, "I'll have a beer," when Cara announced, "Oh I'll have a scotch. Um, make it neat."

Morgan wondered where Cara had learned how to order a scotch drink. Then she remembered seeing Cara's dad watching TV in his recliner chair and holding a glass filled with amber liquid.

Matt reached for a green bottle and filled a glass half-full with scotch. It was Morgan's turn to order a drink. She decided beer was too ordinary and tried to think of something clever to ask for. "I'll have a martini, shaken not stirred."

"What kind of martini?" asked Matt.

"Whaa... What'd you mean?"

"I mean what kind? Gin, vodka, cosmo, or other? Served on the rocks, or straight up? With olives? With lemon? So I repeat: what kind of martini?"

"Matt, don't be a jerk," scolded Katey. "She'll have a cosmopolitan." Katey looked over at Morgan and nodded her head, assuring, "You'll like it."

Matt poured liquids into a jar. First clear, then red, then clear again. He reached a chubby hand into a bucket, grabbed a handful of ice and 'plopped' it into the jar. He swirled the mixture together and then used his fingers to strain the fluid into a glass. With a wave of gusto he squeezed a wedge of lime into the glass and handed the drink to Morgan.

Katey again admonished Matt, but this time for his bar tending ways. "Matt! It was bad enough when you used your hand instead of an ice scoop. Using your hand as a strainer is disgusting! Show some manners PLEASE."

Matt turned red, crossed his arms and snapped, "Well, that shows how much you know. No one in Lethbridge has a problem with it and they're not stupid country bumpkins from a place called Corny Farts."

Cara chimed in, "Oh yah? If Deathbridge is so great why don't you stay there?"

Katey looked like she was about to say something more, but changed her mind and instead said, "Come on, you two, let's get to the real party."

They followed Katey through the hall and down the stairs to the lower floor. Along the way they saw friends and acquaintances from school, and others Morgan didn't recognize. Morgan imagined there were already at least twenty people there and wondered how many more would be coming.

When they got to the lower floor, Katey excused herself to greet other friends who had arrived. Cara and Morgan settled into a sofa in a corner of the room and looked around.

Cara sipped her drink slowly and Morgan suspected Cara didn't really like scotch after all. Morgan's drink, was yummy, in spite of Matt's hands, and she found she was drinking it rather fast. In a low voice, for Morgan's ears only, Cara commented on the people at the party: who they knew, what they were wearing, who was with who.

Morgan, also in a low voice, or so she thought, said Jeff and Cara seemed to hit it off. Did Cara like him?

Cara opened her eyes widely at Morgan. Morgan interpreted the look to mean she was talking too loudly.

"Oops, sorry," whispered Morgan, with a giggle, "Do you think Jeff is cute?"

"Um, he's not available, and he's gay."

"He's gay? I didn't know that."

"He told us, silly, when we were at the door. He said his boyfriend was coming to the party after he got off work. I thought you looked a little zoned-out."

Morgan finished her drink. She put the glass down on the adjacent table. It made a "thunk" sound. Cara laughed, "Oh that was really graceful."

The party got louder, and the lights got dimmer. Morgan looked around. Jeff was playing with controls on the wall. A group of guys were playing beer pong across the room. Based on the cheering and splashing, the game appeared to be well underway. In the centre of the room, some girls were teaching each other dance moves. The way they flipped their hair and swung their hips showed they imagined they were sexy and worth watching. Morgan thought, 'Not!' She spotted a group of classmates standing in a circle and chatting. She got up from the sofa and made her way over to them. This behaviour was unusual for Morgan because she was shy to talk with a group of people, especially if they were not her immediate friends.

As she joined them, Morgan stumbled slightly on the edge of the area rug they were standing on. She flushed red at this embarrassment. The distraction of her arrival caused the group to stop talking, so Morgan felt the onus was on her to say something. She looked at their hands and noticed they were holding beer cans.

"You're drinking beer. So you missed the 'Matt the Jerk Bartender' experience?"

One girl wrinkled her forehead and asked, "Who?"

"Matt. Katey's weird cousin from Lethbridge. What a lummox."

One boy explained, "Must've missed him 'cause we came in the back way and straight downstairs."

The girl who asked 'who?' said, "Speaking of weird, did-ya see what Sally wore yesterday? I didn't think it was possible to have so many fashion faux pas at one time. Hahaha."

Morgan swallowed hard. Even before her Lucid World training began, she never liked mean-spirited talk. Maybe it was because she felt sorry for the person, or imagined she might be the topic someday, or believed in God or Karma, or was compassionate.

Whatever the reason, the comment took Morgan out of her margarita/cosmopolitan-induced happy state.

Disparaging remarks about the girl named Sally, and Sally's mother, lasted several minutes and then they moved on to criticize other classmates. Morgan wanted to say something, and knew she should, but remained silent.

The cruel comments and jokes had livened up the group. Someone made rounds with a tray filled with an assortment of Matt's specialties. When the tray approached the group, Morgan grabbed the closest drink she could reach. The conversation had not yet lost its momentum and Morgan was extremely uncomfortable. She drank fast. It tasted lemony and sweet.

She felt nauseous. She thought she should go back to Cara and sit down. As she turned to go, Morgan began to heave. A slow-motion greenish-red waterfall spewed from her mouth. There was no controlling it. It had a destination: the shoes of the circled group!

"My shoes!" "My new kicks!" "OMG!" "Someone get her out of here!" "No, not like that, now it's on my pants!"

It stopped. No one moved. Then, there was a flurry of activity. They took off their shoes, and Katey quickly arrived on the scene with cleaning supplies.

Cara took Morgan to the bathroom to clean up and put her in Katey's room to lie down.

Morgan slept in the spot Cara placed her and didn't wake until early morning. When she woke, the bright morning light was streaming through Katey's window. No one had thought to close the curtains last night.

The sensation of waking came in stages. First an awareness of the previous evening's events but lack of clear details. Then shards of memories. The more awake she became, the more she remembered.

The embarrassment! How could she ever face them again? Them. Everyone. Everyone at the party would tell everyone. So, everyone!

Maybe it was a bad dream, and if she went back to sleep, when she woke it would be different.

She remembered vomiting on everyone's shoes. Then she

feared what she didn't remember. Morgan buried her head in the pillow. It was because she lived in Nosos. If she lived in Lucid World, it wouldn't have happened. No one in Lucid World would give her strong drinks.

News reports told of people seeking refugee status with 'first world' countries. Maybe she could do likewise and ask for asylum in Lucid World.

She was thirsty. She got up and walked towards the bedroom door. A voice stopped her. "Oh, you're alive." It was Cara. Cara had been sleeping on the other side of the bed. Morgan didn't know she was there.

"Um, how do you feel?"

"Terrible, actually."

"Do you need me to go to the bathroom with you?"

"No." Morgan put her face in her hands. "I'm so so embarrassed … so sorry … really sorry."

"Oh no big deal."

"No big deal! You saw what happened!"

"Yeah, I saw what happened. Someone had too much to drink and put some footwear out of commission."

Cara had a way — a way of putting things so Morgan couldn't imagine things any other way.

Morgan laughed. The crisis had been eased. At least for the present.

CHAPTER 11

OLD NEWS / NEW NEWS

Not everyone was as forgiving and understanding as Cara. When Morgan went to school on Monday, she was the target of jokes and the subject of whispered conversations. Some of the boys filled their cheeks with water and walked past Morgan spewing water from their mouths. She was dubbed with the nickname 'Barfie Doll'. The nickname paved the way for even more jokes.

The whispers lasted only two days, but the jokes and quips continued. Morgan felt morose and detached. She avoided everyone at school except for Cara. She didn't speak to anyone in any of her classes and hid in the library during breaks and lunch. After the school day was done, she left to walk home as soon as possible. She didn't wait for Cara. She messaged that she was already on her way home.

She never told her Lucid World friends about the party and what happened. Lucid World was an escape. She begged for more time during each session. She countered Khyan's concerns regarding the quantity and quality of her sleep with explanations of going to bed earlier so she could spend more time there and learn more. They negotiated and Khyan conceded an extra half hour each evening.

The real reason Khyan conceded to extra time was because he sensed that something in Morgan's waking life was causing her considerable distress. He shared his hunches with Iris and Amasis. They agreed something seemed 'off'. Morgan no longer spoke about her life in Coyote Flats. When asked about family, friends or school, Morgan evaded the subject by saying, "Nothing new. Nothing interesting."

Khyan wasn't the only one who sensed Morgan's silent suffering. Luna sensed it, too.

Luna was a young Egyptian Mau cat with a silver-white coat bejewelled with markings of black spots. She tried to jump onto Morgan's lap. Surprised, like a cat walking on glass for the first time, Luna quickly adjusted to the absence of a corporeal body and made herself comfortable on the chair where Morgan's avatar perched. Avatar-Morgan was semi-translucent, and it appeared as though Morgan had a cat inside her body. This notion, combined with the attention from Luna, delighted Morgan. They conversed, Morgan with warm words and Luna with passionate purrs. Morgan couldn't feel purr vibrations but had no problem hearing purr sounds.

After that, it was a frequent event. Arrangements were made for Luna to attend meetings with Morgan and join her in body and space.

In Coyote Flats, Morgan quarrelled with her brothers and ignored her parents. She rolled her eyes and shrugged her shoulders. She said she had stomach cramps and stayed home from school.

Her parents sent her to their family doctor who said it was not uncommon for a young woman to experience discomfort while her body was changing and maturing. The doctor advised she take ibuprofen and go back to school.

After the doctor provided an explanation, Morgan could sulk and lie around in her room without challenge from her family. But Cara was not so easily fooled. She knew Morgan was not suffering from cramps. The aftermath of the party was the real reason for Morgan's behaviour. Cara tried to end the teasing by admonishing anyone she heard make Barfie Doll jokes, but her efforts only made it worse by drawing more attention to it.

The teasing reached beyond school via social media cyber-teasing. Morgan stayed away from the computer other than to do homework. She blocked everyone on her phone except Cara. After school and on the weekend, she sat in her room playing melancholic music and writing dark poetry. She went to bed early and tried to fall asleep as fast as she could, hoping to accelerate her visit to Lucid World.

Sometimes while she waited for sleep to come, she fantasized about a different life. She imagined she lived in Lucid World with Cara. Along with Iris they were all best friends. Hmmm, what do teens in Lucid World do for fun? She'd ask Iris about it next time she saw her.

She thought about Lucid World's ancestors and empathized with their struggles and decision to depart. She wished her ancestors had been among those who escaped so she could have been born in Lucid World.

She avoided Cara because she was always trying to cheer her up. The only time she didn't avoid her was in the morning so they could walk to school together. Most mornings, her tormentors loitered at the front door to the school building. She felt less vulnerable to their teasing when she wasn't alone.

One morning, while walking to the corner where she routinely met Cara, she looked closely at the details of her surroundings. The buildings, fences, and sidewalks were all so ugly. The sky was overcast and grey. The wind was blowing. A gust of wind blew sand into her eyes. The grass was brown. There were no flowers or leaves. It was spring and too early for foliage. When the grass turned green and there were flowers in the yards, the ugliness would still be there. How did she not see this before? It was a terrible place. Lucid World should not try to unite with Nosos World and all of its ugliness.

The next morning, as she approached the corner, she saw someone was there, but it wasn't Cara.

It was Amasis?! She quickened her steps. It was him! He was dressed the same as the night they first met: blue jeans and a purple T-shirt. Instead of his usual slippers, though, he wore red running shoes.

His dark eyes flashed when he said, "Cara told me how unhappy you are. I've come to take you to Lucid World to live."

"You talked to Cara? How?"

"When we took an imprint of your brain signal, Cara was nearby and our instruments also recorded hers. I've been worried about you, so last night I contacted Cara while she slept."

"How can I actually live in Lucid World? I might spread khaos."

"Most of the time, you'll be quarantined. You can attend virtual school. You'll leave quarantine when we have our usual sessions together."

"That sounds lonely."

"Cara said you spend most of your time alone now and dread going to school. This way you won't have to go where you're tortured. Also…"

"Also what?"

"Also, I can spend time with the real you and not just your avatar."

Amasis held out his hand and Morgan put her hand into his. The contact was both comforting and thrilling. It was also surreal. She said, "I feel like I'm dreaming?"

"You're not dreaming. You're in Lucid World."

"That was fast. It already happened!"

"What happened?" asked Amasis.

"I'm here. I'm actually here!"

"You're here just as last night and the nights before. Here as an avatar."

His T-shirt was yellow, and he was wearing his usual slipper-like footwear, not red running shoes. They were standing on the rooftop balcony above the art gallery with the animal stone carvings, where Amasis had eaten his garguey meal. Luna was sitting in a chair waiting for her.

She had to think fast. She couldn't tell Amasis she'd been dreaming he came for her.

"Um, yah — It's a Nosian greeting. 'I'm here' means you have my attention and I'm ready to learn."

Amasis moved his head to flip his hair out of the way and replied, "Well then, let me say *paratus sum docere.*"

"So what does that mean?"

"It's Latin and means I'm ready to teach."

They settled around a table and Amasis talked about something he referred to as 'victim khaos'.

Morgan was adept at controlling her avatar and able to display body language and facial expressions suggesting she was listening intently. She wasn't. She was watching rather than listening.

Amasis was stocky and muscular, but so gentle. His eyes were so intense, yet kind. When he smiled or laughed, as he often did, it was infectious. The way he flipped his hair out of his eyes with a quick upward move of the head was adorable. Details she had never thought about.

Before now, she never saw him as attractive. Now she could see that he was. Not in a dashing handsome way, but in a charismatic charming way. It was as if she saw him for the first time. Why was she seeing him differently all of a sudden? If she found him attractive, did he find her attractive?

"Morgan, can you see how this is khaos?"

The sound of her name jarred her back to the current conversation. She had seen him gesturing his hands but did not understand what he'd been saying. She said, "Kind of. Though, I'm not sure."

"They see themselves as a victim. The world is out to get them, nothing good ever happens. This defeatist outlook impairs their efforts to succeed at tasks and sets them up for failure. This creates more hardships, and a cycle is perpetuated."

Her thoughts were now turned towards the dialogue, and away from appearances. She wondered if the topic applied to what she had been experiencing since the party. She asked, "So what if something bad actually happened to the person, and kept happening, and they actually tried to fix it but they just couldn't. Is that victim khaos?"

"Unwanted outcomes will happen. It's a normal part of life."

Morgan looked disappointed with his answer. He added, "Having a problem is not really a problem. Expecting otherwise, or refusing to deal with a problem, is a problem. Problems are unavoidable; self-pity is khaos."

The next morning, Morgan reflected on her dream to escape to Lucid World. She remembered what Amasis said about problems and self-pity. She wasn't doing anything to improve her circumstances. What could she do? When she protested the taunting, her tormentors taunted her all the more. When she ignored them, they invented new taunts to get her attention.

When she first met Khyan, he told her about a force which would try to stop her from reaching her goals. Perhaps this force was the meanness of others that had caused her many khaos emotions and thoughts. If only she had a textbook to explain more about the force. When she asked for a textbook, Amasis told her she could find answers relating to khaos no matter where she looked.

She looked through the titles of the books on her shelf, and speculated what book might provide the answer. She spotted a book titled, "The Lives and Times of Cats". It reminded her of Lucid World because of her friendship with Luna.

Morgan took the book from the shelf and with her thumbnail pried it open to a random page. She browsed the two exposed pages. The page on the left-hand side was the end of a chapter and seemed to deal with a cat's fastidious washing behaviours. The page on the right-hand side held a chapter title, 'Why Cats Purr.' 'Purrfect,' thought Morgan, 'Luna often purrs'.

She skimmed the chapter. It included many of the likely reasons cats purr, such as pleasure, communication, and to relieve stress. The last paragraph, in particular, caught her attention and she read it carefully.

Scientific evidence suggests a cat's purr is a healing mechanism to offset long periods of inactivity which would otherwise contribute to a loss of bone density. Cats purr during inhalation and exhalation with a consistent pattern and frequency between 25 and 150 hertz. Such frequencies have been shown to improve bone density and promote healing in both animals and humans.

She put the book down. 'Interesting, that could be the answer: washing and healing.'

She needed to 'wash' away the experience and 'heal'. How? She felt regret and intense shame for having done something disgusting and unacceptable that had been witnessed by so many. She'd lost her dignity and whenever she tried to get it back, she was soon reminded of her shame.

About three weeks after the party, the teasing suddenly stopped. The nickname vanished. The story of Morgan's drunken behaviour was 'old news'. There was 'new news'. Katey was pregnant!

Katey admitted her condition openly and announced her plans.

She would keep her baby and her parents would help her raise it. With such openness and honesty, how could there be much fuel for gossip or blather? To the contrary, there was plenty of fuel: the fuel of speculation. Who was the father? Katey was popular with boys but didn't have a steady boyfriend. So did Katey even know? Did the father know?

Katey's pregnancy had another ramification for Morgan. Meredith decided it was time for them to have 'the sex talk'. That evening, on the phone with Cara, Morgan repeated what she could recall about the 'talk' and they had a good laugh.

Cara told a funny 'sex talk' story she overheard her aunt telling her mother. When Cara's aunt explained to her daughter how babies are conceived, the girl, who was the oldest of three children, said in an alarmed tone, "Oh Mom, you did *that* with Dad three times?!" This story sent Cara and Morgan into spasms of laughter. It was the first time since the infamous party that Morgan allowed herself to let loose and laugh.

Life soon went back to the way it was before the party, with two exceptions. One, Morgan had a greater empathy for victims of the abuse her teen peers could deliver; and two, Morgan had a greater fear of becoming such a victim. So while she felt sorry for the targets of unkindness, she kept away from any attention which might put her back in the spotlight for teasing and gossip. She avoided anyone who was the current favourite target, such as Katey, and she steered clear of any ongoing targets, like Sally.

CHAPTER 12

FRANNY & SALLY

*Kittens' play may be fun for kittens but can be
injurious to human playmates. Scratches and
bites are painful and can easily become infected.*
— from "The Lives and Times of Cats"

Sally rushed into the bathroom and shut the door. She sat on the edge of the bathtub and put her face in her hands. Her wavy black hair fell forward. She reached for a tissue and blew her nose. Then she went to the sink and ran cold water. She cupped it in her hands and splashed her face. After she patted her face with a towel, she inspected it in the mirror. Her short broad nose was red, her cheeks were flushed and her hazel eyes were watery.

She had retreated to the bathroom to hide her face from her mother. She didn't want her crying to be the fodder for another tirade on the topic of the people of Coyote Flats.

Today, on her way home from school, she had passed a group of pre-teen boys. Unlike their parents, these boys had not mastered the social skills of disparaging someone without the person's direct knowledge.

Though her name was Sally, the boys called her other names and made a game of throwing dirt clumps at her. What had she done to bring about this mistreatment? One thing and one thing only, yet it was enough. She had been born to Franny Frey.

Franny was different from other single mothers in Coyote Flats. She didn't care what others said or thought of her, but not because she had lucidity. Franny's way was far from the lucid way.

Her actions were self-destructive. Drinking dulled her pain, but it ultimately made her feel worse. Her sexual activities were unsuccessful efforts to receive and give love, and, like the drinking, made her feel worse. The men did not love her nor did she love them.

Franny was no longer the subject of frequent gossip. She had been judged and labelled long ago. Many of Franny's judges and labellers went to church on Sunday. There, the Reverend preached words of compassion, forgiveness and acceptance to congregants. Some heard the words, but didn't listen. Had they listened, the words could have opened their minds and they might understand that they did not practice what was preached. Some listened and understood, but made exceptions or excuses for themselves. Some neither heard nor listened and only went to church so their absence would not fuel the conversation of others.

THEN THEY CAME FOR ...

There have been times in history when terrible things have happened and people were afraid and didn't speak up, such as during Nazi Germany. Another time, less well known, was when dirt clumps were thrown in Coyote Flats.

Like the others, Morgan did nothing to intervene. One night, she talked to Khyan about it. She and Khyan were seated in cushioned armchairs. Luna had her own chair beside them.

"But what could I have actually done? If I told them to stop, they wouldn't. Or they'd just pick on me instead."

"Your answer can be found in some words from a man named Martin Niemöller[2] who lived in Nazi Germany." Khyan recited the words to Morgan.

> First they came for the communists,
> and I didn't speak out because I wasn't a communist.
> Then they came for the trade unionists,
> and I didn't speak out because I wasn't a trade unionist.
> Then they came for the Jews,
> and I didn't speak out because I wasn't a Jew.
> Then they came for me
> and there was no one left to speak out for me.

He then said, "We shouldn't stand aside and let oppression occur because we aren't a victim of the oppression."

"Didn't the words also say one day we might become a victim and there will be nobody to defend us?"

"I think there's a less selfish reason. Injustices happen not only because people can behave unjustly, but because other people do nothing to stop them."

Khyan reached over to pick up Luna and put her on his lap. He scratched her behind her ears and she purred wildly.

Morgan's avatar attempted a smile but her forehead looked sad. "How do you stop having emotions?"

"I have emotions, many emotions. I just don't have the ones caused by fear in non-threatening situations; like envy, insecurity and anger."

"I get the connection with fear and insecurity. But envy and anger?"

"When humans feel fear, they experience a fight-or-flight reaction. This is appropriate for life-threatening situations."

"Like being chased by a bear?"

Khyan set Luna back on her chair and said, "Most situations are not of the 'chased by a bear' sort."

He stood and grabbed a lint roller from a nearby shelf to remove the fur from his pants and shirt. As he 'rolled' he said, "Envy and anger are old emotions. They once served humans in the struggle for survival. Envy resulted from the fear of not having enough of something. Anger resulted from fear related to a threat. To feel envy or anger, when not necessary for survival, is khaos."

"So if envy and anger are because of a fight reaction, what does a flight reaction cause?"

Khyan sat back down and leaned in towards Morgan, "You mean other than the obvious, like running away from a bear?"

Morgan laughed.

Khyan leaned back, "Using drugs or alcohol 'to escape' is a flight reaction and is khaos. Substance abuse can't solve threats, life-threatening or otherwise."

Morgan remarked that people with khaos don't experience unfounded fear all the time. Different people feel fear in different situations. Was there a way she could identify what situations might trigger an unfounded fight-or-flight response for her?

Khyan suggested she consider what transpired just before the khaos reaction. What was she thinking about? What did she see, smell or touch? Also, early childhood memories might reveal insights into the ways she perceived the world.

Morgan pressed Khyan to share one of his earliest memories. He described when he saw Nosos World the first time. He was seven years old, and he come along with his father as he performed maintenance on the icecap projection field.

"We stood on top of the mountain. Fresh snow sparkled in the sunlight. It was immensely bright, so I turned my eyes away and looked up to the blue sky. When my eyes adjusted, I looked down. I saw rocks, then green valleys and then sweeping golden plains. The air moved past my body and I felt it on my face and in my hair." Khyan stretched his arms out wide, "The wind made me feel so alive!"

He then held his hand above his eyes and said, "I had to shade my eyes from the intensity." He dropped his arms onto the cushioned chair arms. "I thought, 'Nosos World is beautiful' and I knew I wanted to end khaos."

In a sudden move, Khyan slid his arms to the edge of the arm rest, leaned forward and spoke eagerly. "I knew I wanted to pilot a helicopter so I could see more of Nosos World."

Khyan shared that he was studying helicopter instrumentation and navigation. Soon he would fly as a co-pilot.

It was Morgan's turn. She closed her eyes and described a memory of a spring day when she was five years old.

Just like Khyan, she remembered the wind. It was light on her face and brought delicate fresh scents to her nose. She and Dylan moved erratically, like bumblebees, exploring a meadow next to their house. A gentle sun beckoned chartreuse sprouts that reached upwards. The soft blue sky was lined with wispy swirls of clouds.

Dylan, enthralled in his own discoveries, hadn't listened to any of Morgan's calls to come her way. Desperate to gain his attention, she shouted, 'Come see the bird nest I found.' He hurried over.

There was no bird nest. Morgan made it up so her brother would explore the meadow with her. He was panting when he arrived at her side. She pointed, and they started in that direction. They walked only a few feet and discovered a bird sitting on its nest camouflaged by tall grasses. The bird took flight, leaving the nest and eggs behind.

Morgan's mouth shaped into a conspiratorial smirk, "It was like magic. I thought, 'if I imagine something, it can happen'!" Her face became serious, and she opened her eyes, "It was just a coincidence. But I wish there was magic in the world, and I could cure khaos."

"You don't need magic. You already have it. With every decision you make and every action you take, you conjure your own magic. You have great power. We all do."

"What about the power to actually cure khaos and unite our worlds?"

"Yes, I believe we have that power too."

THE CAT WALK

Sally was late for school and tried to go to her seat without disrupting the class. A boy strategically moved his foot in front of Sally's hurried path through the aisle.

Sally stumbled and her shoes made a clopping noise as she righted her balance.

The teacher stopped talking. Looking sternly at Sally, who was finally seated, she said, "Miss Frey, if you're done upstaging my lesson, I'll continue."

As Morgan observed this scene of classroom politics, she reflected on the words 'injustices happen not only because people can behave unjustly but because other people do nothing to stop them.' She wondered what a braver person, free of khaos fears, would have done in the situation.

In Lucid World, she asked Amasis what he would have done.

They were walking along a path through a garden of ferns. Next to the path a stream flowed over rocks into small waterfalls.

Amasis said, "There are two parties who acted mean-spirited:

the bully and the teacher. Let's first talk about the bully. I would speak to the bully after class and explain how his actions were hurtful to Sally."

"I don't think that would actually make him stop."

"It should be said. Bullies should be chastised more often."

"So what about the teacher? What would you say to her?"

"Probably nothing: students should respect and obey teachers. However, if the teacher often belittled students, I would consider talking to the school principal, or my parents, and let them decide what should be done."

"So you wouldn't actually do anything to stop the injustice?"

Amasis stopped walking and faced her. "There's more. I'd tell Sally I saw what happened, and it wasn't her fault. I'd encourage her to talk to me when she needs someone to listen or to help her defuse the bullies."

Morgan thought about how hard it had been for her when she was teased as 'Barfie Doll'. "It's impossible to defuse bullies."

They started walking again and Amasis said, "They are defused when they don't get what they want. If Sally acts shocked or paralyzed and gets upset or cries, the bullies get the reaction they want, a reaction which will set her up for more. Sally could change the pattern and not reward the bullies for their behavior."

"How?"

"She could say something short and neutral and walk away."

Morgan pointed out that Sally hadn't been able to do that when she was tripped in class. Amasis agreed that course of action couldn't be used all the time. But when it could, she could say a simple phrase like 'stop' or 'not funny', something that feels right to her. She shouldn't insult her tormentors or react in any way other than to say the planned phrase and then remove herself from the situation. Not engaging with bullies neutralizes their affronts.

Even though it may be hard to do, she could try to ignore them, by pretending she didn't hear them or by acting uninterested in their insults. Above all, she shouldn't show anger or fear.

"Also, I'd coach her to never allow bullies to lower her self-esteem. I'm sure there are many wonderful things about her. Remembering these things can help her cancel out the taunts she hears from bullies."

Morgan took in the serenity of the garden, and said, "Those all sound like good ideas but you've never gone to school in Nosos. You don't know what it's actually like."

"I understand. Bullying is khaos-driven. If bullies don't get reinforcement, the bullying is negated."

"So Sally should stop worrying about what others think? I've tried to do it and it's not working for me."

"Morgan," Amasis stopped walking so he could face her, "to become the adult you want to be, you need to think and act using your own judgment, and not others' judgements or criticisms. And because different people will have different perceptions, there may be a wide variety of such criticism."

Morgan threw her arms up into the air, "So no matter what I do, someone will think I should have done it differently?"

"There's an Aesop's[3] fable which makes the point rather well."

They sat on a bench looking down into the stream. Amasis removed his neck device from inside his shirt and verbally instructed the computer to display the story. Black letters on a white background appeared in front of them. Morgan didn't recognize the language.

Amasis translated, "A miller and his son were driving their ass to a neighbouring fair to sell him."

Morgan giggled. Amasis stopped reading. "What's funny?"

"You said ass," chortled Morgan.

"It's another word for donkey. Or rather, it was when the story was written. Since the word donkey is more commonly used today, shall I use the word donkey?"

"I'll stop laughing. Go ahead. Read it the way it is."

Amasis touched his device and the story image disappeared. "I'll modernize the story. It'll deliver the same message but you'll be able to better relate to it."

Amasis opened an imaginary book and pretended to read. Once upon a time, there was an incredibly handsome and smart man who lived in Lucid World.

Morgan laughed. Amasis stopped pretend-reading. Morgan quizzed, "So what was the name of this man?"

Amasis grinned. "Let's just call him Amasis." They both laughed.

Amasis noticed Luna sitting on a rock watching the water in the stream. He continued.

One day, Amasis and his friend, Iris, were carrying one of Elder Tabubu's cats in a cat-carrier. They were taking the cat to the cat clinic for a check-up.

Luna, hearing the name "Tabubu" and word "cat", left her vantage point and joined them on the bench.

Morgan said, "Wait a minute. Do you actually have cat clinics in Lucid World?" But what she was really thinking was, 'Wait a minute, you and Iris were hanging out together?' and felt a pang of jealousy.

"Does that surprise you?"

Morgan shrugged and said, "I guess it makes sense you'd have a vet for cats." But she was really thinking, 'I guess it makes sense you'd be friends with Iris and do things with her,' and felt a flash of hope that it was only a friendship and nothing more.

Amasis continued.

They'd gone only a short distance when they were stopped by a man who looked into the carrier and said, "Why don't you take the cat out, put a leash on its collar and let it walk beside you?"

Hearing this, Amasis and Iris took the cat out of the carrier and put a leash on its collar. They walked on with the cat following them on the leash until they were stopped by a woman with her young child. The woman looked down at the leashed cat, assessed the situation and said, "As you walk, the cat has trouble matching your pace. Why don't you take the cat off of the leash and just let it walk beside you?"

The well-meaning friends took the cat off the leash so it could freely walk alongside. They had almost reached the cat clinic. "Pardon the intrusion, but is that cat with you?" asked a young man. "Yes," replied Amasis. "Oh dear," responded the young man. "If a loud noise frightens the cat, it may run away. If that happens, you may have great difficulty finding it."

Not wanting to chance losing the cat, they picked it up and carried it. Amasis held onto the cat's front legs and Iris held on to the cat's back legs.

The cat, not liking the uncomfortable posture, broke free and ran away, but not before scratching Amasis and Iris.

While looking for the cat and calling its name, Amasis and Iris realized that by trying to please everybody, they pleased nobody. Their hands and faces had been scratched and, even worse, they lost Elder Tabubu's cat.

Amasis slammed his hands shut, akin to slamming a book shut, for dramatic effect.

Luna was scared by the sound and jumped off the bench.

Morgan bent down to console her, but her non-corporeal hands passed right through her.

They howled with laughter as Amasis scooped Luna up and put her back on the bench between them.

CHAPTER 13

THE RETURN OF THE HEATER-BUTTON JACKET

Meredith walked to the window and looked out at the street. She sighed. It was the third time in the past five minutes that she'd gone to the window.

"Mere, they probably just lost track of time. When I was a boy..."

Meredith swung around. "Yes, yes, I know. I've heard your stories. You grew up on a farm. This is a town. Now it's sugar beet season and with the extra workers, there are strangers in town." She turned back to the window.

Daniel walked over to his wife, put his arm around her shoulders and said, "Hey, I know you're worried but I'm sure they are fine. They know better than to go off with..."

Meredith cut him off again. "What if they were in an accident? What if a car hit them when they were running across the street?" She sighed and said, "I've told the town council we need more controlled crosswalks."

"Dylan has a phone. One of them would have called. Someone would have called. They aren't all that late. When I was a boy..." Daniel stopped mid-sentence.

"But why don't they answer the phone or text me back? You look for them and I'll phone their friends."

"Mom, let's wait before doing all that." Morgan was sitting in the corner of the room working on her homework. "How embarrassing. Dad driving all over town and you phoning all over town, just because Dylan and Ryan are late getting home. Besides, you make us come home way earlier than other kid's parents do."

"I don't care what the other…" There was a sound at the back door and Meredith flew to it. Daniel and Morgan followed.

Greeted by their anxious mother, the two brothers stood in the entryway. Ryan's heater-button coat was ripped. Dylan had a black eye.

Except for the black eye and ripped jacket, the boys were remarkably similar in physical appearance and stature. Both were an average height and build for their age, with Dylan being taller and bigger because he was older. They both had light brown hair and had been told, by their mother, they were very good-looking. On this particular evening, they shared another appearance characteristic: they looked identically sheepish.

"There you are! We were worried sick. What happened to your eye, Dylan? You were in a fight!?"

"Hope the other guy looks worse than you do," said Daniel.

While still standing in the entryway, Dylan relayed the 'official version' of the events.

Later, when Meredith and Daniel were out of earshot, Dylan and Ryan confided the 'real story' to Morgan.

They were on their way home from hanging out with friends. They'd lost track of time and were afraid they'd be late. To save time, they took a shortcut across a vacant lot where they came across Jimmy.

Jimmy and two other boys were hiding in a weedy patch, smoking cigarettes. Dylan and Ryan passed by within a few feet of them.

Dylan saw them first. He motioned to Ryan. Ryan shook his head and whispered, "Nah, keep going or we'll be late." After the heater-button affair, Ryan worried Jimmy might seek revenge. So he avoided him.

But it was too late to 'keep going' without notice. Jimmy saw them, raised an arm and motioned them over. Dylan and Ryan semi-obeyed and moved a few feet towards him.

"Well, fancy seeing you here. You look like you're in a hurry. Are you going home to your mommy?"

The boys with Jimmy chortled. They were older and larger

than Jimmy. Jimmy and Ryan were in the same class in school. Dylan was two years older. The two boys with Jimmy were in the class between Ryan and Dylan.

One of the large boys sneered, "I wouldn't be hurrying home if I were them. That's where Barfie Doll lives."

Dylan nudged Ryan and said, "Come on, let's go."

Jimmy asked, "Barfie Doll?"

The same boy answered, "She's their gross sister who barfed all over everyone at that party."

Ryan countered, "Oh yeah? I hope you were there and she barfed all over you."

Those were fighting words. The boy jumped up and grabbed Ryan's jacket by the lapels. "Okay, take that back or I'll make you take it back."

Jimmy said, "Be careful, you might rip his heater-button jacket."

"Is that what this is? The famous heater-button jacket! Hahaha, too bad it's not a creep button jacket. If it was, I'd turn this creep off! Hahaha."

Everything happened so fast no one knew who did what first and to whom. Jimmy was the only one not directly involved in the action. This is what appeared to happen:

Ryan kicked at the boy holding his jacket. The boy hollered and jumped back. The other boy jumped up and grabbed Ryan from behind. Dylan screamed, "Whoa guys, that's enough! Stop right now!"

The boy continued to hold Ryan from behind. The other boy who Ryan had kicked, advanced towards him. Dylan jumped in front of Ryan and blocked the advance. Ryan was wriggling. The boy holding him tried to get a better grip. After a commotion of arms flailing about, Dylan made an "ugh" sound and grabbed his eye.

The action stopped. The boys stood still with their arms at their sides and looked at Jimmy. No one spoke. Dylan put an arm around his younger brother's shoulders and they ran off.

They got to the sidewalk and walked until they were certain they were out of range of Jimmy and his thugs. They stopped to assess the damage.

"Whoa, your coat is ripped. Mom will kill you."

"It's nothing compared to the shiner on your eye."

"Let's go sit over there in the park and figure out what we'll tell Mom and Dad. We'd better hurry and figure something out soon though. Mom's been phoning and texting."

In silence, the two brothers sat on a park bench with heads down and hands on foreheads.

Their parents would be angry that they were involved in a fight, but they couldn't explain that they were defending their sister. They both knew about the party where Morgan got sick, and didn't want to get her into trouble. If their parents were angry with Morgan, she would blame them for tattling and their parents would still be angry with them for fighting. If they told the whole truth, everyone would be angry with everyone. They needed a 'truth' they could they tell their parents which would cause the least distress for everyone.

Ryan leapt up from the bench. "I know! The heater-button jacket! We'll tell Mom and Dad I was climbing in a tree, the jacket snagged on a branch and I was stuck. You climbed up to unsnag me. A tree branch ... you pushed it aside to get to me. It catapulted back and 'kapow' you got it right in the eye!"

"Whoa, that might work. But it doesn't explain why we're so late. We were late because ... because... I know! While we were up in the tree, some drunk sugar beet workers came into the park. They sat under the tree we were in, swearing, yelling, and stuff. We didn't want to come down from the tree while they were there. We did the right thing because Mom and Dad are always telling us to stay away from them. We muted the phone so the guys below wouldn't know we were up in the tree. They finally just left and we came home as soon as we could."

And that is the 'truth' Dylan and Ryan told their parents. No one got angry and the only downside was that Dylan and Ryan were told to stay away from the park and not to climb trees. Later that evening, they told Morgan an accurate version of the truth and the upside was that Morgan agreed to do some of their chores to show her appreciation.

DANIEL'S MUSINGS

Daniel stood at the bathroom mirror. He looked down, reached for his toothbrush, applied toothpaste and looked back in the mirror. Holding the toothbrush, not moving, he stood looking at his reflection. It was the first chance he'd had to be alone to reflect upon the events of the evening, and his hurt feelings for the tone Meredith had used with him.

He was thankful the boys were home safe and sound and the evening's drama was concluded. He suspected the events were different from what the boys had described.

He thought about a verse written long ago by one of his favourite poets, William Blake. 'A truth that's told with bad intent beats all the lies you can invent.'

The boys were likely involved in something they knew would upset their parents, so they replaced the truth with fiction. He trusted his sons to be responsible and compassionate. If a fiction had replaced the truth, it wouldn't be to cover up acts of meanness, greed or apathy. It was more likely they avoided an expected problem with a creative solution.

Daniel didn't believe broken rules and lies always warranted punishment. The way he looked at it, before passing judgment, a parent should stop and consider: Which is more important, the aim of the rule, or the actual rule? Which reveals more integrity, following rules and telling truth with no regard to consequences, or honouring the reasons for rules and truth and acting accordingly?

He wanted to share his hunches with Meredith, but decided against it. She was satisfied and relieved by their story. He didn't want her to get agitated again. Also, his suspicions were founded on nothing other than a hunch, based on his own boyhood adventures.

Daniel looked at his reflection in the mirror. His hairline had receded. There were wrinkles on his forehead, bags under his eyes and deep creases between the edges of his nose and corners of his mouth. He realized, for the first time, he looked like his father. He didn't feel like he imagined his father felt. It occurred to Daniel a person has three different ages: a chronological age, calculated based on the number of years since a person was born, a physical age related to the body's health and fitness, and an internal age, the age a person feels and acts. Daniel felt like a young man, fresh out of college, ready to make his way in the world. He wasn't the man he saw in the mirror.

How did others see him? Did they see the man in his forties, reflected in the mirror? Or did they see the man in his twenties, reflected in his heart?

Morgan was their first child, and when he and Meredith were expecting, many people gave unsolicited insights. 'Just wait until you become a parent, it will age you overnight.' Those comments made him determined to be an energetic father and to never blame his children for his own limitations. Had he kept his resolve? Reflecting on his life, and not his reflection in the mirror, Daniel decided yes, and he would continue to do so.

He never tried to be a friend to his children. Children need parents to teach and guide them in their early years. But, there's nothing wrong with enjoying their time together and having fun. He wanted his children to grow up understanding that fun is an important part of life and it makes people feel most alive. He didn't want them to fall into the trap of believing fun was unproductive, and therefore unimportant. The human brain was evolved to have fun. So not only is it instinctive and fundamental to human existence, it helps develop problem solving, adaptive abilities and relieves stress. 'That's my story,' he thought, 'and I'm sticking to it.' He chuckled.

Meredith often complained that because of his carefree and fun loving attitude, she had to take on more of the role of the disciplinary parent. He didn't agree. She chose to be that way. It worked for her. He commanded respect and authority with the children in spite of his twenty-something internal age. He didn't know what Meredith's internal age was, but he suspected it was much older than his. How were they compatible?

When they first met, just holding her hand made him feel happy in a way he'd never felt. As they got to know one another, they realized they had similar values and appreciated each other's humour. Daniel 'got' Meredith's dry sense of humour. He adored her wit and charm. Meredith bloomed around carefree Daniel. She tapped into her playful self.

Meredith often struggled with letting go and just living for the moment. Daniel called her a control freak, in a laughing, loving way. She said she knew it and she owned it. But there was more to it. She didn't need to control everything; she didn't need to control others, just certain situations: like tonight. It's who she was.

He let go of his hurt feelings, forgave her, and turned his mind to the matter at hand—brushing his teeth.

CHAPTER 14

KARLEEN

In contrast to the Coyote Flats hospital personnel in uniform, Karleen wore a tailored dress and high heels. Office file folders poked out of the top of her large designer handbag.

As she stood in front of the cafeteria coffee station and touched her short blonde hair, she said to herself, 'You can't have caffeine this late in the day.'

She reached for the decaf pot and stopped. 'After what happened today, I won't sleep tonight, anyway. I need a decent coffee.'

At the cash register, a woman holding a cafeteria tray was telling a story to the cashier. Karleen imagined the woman telling the story probably worked at the hospital, and since she wasn't wearing a uniform, probably in an office.

The cashier looked past the woman and at Karleen. The woman turned towards Karleen, apologized for holding up the line and stepped aside. In doing so, she knocked a glass of juice on her tray. She attempted to grab the glass before it completely toppled. This was an ill-conceived move that caused the juice to splash out, all over Karleen's legs and feet. The woman apologized profusely and insisted on paying for Karleen's coffee. Karleen escaped and retreated to a table to enjoy her coffee and think.

Her solitude did not last for long. The woman carried her tray of lunch, and refilled glass, to Karleen's table and asked, "Can I join you?"

"Sure." Karleen didn't want any company but couldn't think of anything else to say without sounding rude.

The woman sat and held out her hand for Karleen to shake while saying, "I'm Meredith."

"Karleen — with a K."

Meredith commented on the unusual name. Karleen explained her parents had chosen the name Karl for a boy. It was the name of a friend of her father. She never met Karl but he must have been a pretty good friend since they made her his namesake, in spite of her not being a boy.

Meredith said she'd seen Karleen at the hospital before.

"I sometimes have business with hospital patients. What about you?"

"I work here in the finance department. What type of business are you in?"

"The kind where I have days like today and wonder if anything I do truly makes a difference."

Karleen was surprised at her confession. Did she really just tell a stranger she was frustrated with her job? She was certainly frustrated. Evidently she needed to vent. She was aware of situations in which people admitted to confiding personal information to strangers. She supposed it was because a stranger's input was more likely to be impartial. Also, the prospect of disapproval was less threatening because there was nothing invested in the relationship.

Karleen kept talking. She was a social worker. Funding cutbacks caused a moratorium on hiring new staff, but her department had just lost several senior people. She was pressured to close files before they were resolved to her satisfaction. "What's the point? I'm not helping anyone. All I am is a paper-pusher. If I wanted to do that, I would have become an accountant. Oh, I'm so sorry. You said you work in the finance department, didn't you?"

Meredith laughed and said, "I'm not offended. But you know, you'd be surprised how much an accountant can help people by 'crunching numbers' and 'pushing paper'."

"How?"

Meredith explained how she worked within the budget to operate the hospital. She prioritized spending needs and looked for ways to eliminate unnecessary costs. When there wasn't enough money for essentials, she made herself a nuisance to those in charge of the purse strings and bombarded them with data showing how patient care would be compromised if they did not increase funding. She also used external sources of funding like events and private donations.

Karleen said, "Wow. I wish you worked for our department."

Meredith laughed.

Karleen said, "Today was the same old thing, there's a family who still needs my help but I have to close the file and move on to the next case."

"Oh my, that's frustrating."

"I can't say any more. Coyote Flats is a small town."

Meredith made a scoff-like exhaling noise. "Don't I know it. You should hear some of the gossip that goes around this hospital. Sometimes I think the gossip is more infectious and contagious than any of the diseases the patients might have."

They were no longer strangers. A friendship emerged. They sketched out their lives to one another.

Karleen lived in Lethbridge. Her office was there. Her territory encompassed Lethbridge and the surrounding area including Coyote Flats. She was divorced. They never had children.

Meredith described her family. "My husband Daniel works at the sugar factory. We have three kids: Morgan's fifteen, Dylan's thirteen, and Ryan's eleven."

"Those are active ages, especially for boys. They must keep you busy."

Meredith laughed, "Now that's for sure. The boys are close. They spend a lot of time together and look out for each other. Still, I worry. Just the other night they got home late, I was worried sick. When they finally got home, it was obvious they'd been in a fight. They gave some concocted story about a tree. Dan fell for it. Not me.

"Indeed. What'd you do?"

"I didn't push it. I suspect Dylan got into a fight while looking out for Ryan. That's what I want them to do: look out for each other."

"What about Morgan? I sure remember when I was her age. There was a time…" Karleen sighed and looked down into her coffee cup, "I couldn't grow up fast enough."

"That's Morgan! She says we treat her like a child. I tell her that until she's an adult living on her own, there'll be rules." Meredith put both hands on the table and leaned forward towards Karleen. "It's the other things."

"What things?"

"A couple of months ago, she began acting distracted and superior to everyone. Then," Meredith shook her head sideways, "she went through a moody nasty stage and didn't want to go to school."

Meredith positioned herself straight against the back of the chair, "The doctor said it was probably menstrual cramps. I don't doubt that. But I know Morgan well enough to know something else was going on."

"Did you ever find out what?"

"I suspect it was something at school. Well, whatever it was, it suddenly stopped. One day she came home from school and she was our Morgan again."

Meredith looked up at the clock on the hospital cafeteria wall. She needed to get to a meeting. They made plans to meet again.

As Meredith headed towards her office, their conversation lingered in her mind. In particular, Karleen saying she wished Meredith worked for her department to help with funding and finances.

DID YOU FORGET TO TELL ME SOMETHING?

Indoor cats can suffer from depression if their environment doesn't provide enough stimulation. - from "The Lives and Times of Cats"

Where was it? It was on the back of the chair last time Morgan saw it. Maybe it was in the laundry. She yelled out the door of her bedroom, "Mom! Have you seen my blue sweater?" No answer.

She heard voices. She walked into the hallway and listened. It was coming from outside. She looked out the window and saw Mrs. Byrd and Meredith standing on the front path talking.

Morgan opened the window to listen and heard her mother say, "Thanks for letting me know."

Mrs. Byrd replied, "No problem Mere. It's always nice to see you regardless of the circumstances," and left.

Morgan's heart leapt to her throat, and she exclaimed two words in a whisper, "The fence!"

She heard the front door open and her name called out. Morgan headed back to her bedroom. She hoped her mother would think she'd gone out. It was always best to delay these things until her father got home.

She closed her bedroom door, moved some magazines and clothes out of the way, and sat cross-legged on her bed. How angry would they be? After all, she wasn't the one who stole the truck and crashed into the fence. She would tell them the same story Cara had told her parents. 'It wasn't that bad, was it?' She recited the story in her head. 'Cara wanted to surprise her parents with an anniversary dinner. She needed the truck to go to the store. I tried to talk her out of it, but couldn't. I didn't desert Cara. Friends look out for one another.'

Everything made sense as far as the story went. One detail remained outstanding. Why hadn't she told her parents about the accident?

There was a knock on the bedroom door. Belts hanging on hooks on the back of the door made a clanging sound. Her heart jumped. She grabbed a magazine, opened it and set it in front of her.

"Morgan, can I come in?"

Before Morgan could answer, Meredith walked in. She stood, with her arms crossed, in front of Morgan sitting on the bed. "Whatcha doing?"

"Just flipping through a magazine and thinking."

"'Bout what?"

"Nothing in particular, just thinking."

"Now while you're thinking, you might think about whether there's something you forgot to tell me."

Morgan tilted her head to look up to the right corner of the ceiling and tapped fingers against her pursed lips. "Hmm. Can't think of anything. Like what?"

Meredith shifted her stance and put her hands on her hips. "I'll give you a hint. It was important."

Morgan sat upright. "I forgot to do something important!?"

"Noooo, you forgot to tell me something important."

"So if I forgot to tell you something, I must have forgotten what it was."

"Now that surprises me because you usually have a good memory. In the future, I suggest you write important things down."

"All right, write what down?"

"Honestly Morgan. What's the matter with you? Are you taking drugs?"

Morgan hastily crossed her arms. "Of course I'm not taking drugs." She glowered at her mother. "I didn't tell you about Mrs. Byrd's fence because…"

Meredith threw her hands up into the air and dropped them to her sides. "What does Mrs. Byrd's fence have to do with anything?"

"Ahh, isn't that why she just came over? To tell you Cara's dad's truck hit her fence?"

Meredith's forehead wrinkled, eyes squinted and nostrils flared. "What? Why would she do that? Why should I care about Cara's father's truck and her fence?"

Meredith stared incredulously at Morgan, exhaled and said, "She came to tell me about some town bylaw changes."

Morgan replied, "Oh," in what she hoped was a voice implying indifference. It was difficult to feign supposed indifference because in her head, a voice was screaming, 'Oh no, she knows about the party!'

Meredith sighed, "Morgan. We used to be close. Lately, you've been aloof and detached. I feel like we're growing apart. Now my friend Karleen says…"

"That's it! A lady named Karleen called yesterday. You were taking a shower, so she left a message. Oops! Sorry, I forgot to actually give you the message. So you must have talked to her."

Meredith mumbled something indiscernible and left. Morgan scurried to the bathroom in case she came back to ask questions about Cara's father's truck and Mrs. Byrd's fence and whether there was more to it.

While in the bathroom making running water and flushing noises, and staying clear of her mother's purview, Morgan contemplated the lies and details of events she hadn't shared with her parents. She lied about her motive to go to Katey's house and later never disclosed she got drunk and sick. Before that, there was the truck-fence accident. 'Why? Well, what happened at the party and with the truck weren't technically lies. They were experiences. What about the lie to get permission to go to the party? What about the lie Dylan and Ryan told, to protect me, when they were actually in a fight?'

Her brothers' lie was theirs, not hers. Although she was glad they lied, she didn't ask them to. So the only deception she needed to sort out was the reason she lied about going to Katey's house on the party night. Morgan clearly remembered why. If she had told her parents she planned to go to an un-chaperoned party and stay out late, they would have said NO.

She considered her mother's comment: they were growing apart. She seemed hurt when she said it. Morgan supposed it was true. They weren't as close as they used to be. Why was that? Was it because of her Lucid World secret? No, probably not. It was more likely because she was getting older and didn't want her mother questioning and interfering in her decisions. Morgan didn't want to hurt her; she would make more of an effort to talk with her.

Her mother seemed stressed and irritable lately. Maybe it had something to do with work.

She was glad her mother had a new friend, Karleen, to talk with. Her mother's reference to Karleen suggested they had discussed mother-daughter relationships. Could she, Morgan, cause her mother's cranky mood? If so, it wasn't her fault, was it? In Lucid World she learned happiness is not achieved by outward conditions. Happiness is found within a person's own self. She wasn't responsible for her mother's happiness or unhappiness, was she? Something didn't feel right. What? She thought back to the meadow memory she shared with Khyan when everyone and everything was carefree and happy. Things seemed simpler back when she was younger, and before she had knowledge of khaos.

She turned her thoughts back to Meredith. Maybe she should help her mother find a hobby.

MEREDITH'S MUSINGS

Meredith went to the kitchen, turned on the kettle and sat at the table. She put her head in her hands and sighed. 'Now that didn't go well.'

She'd only gone a few steps down the hall when she realized the error of her ways. She went back to apologize but Morgan was in the bathroom, probably avoiding her.

'Why'd I do that? So what if Morgan forgot to give me a message? Why'd I approach it that way and put her on the defensive?'

And the comment about taking drugs; she didn't think Morgan was taking drugs. She did it to get a reaction in response to Morgan's passive aggressive behaviour towards her. 'That was stupid, stupid.'

She couldn't help but think Morgan had been keeping something from her these past few months. And that upside-down magazine Morgan was supposedly reading on her bed, to hide whatever she was doing, now that was kind of funny when you think about it.

Meredith thought it was probably her own fault. It's human nature for someone who believes rules to be strict, without room to negotiate, to be secretive. The converse is true for someone who is given trust and freedom. She trusted her children. But 'children' was the operative word. They were children and needed to be protected. She never wanted them to feel unprotected and unsafe. She never wanted them to feel the way she had when she was young.

In her earliest memories, her parents fought. Meredith, an only child, was afraid of her father. He had a bad temper and took it out on Meredith and her mother. Sometimes he hit her mother and Meredith felt helpless.

When Meredith was a pre-teen, her parents divorced. Not long after, her mother remarried. Her stepfather had two teenage boys. Meredith had her own bedroom, but no one respected her privacy. Her stepbrothers went in and out of her room as they pleased. It used to be their room, so they resented Meredith having it. They also resented their new extended family because now their father spent his time, and money, on his new wife.

It seemed as though her stepbrothers purposely timed their entry into her room to coincide with when she was undressing.

Meredith complained to her mother and asked for a lock on the door. Her mother told her she would ask them to knock first, but she needed to stop exaggerating and learn to get along with her new brothers.

The brothers knocked before entering but made a game of how fast they could open the door after they knocked. Meredith felt she had no privacy and no one to protect her.

She would protect her own children no matter what. She never wanted them to feel unsafe or unloved.

Privacy, hmmm. In her efforts to protect Morgan, she often asked her a lot of questions to keep Morgan away from unsafe situations. This might make Morgan feel a loss of privacy. If Morgan was keeping things from her that may be why. Morgan needed privacy.

Meredith shook her head. How did she not see that sooner?

The kettle whistled. Meredith got up and fetched her favourite teacup from the cupboard.

CHAPTER 15

SCHOOL DANCE

In May, days were longer and the weather warmer. Spring was Morgan's favourite time of year. But two things diminished her enjoyment of the season.

First, the school year ended in June. Students were required to study for exams and complete assignments. Meredith and Daniel imposed a regimented study schedule on Morgan, Dylan and Ryan. But Cara's parents did not have the same rules for her.

The other 'thing' related to the school spring dance. Most attended the dance with a date. Morgan wasn't romantically involved with anyone, and she didn't have designs on anyone; anyone in Nosos, to be more precise. The boys she'd found attractive before now seemed foolish and immature.

Ever since she dreamed Amasis came to Nosos World to rescue her after the 'Barfie Doll' incident, she viewed him in a different light. Besides thinking of him as a mentor and a friend, she now also thought of him as boyfriend material.

Morgan had an idea. If someone from Lucid World had come to Coyote Flats to register her brain waves and install equipment, why couldn't Amasis come to Coyote Flats for the dance?

WHAT'S A DATE?

Amasis sat on a bench in a park, facing a patch of shrubs filled with birds. Lucid World had many such green spaces. Plants thrived in the spectrum of light waves emitted by the dome ceiling equipment.

The park often attracted indigenous species of birds. The birds could easily navigate in and out of the cave, through bird-friendly passageways. Several rose finch had arrived this morning. The males were red with pink spots. The females were a pale grey-gold with brown markings.

He wanted Morgan to see them. He would show the others, too. Today Iris met with the Nosos youth from the earlier time zones. Morgan lived in one of the later time zones and she was his first meeting of the day.

He heard the song of a rose finch and mimicked its twitter fyu-fyu-fyu-fyu-fyu. He stopped and listened. Had one of the birds replied? He imagined Morgan having a conversation with the birds and smiled.

Morgan and the others from Nosos had changed his view of those afflicted with khaos. Before he met any of them, he imagined they would be afraid and angry. It was not at all that way. Rather, their fears and resultant emotions were often subtle and sometimes hard to detect.

Sometimes he forgot all about khaos and simply visited with the Nosos youth. He was easily distracted from his planned agenda. Morgan, it seemed, was the most prone to get him off topic. During a progress meeting, he discussed this with Khyan. Did Khyan want him to try harder to stay focused?

Khyan suggested Amasis's approach was fine and would serve their objectives. When the Nosos youth were relaxed and off-guard, they were more likely to slip into khaos behaviour unique to them. And that was the khaos each of them would have the most difficulty identifying and reversing.

Amasis checked the time on the device around his neck and instructed the computer to start transmission with Morgan.

Within seconds, Morgan appeared a few feet in front of him. In the distance, a father and young child witnessed the appearance of Morgan's avatar. They stopped for a moment while the father explained what they had seen.

"Sit beside me," Amasis said, "and keep your eyes on that bush over there."

"What are we looking at?"

"Birds. I have an optical enhancement device so I can zoom in. You can tell the computer to do the same with your avatar's vision."

They watched the birds flitting in the bushes and hopping on the ground. They listened for song calls and called back to them.

'Amasis is so much fun,' Morgan thought. 'I have to ask him.' So she broached the subject by asking if they had dances in Lucid World.

In Lucid World, they had events with music. People danced if they felt like it. Morgan explained how it worked in high school in Coyote Flats.

"What's a date?" asked Amasis.

"It's someone you go to the dance with, and then you dance with that person."

"How are dates assigned?"

Morgan frowned. "They're not. If you have a boyfriend or girlfriend, you go with them. Otherwise, you have to ask someone or wait for someone to ask you. The spring dance is actually only two weeks away and I don't have a date."

Amasis looked at her and tilted his head, "Why don't you invite someone as a date?"

"It's complicated. If I invite someone, they might think I like them for a boyfriend, and there isn't anyone at school who I like that way."

"What happens if you go without a date?"

"It depends. It's all right to go without a date with a bunch of friends, but only if no one else has a date. If I go with friends who have dates, it won't be any fun. People on dates pay attention to each other and ignore everyone else."

Amasis shrugged his shoulders, "Then go with friends who don't have dates."

"That's the problem. All my friends have dates." Morgan pursed her lips.

"Do you have to go to the dance?"

"No, but I don't want to miss out."

Amasis again tilted his head. "What would you miss?"

"Seeing what everyone wore, the decorations, and who went together and if anyone ended up together. Everyone'll talk about the dance for days afterwards. I'd be left out."

Amasis nodded assuringly. "I can help with this."

"Great! Yes, you can be my date! We'll have so much fun and you can see my high school and meet Cara. She'll ask where I know you from. I'll figure something out."

Amasis reached his hand over to Morgan's shoulder and stopped when he remembered she was non-corporeal. "Morgan, slow down. I can't be your date."

"Why not? Do you have a girlfriend?" Concerned that her voice may have betrayed her feelings, she casually and cheerfully said as she shrugged her shoulders, "That's all right. Just come as my friend."

"Morgan, my physical body is thousands of miles away from Coyote Flats."

"I know, but someone from Lucid World actually came to Coyote Flats already. He took an imprint of my brain signal."

"That was me, but..."

Morgan had always suspected it was Amasis who Cara saw on the day they hit Mrs. Byrd's fence. His eyes fit Cara's description to a tee.

"That was carefully planned and organized. A helicopter and pilot were deployed. Flight schedules were coordinated to avoid detection. It took several days. The Elders would never agree to such a trip to attend a dance."

"Why not?"

"Because every time someone leaves Lucid World, there's risk of detection and exposure to khaos. We only do it when the benefits outweigh the risks."

Morgan tried to conceal her disappointment when she asked, "So why did you say you could help?"

"I meant help you with the khaos of your problem."

Morgan had been cautious and chose her words carefully when she spoke about the dance. She avoided any reference to worrying about what others thought or peer pressure. "What parts are khaos?"

It turned out, there were several. Morgan listened and understood; but couldn't help but think everything Amasis said would be easy to apply in Lucid World and difficult to apply in high school.

After the dance talk with Amasis, Morgan decided her best option was to tag along with Cara and her date. It wasn't as awkward as she had imagined because Cara's date had single friends at the dance who sat with them. Together, they formed a congenial group and Morgan was often asked to dance.

Afterwards, she admitted to herself that Amasis may have been right and her fears were unfounded. She could see how she overreacted to the situation. Morgan shared her insights with Iris.

Iris told her about the khaos of catastrophizing: believing something is far worse than it actually is. Morgan did this in the lead up to the dance and in her predictions of going to the dance without a date.

Morgan asked, "What's wrong with thinking ahead? Didn't you tell me to be proactive to solve problems?"

"When you catastrophize, you set yourself up for failure."

CHAPTER 16

SCHOOL'S OUT!

On the last day of school before summer vacation, Morgan ran into a very pregnant Katey in the school washroom. Morgan had not seen Katey in any of their mutual classes for several weeks. Katey explained she had finished the semester from home via email correspondence with teachers.

"I didn't know that," said Morgan. "I heard a rumour that your parents sent you to Lethbridge to live with your grandparents."

Katey laughed. "I'm sure there were lots of rumours and some of them better than that."

"Why'd you have to finish school from home? Don't you feel well?"

"Well enough, other than being pregnant and all. The school board was worried parents might not want their darling children corrupted by someone like me."

"That's not fair! Kids from the most religious families are actually the ones doing drugs and bragging about sex."

"I decided it would be easier for everyone if I just went along with it."

Katey put her hand on Morgan's arm. "Listen, Morgan, I never apologized to you about what happened to you at the party. Right after that, I took a pregnancy test and found out."

"Apologize for what? I'm the one who made such a mess at your party."

"I should've known better than to have Matt make you a drink.

And I should have warned you about the drinks my brother's friends were passing around."

"I'm the one who should've known better. I think I was actually just super nervous about being there and everything."

"Oh, I sent you texts, and left you messages. I thought you were mad at me when I never heard back. This is the first time we've talked."

The door opened and someone walked into the washroom. Katey pointed her chin in the door's general direction to motion they should leave, and walked towards the door. Morgan followed.

When they got into the hall, they moved to an area away from the traffic of students moving between classes and clearing out lockers.

Katey continued. "You avoided me, so I assumed you were mad at me, and with good reason."

"I actually avoided everyone. I was so embarrassed, and I got teased and made fun of. So I stayed home in my room. I'm sorry you thought I was mad at you."

"I was so caught up in my own situation. How're you now?"

"The teasing stopped when your news came out. They forgot all about me."

"Then, why'd you still avoid me? Were you still embarrassed, even around your friends?"

"No. I did something really terrible."

Morgan's eyes welled with tears and she hung her head.

Katey put her hand on Morgan's shoulder. "What'd you do?"

"I wanted to hide that we were actually friends because, well, because I was afraid I'd be included in the jokes and mean things they said about you."

Katey moved her 'concerned' hand away from Morgan's shoulder and flung it back at Morgan's shoulder in a playful push. "That's it? That's the terrible thing?" Katey laughed. "You sounded like you killed someone or robbed a bank."

Morgan raised her head in disbelief. "You're laughing?"

"Why not laugh? Morgan, I've had to realize there are bigger problems in life than the stupid things the stupid kids at our stupid school say. I get why you'd want to avoid being hassled and how being my friend might put you in the line of fire. Take it from me, stuff like that just doesn't matter."

WILDERNESS SURVIVAL CAMP (WSC)

> Many cat owners protect their cats by keeping them safely indoors.
> It is difficult for such cats to return to a wild existence and fend for
> themselves. Domestication stifles many wild skills necessary for survival.
> - from "The Lives and Times of Cats"

Morgan and Cara stood looking at the Coyote Flats Community Centre notice board. It was the beginning of summer vacation and the following posting caught their attention:

Teen Wilderness Survival Camp for ages 15 to 18. Seeking wilderness survival skills, an outdoor adventure, or just a great time in the wilderness? A week with us will help you develop a higher level of confidence to enjoy any wilderness environment. Our experienced instructors provide you with training and knowledge necessary to cope in the wilderness while camping, hiking, or if you are confronted with a wilderness survival situation. Wilderness survival is an awareness that not only keeps you alive, it allows you to thrive and find a deeper connection to the natural world.

"Sounds interesting," said Morgan.

"Yeah. Let's do it," said Cara.

"I need to ask my parents for permission, though," said Morgan doubtfully.

"Tell them it'll be educational, supervised and could save your life in the wilderness."

Morgan laughed and countered, "I think they'll be more impressed with 'educational and supervised' than 'lifesaving'."

Daniel and Meredith negotiated they would pay half the cost if Morgan paid the other half using savings from her allowance and babysitting.

The next day, Morgan and Cara signed up. They asked to be assigned to the same tent group, but were told they would build individual tent shelters using naturally available materials. Morgan had assumed she and Cara would stay in a modern tent.

Wilderness Survival Camp (WSC) attendees were to meet in front of the Community Centre at 8:00 AM Saturday morning of the scheduled date, so they could travel together by bus to a remote area in the mountains. When the date arrived, Daniel drove Morgan and Cara to their early morning rendezvous. Morgan was excited to go on the wilderness adventure and hadn't complained too much when she had to rise early for breakfast and to finish her packing.

Packing was quite an ordeal. Morgan packed all the items prescribed by WSC as necessary as well as items recommended by WSC as optional. In addition, she packed clothing and fashion accessories she deemed necessary. When she finished her preliminary packing, she had twice as much baggage as permitted. Meredith tried not to intervene because she and Daniel had in fact considered the outing to have educational value and believed the education began with the packing. After much grumbling, complaining and texting with Cara, Morgan's knapsack resembled the maximum permitted size and she could hoist it onto her shoulders and carry it on her back.

Daniel helped the girls get their gear out of the car, hugged them goodbye, joked about avoiding wild animals and drove away. As Morgan watched him drive away, she felt a strange sense of foreboding for the trip and the unknown. She had been away from home without her parents before. This felt different. She thought about khaos and illogical fear. Was this fear illogical? She was going on a survival trip and would live in the wilderness for a whole week. Her guides were experienced experts with equipment and outside contacts if there was an emergency. She reasoned all would be fine if she followed their instructions.

Morgan and Cara were welcomed and checked-in by guides. After following instructions to leave their gear beside the bus for loading, they stood near the bus and looked around to see if they knew any of the others going on the expedition. There was a mixture of teenage boys and girls. Morgan and Cara knew several of them from school. Morgan was relieved she didn't see any of her Barfie Doll tormentors.

The group of soon-to-be wilderness-trekkers boarded the bus. Morgan and Cara chose seats at the back. Seated and settled, Morgan looked out the bus window and saw a red souped-up old sports car speed up to the bus. The car's tires screeched as it stopped abruptly behind the bus. Sally awkwardly emerged from the backseat of the car carrying a thin knapsack. Sally's mother, Franny, rolled down the front passenger seat window and yelled something at her.

Sally looked uncomfortable as she boarded the bus and sat alone in the front row behind the bus driver. A guide, carrying a clipboard, boarded the bus and addressed Sally, "I'm glad your mother let you join us and the hardship endowment was put to good use."

Sally slumped in her seat and emitted an inaudible reply. Her head drooped towards her chest and her hair fell forward to cover her face.

Morgan watched from the back of the bus. She could only see the back of Sally's head, but could well imagine the embarrassment Sally wore on her face. A conspicuous arrival, followed by a public reference to poverty, would be mortifying.

The WSC week was memorable. Morgan learned how to do things she could never have imagined. She learned how to start a fire without a match, identify edible plants, build a shelter, tell direction without a compass, and much more. She also learned how much she appreciated her home, specifically: bed, bathroom, and kitchen.

At the beginning of the week, Morgan was subjected to discomforts and inconveniences she never wanted to endure again. There were times she desperately wanted to go home. Had the teen participants not been prevented from bringing phones, Morgan would have called her parents and begged them to come for her after the first day. Within the first few hours of arriving at camp, Morgan regretted her decision to be there. After eating a bland burned meal cooked in a pot on an open fire, Morgan was informed she was on pot-scrubbing duty that day. The pot's inside was encrusted with hardened food and its bottom was scorched. Morgan's first cleaning attempt was rejected by a guide leader as unsatisfactory. She was told to scrub the pot again until all food or burnt traces were removed. All the while, Morgan begrudgingly thought that anyone struggling to survive in the wilderness should not be concerned about whether a pot was shiny or not.

Cara didn't seem bothered by the lack of creature comforts or the assigned chores. In her usual style, she made the best of things and went with the flow. Morgan wondered what made Cara and her so different. Did Cara suffer less from khaos than she?

On the matter of khaos, Morgan's visits to Lucid World were suspended while she was at WSC. It was unlikely that the range of the transmission equipment installed in Coyote Flats would reach to the mountains. Also, Khyan thought it inadvisable to communicate with Morgan's sleeping body under such uncertain conditions.

Morgan realized her time in the wilderness would not come to an end any faster by wishing it was over. She applied things she was taught during her visits to Lucid World. Soon she relaxed and enjoyed the experience and the time seemed to pass quickly. By the end of the week, she felt satisfaction for having gained new skills and appreciation for the simplicity and beauty of nature. She chortled to herself, "Haha. That Lucid World stuff really works."

There was one more memorable aspect to the expedition. It felt more disconcerting than memorable.

Some of the teen campers repeatedly played tricks on Sally and laughed at her expense. For example, when Sally practiced building a fire, they added water to her fledgling fire when her back was turned. Sometimes, Sally seemed (or pretended?) to be unaware of such tricks. Other times, she laughed along to fit in.

Morgan was conflicted. She knew she should be a friend to Sally and speak out against her mistreatment; but fearing repercussions to herself, she didn't. She knew she was a coward, and this admission caused her to feel a great sense of failure.

Alone with her thoughts while she lay in her tent shelter waiting for sleep, she listened to the sound of the wind rustling the branches of trees. One night, towards the end of the WSC week, the wind found a voice, and it whispered, 'injustices, bullying, stop them'.

Morgan reached for her flashlight, got out of her sleeping bag and crept out of her shelter into the night.

Careful not to point her flashlight at any of the other hovels, as she didn't want to be discovered, she made her way through the camp.

It was late and no one else was outside. There was no moonlight.

Everything was dark except for the stars in the sky and the glow of her flashlight. It was eerie. The wind in the trees caused the branches to make a creaking sound. Morgan imagined it sounded like a lost soul moaning. She shivered. An owl shrieked. Her heart jumped. Slowly and carefully, she meandering through the sleeping structures and stopped at Sally's hovel.

Each camper was responsible to build his or her own sleeping shelter. As a result, they varied in size and appearance. Sally's was small and rickety. Morgan thought back to the day they arrived at camp and were given the task to erect their shelters before nightfall. Friends shared materials and collaborated to securely tie tree-branch-poles. Sally built alone; no one helped.

Morgan whispered at the opening of Sally's shanty, "Sally, you awake? It's Morgan. Can I come in?"

A small voice emitted from the dark, "Okay, I wasn't sleeping yet."

Morgan crouched down, shone her flashlight inside and entered. Sally was sitting up in her sleeping bag. Morgan found a space on the ground to sit beside her.

"Are you having trouble sleeping too?" asked Sally.

"Kind of, I was thinking about something I want to talk to you about. Let's just keep our voices low so we don't wake anyone up."

"Okay." Sally reached beside her. Morgan could hear the sound of plastic rustling. Sally held a bag towards Morgan. "Do you want some cookies? My mom baked them. I have crackers and fruit too."

"Yah, sure that would be great," Morgan said as she reached for a cookie. She put it in her pocket and said, "I'll save it for later. I don't have any in my tent, since we're not supposed to actually have food in our tents."

"I didn't bring it on purpose. My mom packed it in my bag as a surprise."

"The WSC packing instructions said 'no food' because of bugs and stuff I think."

Abashed, Sally said, "She didn't know. She was just trying to do something nice."

Not wanting Sally to feel bad, Morgan reached towards the bag and joked, "Then I'd better take two to help hurry and eat them. You know, before a bug, or a WSC guide, finds them."

Sally forced a laugh and asked, "So what did you want to talk about?"

"It's about something kind of personal actually."

"Okay."

"How do you feel when people play tricks on you?"

Campers were under strict orders: no visits after they turned in for the night. Not wanting to draw attention, in the event a guide might be up checking the camp, Morgan put the flashlight under her nightshirt so only a small amount of light was emitted. In the dim light, Sally appeared as only a shadow. Based on Sally's changed posture and voice, Morgan could tell Sally was surprised at the question and hadn't expected it.

"Maybe some of the tricks are funny, I guess. But it's not like they're calling me names or insulting me."

Morgan thought back to the reprimand Ryan received, from Meredith, for playing the heater-button-jacket trick on Jimmy and what Iris said about humour and khaos: it depends on the underlying emotions and motivations.

Morgan said, "Humour is just like words. It can be nice or it can be mean. With humour, just like anything, a person can have good or bad intentions, and when it comes to bullying, it's still bullying; humour doesn't change it."

Sally's whispering voice carried a defeated tone when she asked, "So what can I do about it? I haven't done anything to cause it."

"Maybe in a way you have, by allowing it."

"How've I done that?"

Morgan sighed, "Ask yourself: what do they get from playing jokes on you? Do you look stupid so they look smart? Do you look clumsy so they look like jocks? It's actually not too late to change how they treat you."

"How?"

"You could say something short that's not an insult, in a calm voice and just walk away."

"Like what?"

"You could actually come up with some things to say beforehand like: 'stop' or 'not funny'. Say whatever feels right. Just say what you planned, walk away, and don't give them anything to laugh about."

"Okay," she said doubtfully, "maybe I'll try."

Morgan knew there was more she could do. She could offer to help confront the bullies. Instead, she said, "I'd better get back to my tent before we get caught. Good night."

For the rest of the week Morgan kept her interactions with Sally to a minimum. Sally didn't seem to expect otherwise. Tricks played on Sally continued to be a source of amusement for a certain few. Morgan witnessed an instance when Sally confronted her tormentors with the comment, *very funny*, and walked away. There was something about the way Sally did it that fueled their joke and heightened their laughter. Morgan wasn't sure what Sally could have done differently. It may have helped if Sally had an ally to share her indignation and reprimand.

CHAPTER 17

DAYS OF SUMMER

When Morgan returned home from camp, she thought more about her actions, or rather, lack of actions, in helping Sally with the bullies. Khaos emotions are irrational. If her reasons for not being a friend to Sally were rational, did it not follow that they were free of khaos?

Amasis said she already knew the answers to khaos questions and only needed a conduit to discover what she already knew. She grabbed the book, *The Lives and Times of Cats*, and used her thumbnail to randomly open it. Nothing on the revealed pages caught her eye. She flipped through the pages, stopping at a chapter heading:"Choosing a Companion for your Cat" and chuckled at the comparison. She read:

Adopting a companion for your cat requires time and patience. If you do not have enough time for one cat and think two cats will remedy the situation, you are mistaken. Cats want time and attention from their owners and you may end up with two bored and misbehaving pets instead of one.

'That's it. I only have so much time.'

Morgan headed to the kitchen to ask what they were having for dinner and if she could invite Cara to join them. Her mother was there, but not alone. She was having coffee with a woman Morgan did not recognize.

The two women were seated beside one another and reading what appeared to be a letter. Neither knew of Morgan's near presence so she turned and quietly moved to a nearby room within hearing distance.

Meredith said, "It says his name was Karl. Karleen, do you think he's who you were named after?"

"Don't know. I called my parents to ask. My dad said he didn't want to talk about it on the phone."

"Oh my, that's odd."

"Indeed. I'll go see them, after I meet with the lawyer."

The conversation changed. Morgan wished they would talk more about the contents of the letter. Who was Karl?

After several minutes, they did not return to the subject of the letter and it sounded like Karleen was getting ready to leave.

Morgan realized Karleen was Meredith's social worker friend: the one who phoned when she forgot to give the message. Morgan didn't realize they had become so close. It made her think more about friendship and the reasons people become friends.

That night, she met with Iris. Morgan enjoyed their time together. Unlike Amasis, Iris didn't plan special venues or activities.

They sat in a room next to Elder Tabubu's quarters. Iris often chose this room because Morgan could call Luna's name, upon her arrival, and Luna would come running. Morgan and Luna would then sit together on the same chair.

Morgan asked Iris to position the chairs so they could face the wall with the large treasure map. It was a relief map sculpture. When Morgan first asked about it, she was told it was carved by their ancestors and depicts their journey from their old home to their new home. Morgan was fascinated by it and wondered if it might provide clues to the location of Lucid World. She tried to memorize its details and match them to topographic maps on her computer at home. She had not yet been successful. There were too many places in the world with rivers, valleys, forests.

Morgan shared her friendship insights with Iris. With so many people in her life, through school and otherwise, she couldn't possibly be a friend to and help everyone. She understood what Khyan meant when he said injustices happen because people behave unjustly and because other people do nothing to stop them, but did he understand that there was only one of her and many bullies?

Iris nodded and said, "While there is only one of you, you can still make a difference. Not just with an individual action; but also with the example. Khaos is driven by fear. Shedding your fear and standing up for what you believe may encourage others to do the same. Ideas and behaviour can spread like a virus. So while each instance of encouraging someone might not seem extraordinary, it can create change that will lead to a big impact."

"But where do I begin? How do I know who to help with my actions?"

"It needn't be a decision. For starters, when you witness an injustice, act against it."

"You said for starters. What comes next?"

"You are compassionate and resourceful. You'll figure it out."

VERONICA

Khaos wears many faces. Some people adhere to a strict code of values and morals, and without question believe actions should be motivated by duty and self-sacrifice. They may also believe that those who do not follow these principles are not worthy of love. Morgan knew of one such family in Coyote Flats. She'd heard her parents talk about them. Their daughter, Veronica, was in some of Morgan's classes at school.

Few incidents in Coyote Flats are private. Morgan remembered what she thought when she heard the story from a classmate. 'Veronica's parents are awful.'

Veronica and her family lived on a farm. In the winter, the farm pond often froze. One morning, during this past winter, Veronica and her brothers lingered outside after returning from church. The sun was shining, and it was uncommonly warm for the time of year. The pond was still frozen and a recent wind had cleared it of snow.

They stepped onto the surface wearing their Sunday dress shoes. The smooth soles of their shoes slid like skates on the ice. They called to one another, 'Look at me, I'm a bird! Hold my hand. Let's run and slide together!'

Veronica's youngest brother fell and hurt himself. He tried not to cry but he couldn't hold back the tears.

Their father appeared. 'Veronica! What kind of sister are you?

You're supposed to look after your little brothers. Look what you've done! Go to your room and stay there until I tell you to come out."

Now, in light of what she'd learned about khaos, Morgan's perceptions changed. 'They believe they're doing the right thing. Because of khaos they can't see what seems clear to me.'

Morgan realized she'd never had a real conversation with Veronica. 'Why?' she thought, 'It's because she's always quiet and just keeps to herself.'

Veronica needed a friend.

As The Wind Blows

The next few days found Morgan conflicted. Her participation in the Lucid World project to remove khaos emotions from her life was supposed to make her a better and happier person. At the start, she accepted she would need to apply herself and make changes, and it might be difficult. But she hadn't realized the extent of it.

She needed guidance. She reached for *The Lives and Times of Cats* from her bookshelf but stopped, thinking, 'No, not this time. This is a Nosos World problem. There are cats in Lucid World. I need a book about something exclusive to Nosos World.'

Then she spotted the book, *As the Wind Blows*. Perfect! There was lots of wind in Coyote Flats and no wind inside Lucid World. And the wind was a common theme when she and Khyan shared early childhood memories. Another thought struck her. Her mother often told a story about a severe windstorm on the morning she was born. Meredith would always end the story by saying, "Oh my. I can't say who howled the loudest, the wind or Morgan."

A random page in the book revealed:

Hurricane storms begin in ocean waters. When a hurricane meets land, it can produce a surge reaching six meters high to extend one hundred sixty kilometers over land. Its intense winds can cause tornadoes. Torrential rains cause further damage by causing floods and landslides. The best defence against a hurricane is to get out of its way.

Damage! Get out of its way? That's what she read. The aim of looking in random places for answers was not to use the information literally. It was to draw the answer from her subconscious. But this felt like an omen.

Many khaos-related matters she could not resolve were connected with school. Morgan was unlikely to see Sally during the rest of the summer, since Sally would probably be at home looking after her little brother. Morgan was also unlikely to see Veronica during the summer. She lived on a farm and with no classes to attend she wouldn't spend much time in Coyote Flats. With this reprieve, Morgan postponed any decision-making related to Sally and Veronica until September when school started again.

SUMMER JOB

During the first few weeks of summer, Morgan 'hung out' with Cara in the same way they had spent summers for years. They walked barefoot, swam in the town pool, went for ice cream, played baseball and rode their bicycles.

When Cara turned sixteen and got her driver's licence, the girls had an added summer amusement: Cara drove her father's truck, and they shopped.

Swimming, ice cream and shopping required money. Morgan's weekly allowance, doled out on Saturdays, was often gone by mid-week. Her savings were low after the WSC adventure and the families who often hired her for babysitting jobs were away on vacation. When Morgan pressed her parents for more money, they suggested she get a summer job.

Morgan talked over the situation with Cara. While Cara's parents were more liberal with Cara's spending money, Cara was enthused about earning more herself.

They didn't want to be separated from one another, so Morgan and Cara plotted to find something they could do together to make money and not have to work too hard. Their answer came when Cara's father paid them to mow the lawn. They made posters advertising they were available for odd jobs like gardening, painting and delivery, and posted them around Coyote Flats. Before long, phone calls and emails arrived with a myriad of assignments.

Apparently, the people of Coyote Flats had a lot of chores that needed doing.

During the summer nights when Morgan visited Lucid World, she talked about her day's activities with Cara. Her Lucid World mentors were pleased to learn of Morgan and Cara's venture. Morgan recognized that in her descriptions and stories, she might have emphasized helping people and de-emphasized making money.

Their business thrived. Ironically, they started it so they'd have more money for activities; but due to its success, they had little time for activities requiring money.

Their undertakings weren't without incident. As a result, Morgan learned organizational skills from first-hand experience. One of their first assignments involved delivering groceries to customers of a local food store. Cara noticed a grocery bag was heavy because it held several cans of dog food. Intending to make small talk, she said to the elderly man who received the delivery, "Oh I hope your dog likes the dog food."

He replied, "I don't have a dog."

Morgan, wanting to save the man and Cara from further embarrassment, tried to rescue the conversation by offering, "I'm sure it's just as good as, or even better, than regular sandwich meat. Who says only dogs can eat it?"

The man laughed. He laughed so hard tears ran down his cheeks.

The girls didn't know what to make of his sudden laughter outburst. Thinking the man was suffering from delusions or dementia, Cara asked if they should call someone to help.

Finally, he could compose himself enough to say, "I don't eat dog food, though as you say, it's very good. Hehehe... these are someone else's groceries."

Even though the venture was started for financial gain, Morgan realized she liked helping people: especially those who needed it most. Morgan asked Iris about the logic of feeling good when helping strangers.

Iris explained, "Feelings of compassion and empathy played a big part in human evolution. Those who lived in communities where help and support thrived had improved chances of survival. We're 'wired' for altruism. So when we help others, parts of the brain associated with feelings of belonging and pleasure are activated. This releases endorphins and creates feelings of happiness."

"So then, why are there people who don't help others?"

"Most often it's because..." Iris didn't have time to finish her response.

Morgan playfully put her fist to her forehead. "Duh... khaos, of course." She put her hand down. "So if evolution is tied to survival, how does khaos fit in?"

"Do you mean, how did illogical fear start?"

"Yah, logical fear would have helped humans survive, not illogical fear. So why did some humans have illogical fear?"

"That's what we're trying to figure out. And the related question: why is illogical fear contagious? What causes the brain to confuse stimuli and trigger a 'fight or flight' reaction when there is no real threat or danger?"

"When did khaos actually start? I mean, who were the first humans to catch it?"

"We don't know. There are historical reports of civilizations whose members acted with unnecessary violence and anger, a product of illogical fear, long before my people left Nosos World. To go back to the subject of feeling good when helping others, there is one more beneficial aspect."

"What's that?" asked Morgan.

"It isn't just the people who help others who feel good. Those who know about it feel good too. The act of helping people spreads a pervasive positive effect."

"Does it matter if it's done as part of a job, like my summer job?"

Iris laughed. "It doesn't matter. The feelings don't change."

CHAPTER 18

MATT

When we expect a future event with dread, it often seems to suddenly arrive and take us off guard, even when the exact time, place and details are well known to us. Such was the case for Morgan on her first day back at school.

Within the official town limits, Coyote Flats boasted a population about 1,700. Small hamlets and farms surrounding Coyote Flats brought the population up to about 2,000. There was one high school.

During Morgan's last class on this first day back at school, the teacher assigned random pairs of classmates to interview one another. Each student was to introduce their pair-partner to the class the next day. The objectives were to become acquainted with one another and to improve communication skills. Morgan suspected the assignment was more for the benefit of the teacher, to help remember names. There weren't too many new kids, and Morgan and her classmates already knew or recognized most of the fifty-to-sixty students in her grade.

As fate would have it, there was a new student and Morgan was matched with him. At first she didn't recognize him. He was taller, more muscular and less pimply than when she last saw him.

It was Matt — the bartender from the party!

Morgan barely got over her shock and indignation when she heard her name and his name called out together.

Her first reaction was 'flight'. She was seated near the back of the room. Maybe she could slip out and ask the vice-principal to transfer her to a different class. 'Flight' was replaced with a 'fight' reaction. Matt was a jerk, but he was on her turf now.

Morgan looked across the room at Matt sitting at his desk. He was staring down at papers in front of him. His body language said, "I'm reading something so important I can't possibly give anyone my attention."

'Well,' Morgan thought, 'I have nothing to fear except illogical fear.' She got up and walked over to ask how he wanted to go about it.

Matt looked up from the papers he had been fixated on, scowled at Morgan and said, "Go interview yourself."

Morgan marched back to her desk, gathered her belongings and left the classroom.

As she and Cara were walking home, Morgan described the details of the incident. When she finished, she waited for Cara's reaction. She expected Cara to be as incensed as she was. Instead, Cara just said, "Yeah, that wasn't very nice of him."

Disappointed in Cara's lack of indignation, Morgan dropped the subject. She'd already decided how she would settle matters with Matt. When she saw him at school the next day, she would tell him off. Later, she would reveal his true colours to the class when she was called on to introduce him.

Were her feelings and planned actions khaos-driven? She concluded they weren't. An injustice happened, and she needed to speak out against it.

Conversation with Cara moved on to boys who changed over the summer. Some attempted to grow beards with varying degrees of success. Some grew more muscular. Others had deeper voices. Talking about boys was a favourite topic for Morgan and Cara, and it took Morgan's thoughts away from Matt... for the time being.

The next morning, Morgan saw Matt in math class. Before class started, she walked over to his desk to execute 'Part I' of her plan. Matt looked up. His face was filled with sadness. She froze.

Matt said, "I'm sorry about what a jerk I was yesterday. Can we talk in the hall?"

Morgan shrugged. She didn't know what to expect. Matt rose, and she followed him out, moving against the flow of students headed into the classroom. They stood off to the side in the hall.

Matt again apologized. He explained that he was feeling frustrated and upset. His family moved to Coyote Flats from Lethbridge so his dad could take a new job at the sugar factory. The first thing he had to do was fire people! So his dad hates his new job. Also, his mother hates where they live. Now they're constantly fighting and somehow he ends up in the middle of it.

"Anyway, I took it out on you. Can we still do the interviews, maybe next break?"

Morgan was speechless for a moment, accepted his apology, and then offered to be there for him if he ever wanted someone to talk with.

Matt was relieved. "Thanks, but I think it will get better."

As he walked back into the classroom ahead of her, Morgan shuddered at the thought, 'I almost made things even worse for him. I wasn't reacting to an injustice, I was plotting revenge.'

CHAPTER 19

SCHOOL PHOTO

So I'm leaving now!" Morgan called to her mother in the other room. "Don't forget to smile for the camera," came her reply.

Morgan walked out the front door onto the street. Normally she turned left to meet up with Cara at the corner. However, on this morning, Cara texted and said she'd gone early for basketball practice. Morgan turned right to take a shorter route to school.

She hadn't gone far when a car drove past and slowed down. The driver's head turned to look back in her direction. Morgan didn't recognize the driver of the car and thought it unusual for a stranger to look back at her. 'Hmm,' she thought, 'they must have mistaken me for someone else.'

She walked a little further and saw a woman standing in the window of a house looking out onto the street in Morgan's direction. The woman motioned to someone to come to the window. Morgan didn't want to stare back, so she looked straight ahead and kept walking. 'Hmm,' she thought, 'they must be looking at my dress. I told Mom it might be too much to wear to school, even for the school photo. Actually, this dress isn't over-the-top. Maybe they weren't even looking at me. Maybe they were looking at the cat in the yard across the street.'

She walked on and heard her name called out along with the word "dress". She turned and saw Sally running towards her and waving her arms. Morgan called back, "Thanks. It's because we're having our picture taken at school today," and kept walking.

"Stop. I have to tell you..."

Morgan stopped. Did Sally like her dress so much she had to yell it down the street? Why would she do such a thing? It wasn't like they were close friends. They were more like acquaintances. Did Sally think they were good friends because of their talk at the wilderness camping trip?

Sally caught up to Morgan and panted, "I saw you walk past... hurried to tell you."

Morgan stood in a stance with her feet apart and arms crossed. "Tell me what? You like my dress?"

"It's tucked in."

"What does that mean? Tucked in where?" Morgan unfolded her arms and looked down at the front and the sides of her dress.

"In the back, tucked into your panties! The whole back side of your panties are showing."

"Oh my God!" Morgan screamed. "Oh, no! How much can you actually see!?" Morgan reached her arms around her back and to her surprise her fingers met the feel of cotton panties. She pulled down on the fabric of her dress. She pulled and smoothed and pulled until it felt like her dress was in its proper place.

"Is it down now? Is it all right now?" Morgan turned around so Sally could check.

"It's okay now. Sorry I ran after you like that but I thought maybe you'd want to know." Sally turned to walk back the way she'd come.

"Aren't you walking to school, this way?"

Sally stopped and faced Morgan. "I have to get home to look after my little brother, Mikey. Mom's still sleeping."

"You'll be late though and have to go to the office."

"Maybe, but my mom will just write a late-note saying I had a doctor's appointment or something."

"All right, see you around."

Sally turned to go. Morgan's feet stayed planted, and she said, "Sally, wait." Sally stopped and turned around. Morgan continued, "You saved my life. If I'd actually walked into school... I can't even..."

"It would've been awful. I know."

"Have you tried any of the things we talked about at camp?"

"Maybe. Did you do those things when you were called Barfie Doll? Is that how you got them to stop?"

Morgan shook her head abashedly. "Actually the only thing that helped was to avoid them. Eventually, they lost interest and moved on to Katey."

"They never seem to lose interest when it comes to me. I think maybe it's because we're poor and some of the things my mom does."

"What if you spent more time hanging out with friends? You might not notice it as much."

"That's a good idea. I'll try to maybe do that. I'd better check on Mikey. Okay thanks, maybe I'll see you at school."

"All right, bye, and thanks for helping me with my dress disaster."

The girls went their separate ways. Morgan didn't know it straightaway, but she'd just had a life-changing moment. Emotions, ideas and conversations swam around in her head. At first it was dizzying, and when the dizzy feeling stopped it was replaced with clarity.

She knew Sally didn't have friends to hang out with. It was a stupid thing to say. Her conscious mind recognized what her subconscious had known ever since she learned about khaos, and even before. She was selfish, insecure and afraid. She was a coward. Her conscious-self fought this awareness and made excuses. Not anymore.

She felt like a bird riding the wind. A voice in her head said, 'You are free and nothing can stand in your way.'

CHAPTER 20

LIFE IN LUCID WORLD

Visits to Lucid World offered more than lessons to overcome khaos emotions. Visits were adventures! Much was different from Morgan's world, and not just because Lucid World was inside of a mountain.

In Lucid World, she had a cat! Luna was a constant companion to Morgan. Not long after Luna and Morgan became buddies, Iris went to the engineers who installed and calibrated the Nosos youth avatar technology. She asked if they could do something in the way of an interactive robotic cat brush.

There is a saying, 'necessity is the mother of invention', meaning that the driving force for most new inventions is a need. Here, the driving force for an invention was the bond between a girl and a cat. The engineers designed an instrument which could be controlled using voice commands, so when Luna sat with Morgan, Morgan could brush her. Soon the brushing ceremony was an anticipated event for them both!

Morgan's meetings were always with Khyan, Amasis or Iris. Lately, more often with Amasis and Iris, as Khyan was learning to pilot a helicopter. Aside from his desire to experience the natural beauty of the world, he thought it would be useful if the youth program was successful and might be expanded.

Morgan was introduced to others if someone entered a room she was in or passed by in a public space. She observed they were all unique, interesting people. One might have assumed they would be similar and uninteresting because they were so congenial. But because the action of conforming to others is often khaos driven, the opposite was true.

One might have also assumed that after so many years of separation from the rest of the planet's population, their gene pool would have more similarity in their physical characteristics. It is a well-established scientific fact that a gene pool needs a certain amount of diversity for a population to be healthy and thrive. Through the centuries, the Elders of Lucid World have been mindful of this and any time there was an opportunity to expand the gene pool, they encouraged it. In earlier times, young Lucid World women volunteered to venture out into Nosos World to procreate with men on Nosos. Often they went to large festival gatherings where those who attended did not know all others who were there. Of these volunteers, almost all returned to Lucid World except for a few who, sworn to secrecy, stayed in Nosos because they fell in love; or feared they had the khaos. There are many Lucid World legends and stories about these brave women. In modern times, it is much easier to expand the gene pool. Lucid World couples having difficulty conceiving a child can access eggs or sperm from Nosos fertility centers. Over the centuries, many healthy babies have been born to Lucid World, with genes from Nosos, and all have been free of khaos. Genetics has been largely ruled out as a cause for khaos.

Most of the clothing worn in Lucid World was designed for comfort, warmth or ease of washing. When Amasis first contacted Morgan, he was wearing jeans and a T-shirt. This was considered by many of Lucid World to be the preferred clothing just as in Coyote Flats. When Levi and Strauss invented blue jeans, Lucid World adopted them. Some of the people wore bright colours. Purple was popular. No one conformed to a particular fashion. Old, new and original fashions were all brought together. Morgan imagined gatherings of people in Lucid World likely resembled a costume ball without masks.

Morgan knew she wasn't the only Nosian (Morgan's made-up name for those from her world) who visited Lucid World. There were others, but Khyan didn't want them to interact. He said there was enough 'khaos feeding khaos'. He insisted the time Morgan spent in Lucid World was too valuable, and should be spent only with people not infected by khaos.

There was one occasion when Morgan had an encounter with another Nosian.

Amasis and Iris apparently mis-communicated venues and timing. So while Morgan was meeting with Amasis, an avatar named Elvis appeared. While Amasis sorted out the mix-up, Morgan and Elvis had a few minutes to chat. Elvis was a year older than Morgan, from a remote area in Hawaii and an avid surf boarder. He had dimples, a big smile and flirty eyes.

Amasis seemed to be in a hurry to transport Elvis to another room. Elvis seemed disappointed to leave. The encounter with Elvis fueled Morgan's curiosity about the others. Who were they and why were they all from rural areas?

To maintain the protocols established by Khyan, no one would tell Morgan anything about the other Nosos youth. All she knew was the reason they were all from rural areas. It was because the technology used to transmit to and from their sleeping brains was sensitive to interference caused by electro-magnetic fields (EMF). Rural areas have less EMF than cities. Sources of EMFs can be natural or human-made. Human-made EMFs are more concentrated in populated areas and include power lines, electronic appliances and wireless networks.

Morgan was curious about many things.

What about colds and flu? Lucid World has advanced technology. Have they discovered a cure for the common cold? Occasionally people in Lucid World caught colds and flu. Like Nosos World, they vaccinated against strains of flu viruses. The common cold can be caused by hundreds of different viruses, so it's not practical to make a vaccine to protect against all of them. Also, there's less need to create a vaccine for colds because although a cold can make you feel awful when you have one, it typically runs its course with no serious health complications.

Separated from the rest of the world, how did people in Lucid World even catch a cold... or any disease? Don't you have to be in contact with a sick person to catch what they have?

True — their exposure to disease was limited. Since human bodies require exposure to pathogens to develop immune systems, they vaccinated against known pathogens. If they didn't, a non-life-threatening illness in Nosos World could devastate all of them if introduced into their population.

"So then how do babies defend against disease?" Morgan asked.

Morgan was meeting with Iris. Iris laughed and said, "This is turning into a science lesson. Antibodies from the mother are passed to unborn babies through the placenta. Morgan, if you're interested in biology and immune systems, you can research on the internet. We need to turn our conversation to ..."

"Just one more question. It's not something I can find on the internet: how does Lucid World get light and water inside of a mountain?"

Iris gave a brief description. The pressure of the snow's weight on the mountain creates ice that melts into water. Light and air enters through openings in the surface. To retain warmth during colder months these openings are restricted using a large ceiling apparatus moved with pulleys. An underground hot spring is channelled throughout the cavern. Though not suitable for drinking due to its high mineral content, the spring water is used for many other purposes and radiates considerable heat.

"But what about garbage, how do you get rid of it?"

"Oh. Everything is either composted for soil for the greenhouse or sent to an energy conversion plant in a nearby mountain, to power devices in Lucid World."

"So what about regular garbage? You know, junk!"

"We do not have that. Most things can be reused or recycled; and what can't is sent to the energy conversion plant." Iris laughed. "That was three more questions. Let's get to work."

Experiences and information sharing was not one directional. The Lucid World mentors were influenced by their Nosian visitors.

No, they didn't catch khaos. Rather, they realized that some of their views, concerning those infected with khaos, were flawed. Like Morgan, they too had made assumptions about personalities. Khyan had assumed they would be less mature. Iris had assumed they would be more self-absorbed. Amasis had assumed they would be less interesting. All these assumptions proved to be wrong; and if not wrong, too simplistic.

Precautions taken to keep everyone safe from khaos included agendas and time limits for interactions. Also, the mentors, Khyan, Iris, and Amasis, routinely performed self-assessments to check for signs of khaos. Other than one small incident, which was more of an emotion than an incident, there was no reason to believe there was any cause for concern.

What was that incident, or rather, emotion?

When Elvis appeared in the wrong room, and 'chatted-up' Morgan, Amasis seemed not only to want Elvis gone. He really wanted him gone.

Afterwards, Amasis reflected on this. Why did he want Elvis gone? Was it because it was contrary to safeguard protocols? No, that wasn't the reason. He did not like the way Elvis looked at Morgan. Why? He cared for Morgan. Was he trying to protect her? Yes, but was it more? Was he jealous? If so, that was a khaos emotion. He was infected.

He ruminated. No, it wasn't jealousy. He did not feel fear of a threat to a relationship, illogical or otherwise. He felt a type of caring he had never felt before.

FROM LUCID TO NOSOS

Morgan wanted to tell people about khaos and how she knew about it, but she promised Khyan she wouldn't. Besides, no one would believe her. In particular, she wanted to tell Cara. Until Morgan first visited Lucid World, she and Cara never kept secrets from one another. Now, she was keeping the biggest secret she ever had. If she broke her promise to Khyan, and confided in Cara, Cara would never believe her. In fact sometimes Morgan had trouble believing it herself.

Morgan unintentionally let it slip out one warm evening in September. Morgan, Cara, Dylan and Ryan were in the back yard throwing a baseball across the grass. They thought they invented the game, but unbeknownst to them, it was akin to bocce ball. They played with two teams, girls against boys. This resulted in playful rivalry with lots of laughter and cheering.

Meredith called out the back door and told them to come in the house, now! This directive was met with disappointment, negotiations to stay out longer, and demands to know the reason. Meredith was adamant, so the players conceded. When they got into the house, Meredith explained she had received a phone call from a neighbour complaining about the noise they made.

Morgan and Cara went to Cara's house to 'hang out' there. On the way, Cara said, "Your mom wouldn't say who complained but I know who it was."

"Actually I think I know, too. It was probably those old people who just moved in across the lane."

"Yeah let's go ring their doorbell and run and hide!"

"That's mean and childish. Besides, we don't even know for sure it was them."

"Um come on. Let's have fun. Oh if you don't want to do it to the new neighbours, let's ring the witch's doorbell and hide. It's always fun to watch when she comes out of the house and searches behind the bushes."

"It's still mean. You shouldn't call Mrs. Costadinawich a witch. She's just an old lady who lives alone and minds her own business."

"Um, yeah, I know. What's with you? Lately, you've been acting like you're smarter and better than everyone. Everybody says so."

"Oh yah? So what! You all have khaos!"

"We all have what?"

"Kooky ideas, you all have kooky ideas."

The girls walked in awkward silence until they got to Cara's house and the change of scenery gave them a change of mood and a change of conversation.

Morgan couldn't tell anyone about khaos but she could try to live her life without it. One of her priorities was to confront and resolve her conflicting feelings about friendship with Sally. She did this the day after Sally saved her from going to school with her dress tucked in her underwear.

Cara had basketball practice after school and couldn't walk home with Morgan. After the last class of the day, Morgan hurried over to Sally's locker, where Sally was offloading her books and suggested they walk home together. Sally's mouth dropped open, and then she nodded her head and gave Morgan a shy smile.

The girls walked slowly and talked about general things happening around school. At one point the subject of class photos and what Morgan wore for her photo came up. At the reference to Morgan's dress, they exchanged grins and eye contact acknowledging a mutual understanding; Morgan's exposed underwear was their secret.

The seasons were changing, and the trees boasted colours of crimson and gold. Leaves clung to the branches but some let go as a light breeze unseated them from their perch. When Sally and Morgan arrived at Sally's gate, the breeze unexpectedly intensified and sent leaves whirling through the air.

Morgan asked for Sally's phone number. In a low unsteady voice, Sally awkwardly explained she didn't have her own phone and her mother didn't like people calling their house and bothering them. Sally suggested Morgan could email her or she would phone Morgan when her mother wasn't home.

Sally's tone of voice, and the whirling leaves, produced an eerie atmosphere. It gave Morgan the impression that a ubiquitous Franny Frey was opposing Morgan's entrance into Sally's life. This sensation intensified when Sally nervously looked over her shoulder, gave a hurried 'goodbye', and then ran to the house.

While Morgan walked the rest of the way home, she thought about how fortunate she was in her relationship with her parents. She had considered them stricter and less flexible than her friends' parents, especially her mother. For instance, Cara's parents seldom gave her a curfew; and when they did, the consequences of breaking curfew were fairly inconsequential. Looking at what Sally and Veronica had to deal with, Morgan realized she was fortunate.

Morgan emailed Sally, and they got together from time to time. They rode bikes, went for walks or just hung out at Morgan's house. Often it was just the two of them. Cara was occupied with basketball during the autumn months but sometimes she joined them. When Cara asked Morgan about her new interest in spending time with Sally, Morgan answered, "She's lonely and doesn't have any other friends and I like spending time with her." That was a good enough explanation for Cara and nothing more was said about it.

In spite of Cara's mischievous antics like ringing doorbells and truck theft, she was a level-headed and confident teenager. It seemed to Morgan that Cara was less prone to khaos emotions and actions than she was herself. She wondered why she was chosen for the Lucid World project rather than someone like Cara. When she asked Khyan about this he smiled and said, "To quote James Joyce, mistakes are the portals of discovery."

LIFE IN SHAMBHALA — A LONG TIME AGO

The founders' journey to Lucid World was a difficult one. They carried heavy loads of supplies and covered distant and treacherous terrain. The trip was not without fatalities.

When they arrived at the mountain, they camped near the entrance to the cave. The spacious cavity within the mountain needed to be cleared, vented and readied for habitation.

While many mourned the loss of life and loved ones, Kasta mourned the loss of friendship with Djer. Djer's family had the khaos and Kasta's family was distracted with secret preparations for the trek. The boys found love and support in one another. Not brothers in blood; they were brothers in heart.

Kasta vowed he would return for a proper farewell to Djer. If Djer was without the khaos, he would bring him to Lucid World to live.

Kasta had memorized every detail of the journey: rivers, plains, forests, valleys, location of the north star, where the sun rose and set...

Each morning when Kasta woke, he retraced the journey in his mind, but in reverse direction. One morning, he stumbled over a detail. It was fading. He needed to map it.

With the construction going on inside the cavern, Kasta had no difficulty accessing stone carving tools. He enlisted the help of boys older and stronger than he, and together they created a relief map. Several stone slabs were pieced together. The map carving was three times taller than Kasta!

When the inside of the mountain was ready to move into, traces of the camp had to be eliminated as a precaution against invaders. The map could not remain outdoors. It was installed inside the cave.

Kasta grew to be a man. He had children and told them stories of the world beyond the mountain. He often stood in front of the map and stared into it. He never gave up on his dream to go back and find Djer. At the beginning he couldn't go because he had to wait until he was older and stronger. Then there was a time when reports from the outside suggested their survival could be threatened if anyone ventured away from the mountain. When the outside threats lessened, he was a father and a husband, and there was always something to do to survive and improve upon the comforts of life.

One day, when his children were grown and his hair was greying, friends who had gone out into Nosos returned with news of Djer's obsession to find Kasta and the place where he, and the others, had gone when they disappeared in the night.

It was time. Kasta closed his eyes and could see every detail of his journey ahead.

CHAPTER 21

INSECURITY AND BLAME

Not long after Morgan shared the news of her friendship with Sally, Amasis asked whether Sally was still being bullied and if his suggestions had been helpful.

Morgan said she had witnessed no instances of bullying while Sally and she were together.

They were seated beside one another, on a rock ledge, looking down into a clear pond with a white rock bottom. A pair of yellow seahorses propelled themselves through the water looking for plankton in green weeds.

Amasis nodded his head while saying, "That's because those who are prone to bullying are also cowards and less likely to victimize someone who is not alone. What about the teacher who made the joke after Sally was tripped in class? Has that behaviour continued?"

"Nah. She's not actually a teacher at our school anymore. She left because she had an affair with a student."

Amasis looked up from the water and looked at Morgan, "An affair? What's that?"

Morgan continued to gaze into the water, "You know... a love affair."

Amasis was still puzzled. Morgan knew he was looking at her but felt embarrassed to look at him. Still looking down she said, "The teacher fell in love with a student."

"Oh. How do you know this? I wouldn't think it would be openly discussed."

Morgan looked at him, "I heard it from a classmate whose mother's neighbour is on the school board."

"Morgan, gossip is khaos behaviour."

Morgan looked down again, "It's not gossip. I'm pretty sure it's actually true."

Amasis, too, turned his eyes back to the pond. "Whether something is true, or untrue, doesn't determine whether it's gossip. Any conversation about someone else's behavior or personal life is gossip."

Feeling abashed, and sensing discomfort from Amasis, Morgan changed the subject and pointed at another seahorse pair that had come into view. Amasis did not pursue the former topic.

Morgan did, however, pursue it the next day.

Khyan met Morgan in the treasure map room. Iris was still in a meeting with another Nosos project participant and would join them as soon as she could.

Morgan assumed that Amasis probably told Khyan about their gossip conversation. She wanted to tell her side of the story.

As soon as they were in their respective chairs along with Luna, Morgan described what happened, beginning with the teacher bullying Sally. She ended with, "He said I was gossiping. I wasn't. He asked a question, and I answered it. How's that gossip?"

Khyan considered her question and said, "Your reason for volunteering unnecessary personal information is likely a khaos emotion such as dislike for the teacher or low self-image."

"Low self-image?! Me?"

"You may have been feeling doubt or vulnerability."

Morgan sighed and shook her head, "So tell me, does every Nosian have some inferiority complex?"

"I don't think so. Many are confident and feel no need to validate their beliefs or self-worth by disparaging or blaming."

"Blaming?"

"It's khaos to blame others, instead of taking responsibility for one's own actions or inactions."

"What if it actually is someone else's fault?'

"It depends."

Morgan thought back to the incident with Mrs. Byrd's fence.

Mrs. Byrd's reaction was surprise, not anger. She didn't dwell on blame or seek to exact punishment. She recognized it for the accident it was. Her only concern was to have her fence repaired.

Morgan nodded her head in understanding, "So it's khaos when it's illogical blaming?"

Khyan agreed. Blaming doesn't deal with the real problem and can interfere with remedying the situation or preventing a similar event. Also, it creates unnecessary conflicts.

"So when is it logical to blame someone?"

"When carelessness or maliciousness is involved, the responsible party should be held accountable and expected to rectify or mitigate the consequences."

"What does 'mitigate' mean?"

"It means to lessen the seriousness or the extent of consequences."

"So what's an example of mitigating something?"

Khyan though for a moment and then said, "Sometimes I can be loquacious when conversing on certain subjects. Someone might mitigate by changing the subject."

Morgan laughed and asked, "What does 'loquacious' mean?"

Khyan winked and said, "It means long-winded. Are you asking or are you mitigating?"

CHAPTER 22

A BAG DROPS

The next morning was Saturday so Morgan didn't have to go to school. She found Meredith and Karleen in the kitchen having coffee. Engrossed in conversation, neither of them was aware she had entered the room. Karleen was talking, "... considerate and happy. It was truly an act to get me to fall for him. The real Scott was the man his friends and family knew, detached and sulky."

Morgan moved in closer so her mother's peripheral vision would notice her, "Mom, sorry to interrupt. I've finished my room and I'm going to school now to see Cara's basketball practice."

Meredith introduced Morgan to Karleen. Karleen seemed very nice. Meredith didn't encourage Morgan to stay and visit with them.

As Morgan walked away, the conversation started up again. While at the back door, putting on her shoes, Morgan heard Karleen say, "He insisted 'he was who he was' and 'I' was the one who needed to change. Yet, I was the same woman he married, who he didn't seem to have a problem with when we dated. Unlike him, I never pretended to be someone else."

Morgan opened the door and left. It was a hazy sunny autumn day. There were still a few leaves left on the trees. Some of the landscape shrubs in neighbour's yards had crimson red leaves. The air carried a hint of smoke from the burning of grass or leaves.

Morgan walked at a slow pace. The scenery was too lovely and tranquil to rush through it. She thought about the conversation she heard. It sounded like Karleen was talking about her divorce. Did it have something to do with the mysterious letter?

She walked behind Mrs. Enid Meany and Mrs. Winifred Bittar. The sun went behind a rogue cloud and the air became cool. Morgan was wearing only a jean jacket and felt cold, so she picked up her pace.

Now walking faster than the ladies, Morgan was just about to pass them, when Mrs. Bittar touched Mrs. Meany's arm to get her attention to stop and look at something in the distance.

Mrs. Meany, who was carrying grocery bags, stopped and shifted some of the bags to change her grip. She dropped a bag and the sounds of a thump and then a crack were heard. Bending to pick it up, she looked up at Mrs. Bittar and admonished, "Winnie, look what you made me do!"

'Ah ha! Khaos!' thought Morgan. She considered her words carefully and interrupted, "Mrs. Meany, I'm sure you must realize Mrs. Bittar didn't make you drop your bag. When something bad happens, blaming someone doesn't help. Maybe you were feeling insecure, and that's why you blamed her."

Enid Meany and Winifred Bittar were utterly shocked! For a moment, they appeared frozen as a video in 'pause mode'. They quickly recovered and changed to 'attack mode'.

Mrs. Bittar, coming to the aid of her friend, said, "I know you. You're the daughter of Daniel and Meredith Kith. I can't believe how you speak to adults. As soon as I get home, I'm calling your mother." It was Morgan's turn to go into 'pause mode'. What went wrong? She was only trying to help. She tried to apologize but her words made little sense. The two women stormed off discussing Morgan's insolent behaviour and the obvious parenting failures of the Kiths.

That night, in Lucid World, Morgan was still disheartened by the two women's admonishment. They had called her mother, so she then received a lecture on manners and respect for adults.

Morgan recounted the morning's events to Iris, while brushing Luna using the voice-activated brush. The special cat brush was attached to a swing arm suspended over an oversized sofa chair which Morgan and Luna shared.

Iris consoled Morgan and suggested enthusiasm had clouded her judgement.

Morgan straightened her posture, "So how was my judgment clouded? I thought I was supposed to help spread the lucid way and stop khaos."

Luna didn't care for the tone of Morgan's voice and left. The brushing arm stopped.

"Yes, but it's not up to you to tell people what they're doing wrong or right. Even if it was, people reacting to khaos emotions will go deeper into khaos to defend themselves."

"Then what good is it for me to even learn about khaos?"

"So you can teach by example."

Iris smiled. While leaning back in her chair she said, "People with khaos are better at seeing khaos in others than in themselves. If you live and react to life using the love emotion, you will set an example for others. Love is contagious in the same way khaos is contagious."

Morgan mimicked Iris's posture and leaned back in her chair. "So if love is contagious, does that mean falling in love is contagious too?"

"No, I mean love in a general sense: feelings of compassion, kindness and understanding."

Morgan thought about Amasis. She still had a crush on him even after he declined her invitation to the school dance. Did he have a girlfriend? She didn't know why, but she imagined Amasis and Iris together. Perhaps she could find out from Iris.

Morgan asked, "So if you love or like someone, will they like or love you back? Is that contagious?"

"Maybe. It depends. Romantic love is complicated. Especially for those with khaos when what appeals to them most about a relationship is that they imagine themselves happy. With their happiness on 'hold', they reject possible relationships because the 'happy' feeling is missing. They find fault with every prospective partner; or the prospective partner finds fault with them."

"Huh?!"

"Let me give you an example. Have you ever heard about people who spend their entire life looking for love; then when they decide to just be happy with their life the way it is, they meet someone and fall in love?"

"Actually, I have."

"Well, that's because when a person feels happy they see the positive in others."

"So someone is more likely to fall in love when they feel happy? Isn't that only half of it though? The other person has to actually love them back, right?"

"Yes, but it works both ways. People feel good when they're with someone who's happy, so they're more likely to fall in love."

"What about physical appearance and attraction? Aren't they important too?"

"To some people they are. But often someone may not be attracted to a particular person until they get to know them."

Morgan thought about what she heard Karleen say about her ex-husband Scott. "Is it khaos to pretend to be happy so the other person will like you?"

"Yes."

"Why? What's wrong with pretending to be happy, or to like something, to make someone feel happy?"

"Pretending is an illogical foundation for a meaningful relationship. Eventually, true feelings will surface."

Luna returned. She must have been at her food dish because she was licking her lips as she settled onto the chair beside Morgan. Morgan adjusted her posture so she could watch Luna, then looked over at Iris and said, "Really? Why?"

"In the long run, people can't be content pretending to be someone they're not. They'll want to be themselves."

"So people like people who are happy; but if one of them is only pretending to be happy, neither of them can stay happy."

Iris laughed. "Yes, that sounds right."

They talked about other qualities people like in others. People enjoy speaking to a listener who values what they say. People don't like being interrupted because it seems the interrupter is not listening and may not be respecting what they say.

"How do people in Lucid World get together?"

"It's not that different from the way it is for healthy relationships in Nosos. People have varied interests and priorities. People come together when they feel attracted to one another and enjoy spending time together."

"Is an unhealthy relationship based on illogical emotions?"

"Yes, I think that sums it up."

"Chemistry and pheromones, logical or illogical?"

"Interesting question. Scientists in Nosos have been conducting studies for years to establish links between body chemistry and human attraction. But it's inconclusive. As humans evolved, they lost the gland that other mammals use to detect pheromones. Perhaps there may be other ways we perceive pheromones."

Iris grinned and continued, "There is, however, one thing that evidence supports conclusively."

"What's that?"

"We are completely off-topic from the studies I planned for tonight."

"Do you have a boyfriend?"

"I have lots of friends who are guys."

"You know what I mean."

"Yes, I know what you mean. Let's get back to our studies."

CHAPTER 23

TRYPTOPHAN

Every October, a local church group sponsored a Harvest Dinner featuring a full turkey meal at a reasonable price. Morgan's family's attendance was an annual event. Unlike many of the Kith family outings, there were no complaints from anyone. Roast turkey when it wasn't a special occasion such as Thanksgiving or Christmas appealed to everyone.

Long tables, covered in white linen, were arranged in the brightly lit community hall. Dinner attendees sat on chairs tightly crammed together around the tables. The room buzzed with multiple conversations.

Morgan sat beside her brothers, across from her parents. She had just finished and was contemplating what type of pie she should have for dessert when she noticed Veronica across the room with her family. She seldom saw Veronica outside of school and hoped the occasion might be an opportunity to talk with her.

After dessert, Morgan looked down at her empty plate. Her stomach felt full, she reckoned she had overeaten. She also felt sleepy. She looked at her parents drinking coffee and talking to other adults seated at their table. It looked like it would be a while before they would be ready to leave. Dylan and Ryan made the same conclusion and excused themselves to go outside and hang out with some of their friends.

Mid-sentence, in a conversation with a woman seated beside her, Meredith looked over to Morgan and said hurriedly, "Now, why don't you go outside and play with your brothers?"

"Mom!" blasted Morgan. "I'm not a child. I don't play. I'm not going outside to do whatever stupid thing Dylan and Ryan are doing."

"Oh my. Yes, yes, sorry dear. I meant, why don't you find some of your friends to visit with?" Meredith returned to her former conversation. Morgan recognized the story. She'd heard it before and it wasn't any more interesting this time than the first time she'd heard it.

Morgan looked in Veronica's direction. Her table also revealed the aftermath of a meal. Veronica sat with her shoulders slumped and her straight dull-brown hair falling in her eyes. She wore a plain white blouse and an impassive facial expression. Combined with the white linen tablecloth, her image made Morgan think of a patient in a hospital. Veronica appeared to be waiting for her parents while they talked with others at the table.

Morgan got up from her seat, took her jacket from the back of her chair, and wandered over to Veronica's table. When Morgan approached, Veronica perked up.

"Hi!" Morgan didn't wait for Veronica to speak. "Want to go for a walk?"

"Err, umm, I guess so. Let me check." Veronica stood up and walked around the table to where her father sat and whispered in his ear. He looked discerningly at Morgan, nodded and said, "All right, twenty minutes and don't be late." He looked at the watch on his wrist.

Veronica grabbed her coat from the back of the chair and followed Morgan outside to the street.

"So where should we go?" asked Morgan.

"Not too far," replied Veronica, "You heard my Dad."

The sun had set a few hours earlier, and it was dark out. The community hall was in a residential neighbourhood. Most of the houses were dark because everyone was at the Harvest Dinner. The sidewalks were lit by street lamps.

The girls began their walk. Morgan started the conversation by confessing she must have eaten too much and was feeling sleepy.

"It's not because of tryptophan," offered Veronica.

"Do you mean how everyone always says turkey has something in it that makes people sleepy?" asked Morgan.

Veronica said, "Yes," and explained. The body uses tryptophan to make serotonin, a brain chemical which helps people sleep. It's a misconception that turkey contains high levels of tryptophan. Turkey has less tryptophan than chicken and there are many other foods which contain much higher levels of tryptophan.

"How do you know so much about chemistry?" Morgan asked.

"My parents make me study. I have to get good grades or else they make me study even more. When it comes to chemistry, I don't mind so much."

"So why do people get sleepy after they eat turkey?"

"Most likely from the carbohydrates eaten during a typical meal that includes turkey," Veronica hesitated and then finished her sentence, "and the sequence of things that happen after we eat carbohydrates."

"Sequence of things?"

"Well, it gets complicated because of everything happening in the body with glucose, the pancreas, insulin, amino acids and so on. I doubt you want to hear all the details."

Morgan agreed it was probably too heavy of a conversation topic for what time they had left of twenty minutes.

The girls turned and headed back. The dark sky was overcast and had a pink hue. Large fluffy snowflakes fell. Morgan remarked it was the first snowflakes of the season. Veronica agreed. Winter was coming.

There was an interval of silence. Veronica was shy and likely couldn't think of anything to say. Morgan was thinking about an idea.

STUDY DATE

Meredith was in the kitchen hunched over the dishwasher. From behind, Morgan said, "Hey Mom, I went for a..."

Meredith jumped and put her hand over her heart, "You startled me."

Morgan rolled her eyes and continued, "... walk with Veronica Wagler last night. She's smart and gets the best grades in class. So would it be okay if she came over so we can study chemistry together?"

Meredith resumed loading the dishwasher, "Hmm, it's not like you to come up with plans to study, and you certainly don't need my permission to do it. There's got to be more to this than what you're telling me. Out with it."

"Veronica actually has to study all the time and her parents won't let her come over otherwise. They'll probably even want to talk to you to first."

Meredith stood straight and put her hands on her hips, "I'm not telling them you girls are studying if you're just fooling around."

"That's the whole point of my idea." Morgan handed her a bowl. "We will study. Veronica actually likes chemistry. I might even get to like it too."

Still holding the bowl, Meredith said, "As long as I don't have to lie to her parents. Now don't the Waglers live on a farm? How's she going to get here and get home?"

"She can come home with me after school and I was thinking you or Dad could drive her home."

"I see. Now is there anything else I should know?"

"Nope, that's everything."

"I'll make you a deal." Meredith bent down to place the bowl on the bottom rack. She stood back up and said, "Let's try it and see how it goes."

Morgan said, "Great, do you want me to rinse the plates and hand them to you?"

Meredith answered, "Yes please," and thought, 'Oh my, I think she's growing up.'

CHAPTER 24

RITUALS

Cats love routines and consider them tantamount to rituals.
Such rituals can help cats and humans bond or deepen an
existing connection. - from "The Lives and Times of Cats"

Morgan and Veronica were on their second study date. The first time, Meredith promised Veronica's parents she would keep a close eye on them to be sure they were working on chemistry homework.

During this second study date, Meredith left them alone more often, and they made good use of the unsupervised intervals. In one break, Veronica asked Morgan about the jack-o'-lantern pumpkin carvings sitting on the dining room sideboard.

Morgan explained that she, her father and her brothers carved them so they would be displayed in the window for Halloween.

"Did it take you long to do it?" asked Veronica.

"No actually. Why? How long does it take you?"

Veronica sighed, "I've never carved one. My parents don't believe in Halloween. They say it's sacrilegious. I think it's fun and healthy to celebrate rituals like Halloween."

"What! Halloween is a ritual? That's kind of creepy. We don't worship Satan or anything like that. We carve pumpkins, wear costumes and give out candy to the little kids."

Veronica laughed and said, "I'm talking about the other kinds of rituals, like celebrating special occasions." The pace of her words slowed as if she was reading from a script. "The actions and symbols in rituals stimulate our emotions. Plus, through rituals we can achieve desired outcomes."

"Like when our basketball cheer-squad gets the crowd to cheer for our team to win?"

"Yes, exactly. The colours, the songs, and even the mascot all stimulate emotions. When we rally to cheer for our team, we are taking part in a ritual."

"What about Halloween? What outcome are we trying to get? Isn't it just for fun?"

"Well, fun, as you mentioned. Also, celebrating events with ritualistic actions and symbols creates feelings of unity and common purpose. But some people, like my parents, think rituals are primitive and unnecessary. They don't realize that rituals enrich our lives."

"So how do you know this? Did we learn it in school when I wasn't actually paying attention?"

Veronica laughed. "It was part of the research I did for my sociology essay."

"That's not due for another two weeks though."

"I'm glad for that. I have to do it over. Mom saw it and showed it to my dad. He said it was blasphemous and made me find another topic."

Morgan admitted she hadn't started her paper yet, and she didn't even have a topic. She thought for a moment, and Lucid World came to mind.

Morgan's eyes widened, and she said, "I just had an idea for my essay. I think I'll write about legends and ancient civilizations."

LOTUS FLOWERS

Amasis and Morgan were back at the pond, looking into the water. The seahorses were mating. Their courtship could go on for several days. All that time they would swim side by side at the same pace attempting to mirror the movement of the other in sync.

"It's like they're having a dancing ritual," said Morgan. "Is it khaos to not believe in rituals?"

"It's always khaos to reject something due to illogical fear. I think all people practice rituals whether they know it or not. A ritual is any activity that has symbolic or emotional meaning. So while not every ritual is suited to every person, a meaningful experience from practicing a meaningful ritual is suited to every person."

"What are some of the fun rituals you celebrate in Lucid World?"

"What do you mean by fun rituals?"

"You know, like Halloween or Valentine's Day."

"We don't celebrate either of those. We have a ritual, unique to Lucid World, that I think you'd like. It's called Lotus Day. We grow lotus plants in a greenhouse and they all bloom around the same time. Once a year we decorate Lucid World with lotus flowers. Visually, it is stunningly beautiful. Aromatically, it is marvellously fragrant."

"So do you do anything else besides just decorating and smelling?"

Amasis laughed. "There's special food and music. The music flows with the energy of the celebration as participants join in with various instruments. Some people meditate, to reflect on the meaning of Lotus Day."

"So what's the meaning of Lotus Day?"

"The meaning is taught to even the youngest of children. They learn that a lotus flower is beautiful and then withers. Due to its fleeting nature, it cannot provide real happiness. The symbol of the lotus flower reminds us that true happiness comes from within and does not come from external objects."

CHAPTER 25

POTATO CHIPS

Morgan had planned to write about legends and ancient civilizations for her sociology essay assignment. But when she wrote, she realized the topic was of interest to her only where it involved Mountain Lucid World or Island Lucid World. She narrowed her topic to the mystery of the Nazca Lines. In her essay, she explored various documented theories on the origin of the ancient geoglyphs, and introduced an additional theory. She postulated that the creation of the geoglyphs was inspired by a drawing that had been made by an advanced civilization to function as a marker to find a particular location again.

Morgan researched her topic thoroughly and put a lot of effort into her essay. Nothing in her paper supported her new theory and when her paper was graded, she barely received a passing score. Further, the teacher wrote a comment on the cover of her essay admonishing her for not following the assignment. In the teacher's words, "The assignment was to research a topic and hypothesize with well-founded arguments and reasoning, not to write a fictional story."

Morgan's parents knew she had worked diligently on her essay. When Morgan told them about her grade, their reactions differed.

Her mother told her she should view the situation as an important life lesson. Namely, in order for her efforts to result in success, Morgan must stay focused on the aim.

Her father told her that whether others appreciated imagination or not, imagination was a wonderful ability, for without imagination there would be no innovation.

Morgan felt that while both were supportive in their own ways, her parents were both wrong. What happened with her essay was another instance of her judgement being clouded by her enthusiasm to apply what she learned in Lucid World. The real lesson, in Morgan's mind, was that enthusiasm alone isn't enough to succeed. Understanding, intuition and pragmatism are also required.

Morgan fared much better academically with her chemistry grade. Studying with Veronica translated into a high score in the mid-term exam. For Morgan, the real benefit wasn't the high grade, it was the experience of enjoying the study of a school subject and getting to know Veronica.

Meredith viewed the high grade differently. It reinforced the importance of studying and motivated her to encourage the girls to continue to study together. She became an advocate for the weekly study night and assured Veronica's parents the girls were studying. She also allowed Morgan and Veronica more freedom and privacy during their time together.

As Morgan became increasingly influenced by Lucid World, school work was not the only area she put more effort into. Still, just like removing an impression left on a carpet after a weighted object is set upon it, more time and effort were required. It was more than simply removing the 'impressor'.

Daniel was in the backyard raking the lawn. Morgan offered to help.

"Hey, is this about an advance on your allowance?" asked Daniel.

"I just want to help. I don't actually want anything for it."

"Uh. Did your mother send you to help me? Is she punishing you for something?"

"Mom didn't send me to help you."

"Well, okay, Small Fry, grab a rake from the tool shed. You can start over there."

While Morgan raked, she felt her father was still suspicious of her motives. She recognized that his scepticism could be khaos behaviour. But she also recognized that the complete opposite, naivety, could also be khaos. She thought about the phrase, healthy scepticism, and the concept of not accepting an assertion unless justified by evidence or reason. Was he displaying healthy scepticism? Had her past behaviour given him reason to believe she had ulterior motives?

That evening, watching television with her brothers, Morgan experienced another instance of mistrust of her motives.

During a commercial break, she went to the kitchen to get potato chips. Back at the couch, she passed the bowl filled with chips to Dylan, and said, "So guys, you can put the chip bowl on your side."

Dylan looked at Ryan and said, "Whoa. There must be something wrong with the chips. She usually puts the bowl closest to her."

Ryan asked, "What's wrong with the chips, Morgan?"

Before Morgan could respond, Dylan said, "She probably licked some of them."

Ryan grimaced. "Here, you have this bowl, Morgan! I'll tell Mom what you did and get our own bowl of chips."

Morgan replied, "I didn't do anything to the chips. I promise. See, I'm eating them."

Dylan said, "Well, if you licked them, it wouldn't bother you to eat them."

"But I didn't lick any of them. Other times when we share chips or something, you say I hog the bowl. I'm sharing. You're my brothers and I love you."

Dylan and Ryan replied in unison, "Yuck!"

Dylan asked, "Whoa. What's all this love talk? Have you been watching mushy girl movies?"

Ryan said, "I'm not taking any chances. I'm going to get a new bag of chips and open them myself."

Morgan thought, 'I won't let this discourage me. I won't give in to khaos. But first, I'd better get to Mom before Ryan does and say I didn't lick the chips.'

CHAPTER 26

CLOSURE

Winds can change the weather to bring clear sunny skies
or clouds. Strong winds can bring storms and hurricanes.
– from "As the Wind Blows"

Daniel followed a routine each day when he got home from work: first, hellos to the children and then a kiss for Meredith.

One Friday in November, Daniel arrived home from work and went straight to the bedroom and shut the door. Concerned about his strange behaviour, Meredith joined him.

Morgan, Dylan and Ryan sat at the kitchen table working on their homework. They noticed the change of routine, too. Morgan volunteered to listen at the door.

Standing outside the door, Morgan heard the volume of her parents' voices rise and fall. Meredith's voice was the loudest, "How could they?" Daniel's voice was angriest, "Kept everyone in the dark."

Morgan had only ever heard her father sound so angry once before. It was a time when she was much younger. She had been curious about what would happen if a metal clothes-hanger was inserted into an electrical outlet. She talked the neighbour boy into trying it. Daniel caught them in the act, just seconds before the experiment was to begin. He was angry!

The voices got closer to the closed door. Morgan hustled back to the kitchen and sat at the table. She and her brothers looked down, pretending they were doing homework.

Daniel and Meredith walked into the kitchen together. Meredith's arm was around Daniel's waist.

They took seats at the table.

Daniel said, "Hey, take a break from your homework. We need to have a family meeting."

Daniel saw the alarm on their faces and tried to break the ice, "Relax guys, no one's in trouble. I got some pretty bad news at work today. The factory's closing."

Daniel crossed his arms, placed his elbows on the table and leaned forward as he provided details.

It was more cost effective for all the sugar beets go to the Taberville Sugar Factory for processing. The Coyote Flats operation would be shut down.

"Whoa. Do we have to move to Taberville?" asked Dylan with disdain.

"They've offered me a job there. But uh, not in my field."

Alarmed, Ryan asked, "So what're you going to do?"

"I'll look for another job. Until I find something I guess I'll commute."

"What if you can't actually find another job?" countered Morgan.

Daniel leaned back in his chair, looked at Meredith, who was silent. He exhaled. "There's no need to worry, let's wait and see." He looked worried.

THE WISDOM OF THE DALAI LAMA[4]

While strolling through the bird park, Morgan told Amasis about the factory closure. After she finished, she added, "I'm worried."

"About what?"

"I'm worried about Dad driving to Taberville every day. I'm worried he'll hate his new job. I'm worried he'll like his new job and we'll have to move there. I'm worried we might have less money." Morgan remembered who she was talking to.

Amasis didn't comment on her reference to money. Instead, he said, "Worry is unproductive and caused by illogical fear."

"This isn't illogical. This is real."

"Have you heard of the Dalai Lama?"

"The Buddhist monk?"

"Yes. He seems unaffected by khaos."

Amasis stopped walking and faced Morgan. "The Dalai Lama says: if there's a solution to a problem," Amasis gestured with open palms, "there's no need to worry." He raised his shoulders and shrugged as he said, "If there's no solution," he dropped his shoulders and went back to open palms, "there's no need to worry."

Morgan thought for a moment. "So if things can be changed, there's nothing to worry about. If things can't be changed, then worry won't help."

They started to walk again. Amasis teased, "And you thought I would say something about money and khaos."

Morgan laughed nervously, feeling embarrassed and humbled. She was not as clever as she thought and Amasis was more perceptive than she supposed.

TOWN MEETING

Farmers and employees of the sugar factory pressed the Coyote Flats council to schedule a town meeting to discuss the factory closure.

Though there had been a severe snowstorm the day before, there wasn't a cloud in the sky when the meeting was held. But even December sunshine intensified by newly fallen snow could not brighten up the dark mood inside the community hall.

The room was set-up theatre style, with a podium at the front. In spite of the difficulty of getting into and around Coyote Flats after the snowstorm, every chair was taken and several people stood at the back of the room. To the side, near the front of the room, three men and one woman, all dressed in business attire, sat at a table.

Most of the people there were acquainted with each other, but only a few whispered conversations could be heard. The soft voices tapered off as a middle-aged man wearing a charcoal-coloured suit paired with a striking ruby tie rose from the side table holding an opaque jar. He walked to the podium, set the jar in front of him and adjusted a microphone to the level of his mouth. His receding hair was dark, greying at the temples. After he adjusted the microphone, he said, "Attention everyone. I need your focus." He surveyed the group before he continued.

"I'm Antonio Marco. I've been asked to chair this forum to focus on the factory closure and the future of Coyote Flats. Most of you know me. For those who don't, I'm the mayor here in Coyote Flats."

He explained the meeting format. Executive officers from Wilco Sugar, owner of the Coyote Flats Sugar Factory, were there to answer questions. Attendees who wanted an opportunity to speak, registered at the table by the entrance and received a number. He would draw numbers randomly. After that, the party to whom the comment or question was directed would respond.

Mayor Marco reached his hand into the jar, pulled out a slip of white paper, read it and called out, "Number 76."

A stout balding man stood up. Mayor Marco said, "Hey Sam, come on up to the microphone."

Sam grabbed his belt at both sides of his hips and hiked his brown trousers up onto his bulbous belly. This wardrobe change puckered his white shirt; with his right hand he tucked the excess fabric into the front of his pant waistband. He bumped his way past the people seated beside him and lumbered to the microphone. Mayor Marco moved aside and sat near the podium.

"I don't work at the factory. I own the hardware store and it depends on the support of the community. It seems to me, if everyone moves to Taberville, no one will be left in Coyote Flats. So I want to say it's not just factory workers and farmers who'll be hurt."

The man left the microphone and returned to his seat.

The people seated at the table, whispered among themselves. A tall man, wearing a navy blue business suit, walked to the microphone. His stiff manner suggested a rehearsed speech as he addressed the audience with polite formalities and thanked the council for organizing the meeting. He then said, "For several years, Wilco has lost money at the Coyote Flats plant. We tried to turn things around. Now, with sugar prices so low, we have no choice. We need to reduce expenses by combining the operations of Coyote Flats and Taberville. Taberville is the larger of the two plants. It is more centrally located in the sugar beet agricultural region and so is the natural choice. Everyone at Wilco is very sorry, but there's nothing else we can do."

The man returned to the table and joined his Wilco colleagues. They resumed whispering.

Mayor Marco, holding the opaque jar, stood, reached for a number and called, "Number 23".

Number 23 was a tall blond man dressed in the fashion popular with farmers in the area: blue jeans, a denim shirt and a mesh trucker cap. When he got to the microphone, he turned to the Wilco people and reproached them, "Every year it gets harder and harder to make a living farming. I'll need another truck and another driver to get my beets to Taberville if I want to get them there before winter freezes 'em. I don't believe you're losing money. You just want more money."

The man's face was angry and red. He wasn't done. "You said you've known this for many years. Why didn't you warn us? Last year I bought more land to grow beets. Hell, I may as well just sign it over to the bank. I can't make a go of it now." Now he was done. He stood and stared.

Mayor Marco approached and touched the farmer's elbow. "John, why don't you take a seat and let the Wilco people respond."

As John took his seat, whispers emanated from the crowd and the Wilco representatives.

This time a slightly plump, kind-faced woman rose to take the microphone. In her sensible and professional soft blue dress, she did not give the polished and arrogant image of the first Wilco representative. She spoke softly and clearly as she addressed the audience and requested their attention.

There were "shushes," and then it was quiet. The kind-faced woman began, "John, may I call you John?" She didn't wait for his permission. "I understand your anger and frustration. You've every reason to feel as you do. In fact, I'm glad you feel that way because it means you believe in something important. Important to everyone in this room. Important to Wilco Sugar Company. Wilco believes in the local sugar industry. We waited to announce the plant closure because we were looking for other options. We cut costs and waited for sugar prices to go back up. Then last month, we lost a big percentage of our sales when our major supermarket customer imported more sugar made from sugar cane."

She paused, presumably to add dramatic effect to her next words. "If we keep the plant open, Wilco will go bankrupt and we'll all have hardships worse than travel and relocations."

She paused again. This time it seemed she did so to study the effect her words had on the facial expressions of her audience. However, her face was the only one that revealed any sign of changed emotion. Her former expression of empathy was replaced with disappointment.

She continued. "Employees have been sent letters explaining their options. Some have been offered jobs at Taberville. Severance payment packages are more than the labour laws require. Farmers from the Coyote Flats area will be paid extra for each truck load to compensate for the longer trip. What more can we do? If anyone has any ideas, we'd like to hear them."

The kind-faced woman extended her arm, holding the microphone, towards the audience.

Mayor Marco joined her at the podium. He took the microphone from her hand and said, "If anyone has any ideas, it's unnecessary to wait for your number to be called. Just raise your hand."

A woman with dark brown hair bound in a tight pony tail raised her arm. Mayor Marco nodded, pointed in her direction and said, "Go ahead."

The woman stood at her chair. She placed her hands on her hips and looked at those seated near her before fixating on Mayor Marco. "Sugar is a health menace. It's associated with heart disease, obesity, diabetes, cancer and cavities … to name a few. I could go on. Why are we looking for ways to continue making sugar? We should look for ways to make healthy products." Before she sat down, she looked around and waited for a sign of acknowledgement.

No one gave any indication of agreement or disagreement until finally a half-raised arm was visible. The arm belonged to Mrs. Vanderkloot, the wife of a farmer.

Mrs. Vanderkloot, a blonde woman with a girlish face, spoke without waiting for an invitation. "I agree with the ponytail lady. Too much sugar is not good. Except I don't agree that it causes diabetes. Type 2 diabetes is caused by genetics and being overweight; and too much food of any kind makes people fat." She paused and then emphasized her next word by raising the volume of her voice, "But it's up to individuals to decide how much sugar they want to eat. Not us. We already have our farms and equipment and we need to make a living to support our families. The sugar company man said sugar prices are too low. Why doesn't the company raise the price it sells the sugar for?"

Mrs. Vanderkloot's husband was sitting beside her. "I told you that won't work. The price is based on supply, demand and world economics."

Neither of the Vanderkloots said another word. Both sat looking straight ahead with their arms crossed and lips pursed. The room was silent and still. It seemed everyone was afraid to talk or move, for fear they, too, would be embarrassed.

Morgan sat quietly and attentively beside her father. Unlike the others, Morgan didn't think Mrs. Vanderkloot's suggestion was ill-conceived. Rather, it sparked her imagination.

She thought back to one of her first visits to Lucid World when Amasis told her Elder Tabubu invented the lint roller. The lint roller, a roll of sticky paper with a handle, a simple concept made from simple materials. Yet, it sells in stores for a price far higher than the cost to make. Was there something the sugar factory could make and sell for a price higher than the market price for sugar? Another memory ignited an idea. She had to speak.

Slowly, Morgan raised her hand. She looked around the room to see if anyone else had their hand up. No one else did.

Mayor Marco's voice rang through the microphone. "I see a hand raised." He pointed at Morgan.

"If we make something different, we could actually charge more money," blurted Morgan from her seat. All heads turned to look at her.

Mayor Marco said, "Your name is Morgan, isn't it? You and your friend painted my fence this summer. It's tremendous to see our young people focused on community matters. Well, ha-ha, I can't hear you very well," he chuckled, "come up to the microphone." Everyone in the room chuckled, too. The tension was lifted, for everyone except Morgan.

Antonio Marco continued as Morgan approached the microphone. "The factory closure impacts the entire community. Our young people should have a chance to speak."

From the podium, Morgan said, "I have an idea." It felt as though her heart was beating in her ears. When Morgan was nervous, she spoke rapidly. Quickly, she continued.

"Yesterday, in cooking class, my friend Veronica, who's a whiz at chemistry, melted sugar and added other things and poured it into a mould. When it hardened, it was amazing! It sparkled just like fresh snow when the sun is shining."

Morgan caught her breath. "The factory could use Veronica's invention to make things and charge more for them. Things like sparkly edible snowflakes."

Morgan was interrupted by a loud voice from the side table. "Thank you for your suggestion err ... young miss." It was the Wilco man who previously spoke to the crowd. "Wilco looked into specialty items like what you suggested but the volume required to break even is more than the market can support."

He was interrupted by Mr. Hunter, the head accountant for the factory, who was also seated at the side table. "Ah yes, if only specialty items are produced."

Robert Hunter rose and moved to the centre of the room near the podium where Morgan still stood. He directed his words to the Wilco man and woman. "Regular sugar products could still be produced. And the new line of specialty items would have a much higher gross margin. It's all about fixed and variable costs. I don't need to get into the details here. Trust me, it could work."

John, the farmer who spoke at the podium previously, yelled from his seat, "Why should we trust you? You work for the factory."

Robert said, "Let me explain. Regular sugar products currently cover their own variable costs and contribute towards the fixed costs, but not enough to cover all the fixed costs. The specialty items could cover their own variable costs and take care of the rest of the fixed costs and may even add profit to the bottom line."

Conversations broke out throughout the room. People rose and stood at their chairs all over the room, talking.

"Sparkly coffee sweeteners... diamond shapes... fancy restaurants would buy... kids would love..."

Mayor Marco called 'order' and the roomed quieted. The Wilco woman addressed Mr. Hunter from her seat. "Bob, I'm not so sure I can convince our shareholders. Any invention and specialty items are all very risky."

Morgan still standing at the podium asked, "What's Wilco actually going to do with the Coyote Flats factory building and land?"

The Wilco woman rose and in an insolent tone said, "We'll salvage as much as we can. The empty building and land will be donated to the Town of Coyote Flats so we can save the cost of property taxes."

A factory employee leapt to his feet. "What if Wilco leaves the entire factory to us?"

The Wilco woman replied. "We need the money from the salvage to pay employee severances."

Fred Bell, the manager of the local Poultry Cooperative, had been seated in the audience. He stood and said, "If Wilco doesn't have to pay severance, it doesn't need salvage money." He moved to the front of the room and joined Robert Hunter in a manner denoting an alliance. Fred looked at him for permission to continue. Robert nodded.

Fred said, "Farmers, employees and businesses could form a cooperative and Wilco could leave the entire plant to the co-op. The co-op can run the factory and it can be business as usual, except for the new specialty products to be added. Breaking even is enough for cooperative members but shareholders of companies like Wilco have much higher profit expectations. Since members of the co-op get rewarded by keeping their jobs, farms and businesses, there's less pressure for a profit."

Mayor Marco interjected. "Fred, could you explain more about a cooperative for the folks who don't know."

"Well, it's an organization owned by its members: suppliers, employees and even customers. If the organization makes profit, the profit is distributed to the members based on the amount of business or work each member had with the organization."

Enthusiasm filled the room and produced an infectious energy. Everyone felt it. Everyone except the Wilco people. They seemed confused and perplexed. They hadn't expected the people of Coyote Flats to come up with a solution.

Mayor Marco helped Morgan down from the podium and asked everyone to return to their seats. He resumed his role as chairperson and asked Robert Hunter to outline the next steps.

Mr. Hunter then suggested that they form a committee with representatives from the growers, the employees, local business and Wilco. The committee would determine the feasibility and marketability of Veronica's sugar invention, and whether there were any other possible specialty products. After that, numbers would be crunched and negotiations entered into with Wilco.

When Mayor Marco resumed his position at the podium, he asked, "Would those in favour raise their hands?" He didn't need to do a count. He said, "It looks like it's unanimous!"

Members of the crowd clapped their hands in applause and nodded their heads in approval.

Mayor Marco quieted the crowd and said, "We've all done a tremendous job today. It's most wonderful to see everyone focus on a problem and work together for a solution. Also, we can be tremendously proud of the youth in this town."

ON THE FARM

Morgan couldn't wait to give Veronica the news. Then a thought struck her. How would Veronica's parents react? Would she get into trouble for fooling around in class? Was it fooling around? It was more like combining two school subjects: chemistry and cooking.

The town meeting had been held on Saturday. Morgan didn't want to wait until Monday to talk to Veronica, in case the news got to Veronica's parents sooner.

Morgan emailed her. Veronica emailed back. Morgan's worries

were unfounded. Veronica had told her parents about the invention because she considered it a scientific feat. She and her mother had already made a batch of the sparkly candy together.

On Monday, when the girls talked at school, Veronica said her father was happy about the news of the cooperative idea. The factory closure had been upsetting to him for the same reasons it was upsetting to all the farmers. Besides the usual challenges related to farming, last year the crop on Veronica's family's farm was destroyed by a severe hail storm. Her father had to use the farm as collateral for a large operating loan and worried he wouldn't be able to provide for his family and make loan repayments.

"He thinks God is punishing him for something," Veronica said. Her eyes looked sad.

"Why would he think that?"

"I know. It doesn't make sense. Especially since," Veronica shook her head, "he never even wanted to be a farmer."

"Then why is he?"

"Obligation, responsibility, to do the right thing. He wanted to be a doctor, but when his older brother Karl left home to join the RCMP, that was the end of his dream. There was no way he could help on the farm and at the same time work to save money for university."

Veronica added, "That's why they make me study so hard, so I can get a scholarship."

Morgan said nothing and had a wondering expression on her face so Veronica elaborated, "You know, to pay for tuition and stuff."

"Oh, right." Morgan had been thinking about the name 'Karl'. She didn't know anyone by that name, but she'd heard the name before, and recently. Where? Then she remembered. Karleen had a letter that had something to do with someone named Karl. It was probably just another example of life's coincidences. Or an example of how the subconscious notices things related to previous thoughts.

CHAPTER 27

WHO'S SINGING?

Morgan stopped to listen. Sounds of a melodic female voice, and the soft strumming of a guitar, emanated from the Frey house. Morgan was walking by when she heard it.

She stayed on the sidewalk and listened at a distance. Sally had never invited Morgan to visit her at home. The playing started and stopped in the manner of someone learning a new song. Whoever the musician was, she was talented.

Later that day, Morgan walked by the Frey house again, this time with Cara. Sally was outside with her toddler brother, Mikey. Morgan called out, "Sally, so who was singing before? She actually sounded like a real singer."

"Hi Morgan, Hi Cara," said Sally hurriedly, "sorry have to go. Mom's calling." She grabbed Mikey's hand, and they ran into the house.

The next day, at school, Morgan saw Sally in the hall between classes.

"Hey, who was singing at your house yesterday? Was that your mom?"

Sally looked around to see if anyone could hear their conversation. In a low voice she said, "No, that was… me." She put her palms together to illustrate praying hands, "Please don't say anything to anybody."

"Wow! Why not?"

Sally exhaled loudly and said, "My mom'll get mad."

"Why? You're actually fantastic."

Sally shrugged, "She says it'll ruin my life, like it ruined hers."

"How'd you learn to play?"

"My mom's boyfriends taught me. A lot of them are guys who play music in the pub."

"If you could sing in public, you might get discovered. You could be rich and famous."

"Maybe but my ..." Sally didn't finish.

"How can music ruin someone's life?"

Sally shook her head, "I don't know, she won't tell me."

CHAPTER 28

A CAVE

Morgan couldn't stop thinking about it. Sally was exceptionally talented at music. Khaos often passed from one generation to the next so Sally might be destined for a life like her mother, Franny. Morgan knew she shouldn't judge someone's life. But she saw the disrepair of the exterior of the Frey house and condition of the yard. Also, Franny Frey didn't look happy, especially when she scowled and mumbled profanities, as she often did.

Visions of Sally's future if she followed her mother's path troubled Morgan. Well, it didn't have to be that way, did it? Sally, like everyone, could beat khaos and be happy. However, she could use a little push in the right direction.

That night Morgan had a vivid dream before her visit to Lucid World. She was in a cave where an underground spring surfaced and pooled. Others, strangers, were there. The air temperature dropped, but it was of no concern because the underground spring was warm. Dream-Morgan believed she remembered she had been in the situation before, and that time everyone froze to death. 'How?' she wondered, 'if the water in the spring provides warmth.'

The water temperature dropped. It would happen again!

Dream-Morgan tried to build a fire, but it kept going out. The others seemed oblivious to the situation. 'That must be how they froze last time!'

If they wouldn't tend the fire, she would. She looked around for flammable material to burn; and found chairs and books. Such items wouldn't normally be found in a cave, but it was a dream.

Dream-Morgan stopped to consider the value of the items. It didn't matter. She couldn't let people freeze to death. Not this time. As she fed the flammables to the fire, she noticed she was no longer tending it alone. Others helped.

"Morgan, can you hear me? Hello. Hello. It's Amasis."

She was in a kitchen? In Lucid World? She was no longer Dream-Morgan. She was Avatar-Morgan.

Amasis was standing over a mound of grey-brown roots piled on a counter top.

"Amasis! What a dream! It felt as real as when my avatar is here."

"Perhaps the dream related to something you've been thinking about lately."

"Don't think so. There was a cave and a fire and people freezing to death. What're you doing?"

"I'm making garguey." Amasis scooped the roots with his hands and dropped them into a pot of boiling water on a stovetop, saying, "Dreams can be symbolic. Why don't you tell me the whole dream and if anything different or unusual happened recently."

"Who's the garguey for? You haven't figured out a way for my avatar to eat, have you?"

"No, but I wish I could." His dark eyes twinkled, and he winked. "I wanted you to see how it's made and that it's not worms or whatever you think it looks like."

While they waited for the roots to cook, Morgan described the dream and then described her discovery of Sally's talent.

Amasis said, "I think you'll be able to figure this one out."

"How? I don't actually know anything about dream interpretation."

"What does the cave with an underground-spring remind you of?"

"Lucid World?"

"Perhaps to you it represents Lucid World."

"The water cooling, could that be khaos? Khaos patterns

repeat, but not this time. I started the fire, and we kept it going together. I fought khaos; and others fought khaos too!"

"Perhaps."

"Perhaps! Is that all you can say?"

Amasis dipped a utensil into the boiling pot and pulled out a root. He set it on a dish to cool and said, "I say, I think the garguey is ready. And dream interpretation is about what the dreamer takes from the dream. How do you think the dream ties in with your recent thoughts of Sally?"

Amasis picked up the root with his fingers and waved it in the air. It was pliable, like a worm.

Morgan watched and scowled. "Should I interfere in others' lives? What if people want to freeze to death? Should I build a fire for them? What if Sally doesn't want my help?"

Amasis turned back to the pot, turned off the flame under it, and used a broad scoop with holes to transfer the garguey to a blue-green ceramic bowl.

Morgan watched. So far, the concoction didn't look too bad. "Besides, even if she wanted my help, how could I help? I'm just a teenager."

Amasis reached for a squirt bottle and bathed the garguey in a milky slimy mixture. Now it looked gross! He said, "Let me tell you a story."

"Okay. Ewww, you're not going to eat that in front of me?"

"It's best when it's fresh. Besides, I think it may be a good prop to use to tell the story." Amasis sat at a stool at the counter and Morgan joined him.

"Imagine creatures, which look like this garguey, living in a large river."

"That won't help me watch you eat it."

Amasis laughed. "The garguey-like creatures clung to the river bottom so the current wouldn't sweep them away. They did this from generation to generation because it's what their roots taught them to do."

"Good one: 'roots' hahaha."

"One of the garguey, tired of clinging, decided to let go and allow the current to take it where it would. The other garguey predicted it would be thrown and smashed to death on the rocks. When the current first carried the garguey, it got bumped and gashed on the rocks. In time, as the garguey continued to refuse to cling, the current lifted it off the river bottom and it smoothly glided away."

"I don't think it needed the current to slide along. I would think some of your slimy sauce would do the trick."

"True. Hahaha. So as this garguey floated above them, other root creatures looked up and saw one that was like themselves but it was flying, so they believed it possessed special powers. The flying garguey called out, 'The river will set you free if only you dare to go.' The others continued to cling. They looked away, and when they looked back, the flying garguey was gone, and they were left with a legend."

"So I'm one of the garguey clinging to the bottom of the river. Still, I'm only just a teenager going to high school. I don't have my own money. Even if I did, I don't actually know anything about the music industry. I don't want to end up like your garguey: in hot water, then devoured."

"I'll have you know, I cook only the best garguey. But seriously, it sounds like you have khaos manifesting as a distortion of reality."

"Really!?" Morgan feigned a dramatic exasperation with her arms up in the air, "There are even more kinds of khaos?"

Amasis feigned dramatic sympathy by nodding his head and looking to the ground. He then pretended to quickly recover, and said, "Yup, beliefs are based on environment and experience. When new information is compatible with existing beliefs, it's accepted and absorbed. But when it conflicts, it may be ignored or even distorted."

"Huh. I don't do that."

"Think about it. You hope you can help your friend, and you fear you can't. If your fear causes you to abandon your hope, you are processing new information distortedly. Your fear is the distortion of reality. Not your hope."

"It sounds good when you say it, but I actually can't help Sally with her music."

"What about the Sugar Factory meeting? You may have helped save the factory and people's jobs and businesses."

"All I did was come up with an idea. This is different. People I know aren't music producers or famous people. They can't do anything other than say, 'That's nice, maybe someday she'll be discovered'."

"Remember the garguey living in the river. Let go and watch what happens."

CHAPTER 29

INCIDENT AT THE COYOTE FLATS GARAGE

All that is gold does not glitter,
Not all those who wander are lost;
The old that is strong does not wither,
Deep roots are not reached by the frost.
- A verse by J.R.R. Tolkien

Franny stood in line at the cash register, behind a farmer who was paying an invoice. 'Humph,' muttered Franny, 'Just pay the fricking bill and quit asking stupid questions, or we'll be here 'til Christmas.'

The Coyote Flats Garage was the only place in town that carried her brand of cigarettes. Otherwise, she would have left to go elsewhere. She crossed her arms and tapped her right foot. Christmas music was playing in the background. Could this be any more painful?

Tired of looking at the farmer's back, she looked around the room. In the corner, there was a Christmas tree with wrapped presents underneath it. Her mood softened as she thought how much Sally and Mikey would love their gifts this year. She had worked extra shifts cleaning rooms at the hotel, for extra money for Christmas.

Her toddler, Mikey, was tugging at her hand. She loosened her grip and pointed at the tree. He walked towards it. She caught her reflection in the two-way glass-mirror to what was probably the office. 'Not bad, not great,' she thought. She sucked in her tummy.

'Collateral damage from having kids. Otherwise, I'm still working it.'

The door to the outside was a swinging door. Mikey was finished looking at the tree, which was much like the one at his home, and pushed against the door. It easily, and soundlessly, opened.

He walked out onto pavement that was sheltered by an overhang. A large oil stain was covered with sand to soak up the oil. 'Just like the sand box at the playground!' imagined Mikey.

The farmer left and Franny addressed the cashier, "Finally! Gimme two packs of the usual."

The farmer's tractor was parked parallel to the garage. He climbed up into the driver's seat. A vehicle was parked in front of the tractor. The farmer shoulder checked behind him and put the tractor into reverse.

Mrs. Costadinawich stood across the street. Her eyes were fixed on Mikey playing. A faint smile shaped her lips. Sounds of the tractor motor and transmission changing gears jarred her out of her trance. She saw the tractor's backup lights.

'Oh my God!' she thought, 'he can't see the little boy! He doesn't know he's there.' She froze. 'There's no time!'

She jerked her body into motion. 'There has to be time!' She ran to the driver's window of the tractor and flailed her arms about. The window was high and the farmer couldn't see her.

She saw a tire wrench on a tool stand. She grabbed it and hurled it at the tractor door. The tractor stopped. She flailed her arms again.

The motor turned off. A very confused farmer stepped down from the tractor cab.

For years to come, Coyote Flats people will still talk about how an old, old woman (she gets older every time the story is told) mustered the strength to get the tire wrench airborne to hit the tractor door.

Mrs. Costadinawich trembled and cried. The puzzled farmer approached her.

Franny walked to the rear of the tractor and yelled, "There you are you little brat." Mikey continued playing in the sand. Franny was oblivious to what almost just happened, or was in denial.

She grabbed Mikey by the arm, yanked him up and they trotted off.

It wasn't until then that the farmer realized what almost happened. His face turned pale, his eyes widened and his mouth gaped. When he recovered enough to speak, he said, "You're a hero. If it wasn't for you..." He couldn't say the rest.

SUSAN COSTADINAWICH

A hero. The man called her a hero. She didn't feel like a hero. She felt like an orange with the juice squeezed out of it. Her legs, arms and shoulders ached. Her head ached. She couldn't stop imagining what would have happened if the tractor hadn't stopped.

After the owner of the garage drove her home, she sat in her favourite chair for a long time, thinking.

'The world can be a very sad place.' The time leading up to Christmas was always an especially sad time for her. She still missed her husband, Aylmer. Last month was ten years since he passed away.

'Mikey. Mikey. Just a little boy.' She had been watching him play in the sand because when she first looked in his direction, he returned her gaze with a big chubby-cheeked smile. For an instant, she felt a stab at her heart.

Something about his smile reminded her of a friend from long ago. Margie and she met in grade one and were best friends until Margie's daughter, died in an accident. Margie was grief-stricken. To make matters even worse, a few days later, her other daughter ran away from home. Things were never the same after that. Margie needed consoling and guidance that, she, Susan Costadinawich, didn't know how to give. Margie must have felt this, too, and the two long-time best friends drifted apart.

A tear ran down Susan's cheek, 'Yes, the world can be very sad and lonely.'

She and Alymer moved to Coyote Flats when Alymer was transferred from the Taberville Sugar Factory. Most Coyote Flats townspeople were born and raised in Coyote Flats and had well established social connections. They were polite to Alymer and her. Yet, it seemed they were always considered to be outsiders.

After Alymer died, she tried a little harder to 'fit in' and make friends. After a while she gave up. Maybe she should have tried harder. 'Too late now. Too tired for parties and social clubs and such. Still, it would be nice to have a friend to talk to.'

The town kids called her a witch, and every Halloween they threw eggs at her house. Mostly because of her name, Costadina-witch. And probably because, after Alymer passed away, she quit dyeing the grey out of her hair and grew it long so she could tie it up.

A friend might suggest they dye her hair together. Or go to the beauty salon together for a short easy-to-style haircut. Even better, and Susan made herself laugh at this thought, plan a trick to play on those egg-touting brats to scare the pants off them, hahaha. She and her friend wouldn't do it but they'd have fun thinking and talking about it.

A smile lingered on her lips as she fell asleep in her favourite chair.

CHAPTER 30

YES AND NO

Khyan, Iris and Amasis sat in Elder Tabubu's chambers awaiting her arrival. She had summoned them to a meeting. None of them knew the reason.

Khyan thought back to the first time he'd been summoned by Tabubu and waited for her in this same room. It was over a year ago. Amazing! During the first few months, they worked long hours to select and prepare for the group of Nosos adolescents. In February, they made first contact. Now it was already December!

One of Tabubu's cats, a big-eared, cinnamon-coloured beauty, rubbed against Khyan's leg. He reached down and placed her on his lap.

The cat heard the sound of footsteps, in the distance, long before the humans did. She leapt off Khyan's lap, scratched his thigh in the act, and ran towards the sound.

Khyan winced and let out a small howl just as Tabubu entered the room.

Tabubu addressed Khyan and said, "I hope your wait wasn't too painful."

Amasis and Iris laughed. Khyan seemed lost for words and stuttered, "Ahhh, yes, I mean no, hahaha."

Elder Tabubu went to her chair. The cat leapt onto her lap in a single bound and purred loudly, as Tabubu's fingers caressed its head.

"Tonight is the Council Assembly. I need to provide a status report on the Nosos World youth program. It has been almost ten months and by now you must have made progress."

Khyan answered, "Yes and no, Elder Tabubu."

"Yes and no, again?" Elder Tabubu teased.

Khyan laughed. "In this context, it's an expression I picked up from the Nosos World youth. It means the answer is not straightforward. Rather, it's complicated and involved."

"In that case, I will listen carefully."

Khyan began. "We are working with five adolescents. We started with six but one had to leave the project."

"Why was that?" asked Tabubu.

"Our project participants need to live in a rural area with minimal EMF interference. One boy's family moved to a large city. We could not adapt our transmission equipment problem. As a result, he couldn't continue with the project."

"How goes it with the remaining five?"

Khyan answered. "All of them understand and can identify khaos emotions and actions. Still, they often have difficulty applying what they know."

"They are getting better at it, though," interjected Amasis. "They've all shown great improvement in the last two or three months."

"Improvement, in what way?" asked Tabubu.

Khyan said, "For example, one boy had strong feelings of guilt, anger and resentment related to his parents' divorce. Now, he realizes the divorce was not his fault and it was his fear that fueled his anger and resentment."

"Superb," said Tabubu, "tell me more."

Amasis volunteered the next example. "One girl was often influenced by acceptance of others. She recognized the khaos of this very early in our sessions, but changing this behaviour proved very challenging for her. In September, seven months into our program, she overcame many of her fears related to rejection and judgment."

Enthusiastically, Iris added, "Amasis is talking about Morgan. That's not all Morgan has accomplished and I think there's more to come."

"Do the others show similar encouraging signs of reversing khaos?"

"That brings us back to the 'yes and no' answer. All of them have changed how they think, act and react. Often the changes are short-lived; or when a different situation comes along, they revert to khaos without realizing they are doing so."

"Do you think in time the changes may be more permanent and they will learn to deal with new situations without khaos?" asked Tabubu.

"Yes. That's why I believe we should continue our work," replied Khyan.

"Iris, Amasis, do you agree with Khyan? Do you want to continue with the program?"

Iris answered first. "Elder Tabubu, I wasn't as optimistic as Khyan and Amasis when we began."

She looked at Khyan. He nodded, he knew.

With enthusiasm, she addressed Tabubu, "From what I've seen, we've already made enough of a difference to justify our efforts, regardless of whether we ultimately reverse khaos in an individual or a global level." Iris moved her eyes back to Khyan, "I think the program has a lot of potential, and I'd like to continue to be involved."

Khyan beamed and asked, "Amasis, do we have your support?"

"I think you already know the answer. Yes, of course."

Tabubu lifted the cat from her lap, set it on the floor, and rose from her chair indicating the meeting was coming to a close. She said, "I am encouraged by your progress and I share your enthusiasm."

Khyan, Amasis and Iris exchanged respectful goodbyes with Tabubu and filed out of the room.

'TIS THE SEASON

When Avatar-Morgan arrived in the treasure map room, the first thing she noticed was a big grin on Iris's face as she sat back in one of the comfy chairs.

Morgan sat down beside her and asked, "What's up? You look like the cat that swallowed the canary."

"What? I look like a cat that ate a bird?"

Morgan laughed. "It's just an expression. You look pleased with yourself."

"Oh, it's an idiom."

"What?"

"It's an expression with a meaning not deducible from the individual words."

"Like, 'it's raining cats and dogs'?"

"Yes. That one I know," said Iris. "I'm pleased about the project progress meeting we had with Elder Tabubu."

"That's good to hear, especially coming from you."

Iris straightened up and asked, "What'd you mean?"

"You weren't very positive when we started."

"True." Iris nodded, "I think we need to continue looking for a more scientific solution. This project is worthwhile if we can make even a small difference."

"Rome wasn't built in a day."

"Another idiom?"

"Yup." Morgan smiled at Luna falling asleep in the chair next to her.

Iris considered the expression on Morgan's face and said, "You look pleased today, too. What canary did you swallow?"

Morgan laughed, "I'm always in a good mood leading up to Christmas."

"Ah, I have heard the ritual of celebrating Christmas is a favourite for many in Nosos."

"It is for many, but not for everyone. Some religions don't celebrate Christmas. Also, many who celebrate it complain that it's too commercial, too expensive and too much work. And it can be sad for people who are lonely and have no one to share it with."

"It sounds like there's a lot of khaos associated with it."

"There is. I've been thinking about Christmas and khaos and whether it's true that the meaning of Christmas has been lost." Morgan put her hand close to her chin, "Why can't Christmas mean different things to different people? It shouldn't matter why Christmas is, or isn't, important to someone. People who celebrate it should decide what the ritual means to them and celebrate it in a way that feels right for them. Why are you grinning again? You look like you swallowed another canary."

"I'm just so proud of you. I agree with your insights about the meaning and celebration of Christmas."

"Good to know khaos didn't creep in. I guess I hit the nail on the head." Iris and Morgan both laughed.

CHAPTER 31

LET GO AND WATCH WHAT HAPPENS

*When the wind powers a vessel through water it is termed
sailing. Proponents of sailing say it is relaxing, fun and
exhilarating. Opponents of sailing complain of becoming
stationary because of lack of wind or being blown off course
by severe winds. - from "As the Wind Blows"*

Amasis's garguey story had made convincing points. Soon
Morgan set out to help Sally in spite of the obstacles
she perceived. Morgan met with the school career
counsellor, Mrs. Kyatchi, who suggested a scholarship fund could
be established for Sally to go to music school.

What ensued gave Morgan an important insight. Not only
did Morgan have to overcome her distorted perceptions of
her resources and abilities, she had to overcome her distorted
judgements of motives and abilities of others.

It was Lucid World that created this judgemental flaw in
Morgan's world view. She had been chosen by Khyan's team to
help with an important project and was a student in the study
of khaos. Morgan often identified khaos in others. Because khaos
in others is easier to detect than khaos within ourselves, Morgan
had a superiority complex. She believed herself less "khaosy" than
others.

Morgan went door to door asking neighbours for donations
to the scholarship fund to help a girl who had an exceptional gift
which, due to financial circumstances, she may never develop.

Morgan skipped the Byrds' house. She preferred to avoid Mrs.
Byrd after the fence incident.

One day after school, there was a message waiting for Morgan: Mrs. Byrd would like her to come to her house. She didn't say why.

Morgan called Cara. Did she know anything? She didn't. The fence was fixed several months ago and as far as she knew the matter was resolved.

Morgan rang the doorbell. She waited. Maybe she didn't hold the button long enough. She pressed it again.

"I'm coming! I'm coming, hold your horses." Mrs. Byrd opened the door handle using a hand held under the cloth at the front of an apron she was wearing. "Come in and close the door. My hands are messy." She turned and walked up a short flight of stairs. Morgan followed.

They went to the kitchen. Mrs. Byrd rinsed her hands at the sink and wiped them on a towel. A strand of red hair was touching her cheek. She brushed it aside with the back of her hand to return it to the rest of her loosely-curled short hair. A few grey roots betrayed the authenticity of her dramatic hair colour.

Mrs. Byrd removed a cutting board with partially chopped vegetables from the table and placed it on a nearby countertop. "Please sit. Want something to drink?"

Morgan declined refreshment and sat down. Mrs. Byrd sat across from her and eyed her through the thick lens of her glasses while saying, "I know what you've been up to."

"Huh? What?"

"With the Frey girl. I know it's all anonymous and hush hush so no one has to deal with Franny. I've seen you with Sally and you're not the only one who knows about her talent."

"How do you know about this?"

"I have ears, don't I? Their house is directly across from the empty lot out back."

Mrs. Byrd motioned towards a window facing the back of the house. "Go and look. The Frey house is right there."

Morgan got up to look. She hadn't realized how close the two houses were. The Byrd's house was on an angular lot and the street behind curved towards it, resulting in the Frey house being a stone's throw away.

Morgan sat back down. Mrs. Byrd leaned in towards her. "If

Franny knew what that girl does when she's gone, there'd be a hullabaloo." She leaned back in her chair, "I hear her mostly in the summer, when the windows are open."

"Are you going to tell Franny? I mean, Mrs. Frey?"

"Of course not! I'm not a blabber mouth. I never said a word that you were with that Cara girl in the truck. Meredith mentioned nothing about it when I saw her, so I'm sure she doesn't know. Oh, don't look so surprised. You think I was never young and adventurous?"

"I'm sorry that Cara and I hit your fence. I didn't tell my parents. I guess I should have. But I didn't want to get grounded."

"Yah, I know. Like I said, I was young once. I didn't ask you to come over so I could hold it over you or get an apology or anything like that. I think what you're doing for the Frey girl is nice and I want to help."

"Help? Okay, how?"

"You will need more than a scholarship fund to convince Franny to let Sally go to music school. I know what people say about her and all but she loves her kids fiercely. They're all she has. Mr. Byrd's sister works for that Talent Scout show. I can ask her to help us."

IT'S SHOW TIME!

It was a Saturday night in January and Morgan was so excited she could barely contain herself. For several weeks leading up to the anticipated event of the evening, she had worked obsessively on plans and arrangements.

Mrs. Byrd's sister-in-law arranged for an audio recording of an original song, sung and played by a 'Miss Terry', to go to the producer of the popular television show 'Talent Scout'.

The career counsellor at Coyote Flats High School contacted the Music Foundation, also known as MF, to make arrangements for...

"Quit talking everybody! It's actually started!" commanded Morgan.

Morgan, her parents, her brothers and Cara anxiously settled around the TV.

The announcer appeared and explained the premise of the

show. Contestants perform and a panel of independent judges score each performance. The performer who achieves the highest score is the winner of a monetary prize.

The first few contestants performed. Morgan wished each one would hurry and finish. And then, "Ladies and Gentlemen, we have an unusual entry tonight. We have audio only from a contestant referred to as Miss Terry. Oh I get it, 'Mystery'."

It was a sad song. The voice was clear and strong. The guitar strumming was enchanting. As the melody rose and fell it sent shivers up Morgan's spine and neck. Morgan had heard the song many times in the past few weeks, but she never tired of it and it never failed to make her feel shivery.

With no contestant on stage to focus on, the television camera panned through the audience. Everyone was still. Everyone listened. Some had teary eyes. When the song finished, the audience appeared momentarily frozen; and then simultaneously broke into a voluminous applause. Some stood at their seats.

The announcer returned to the stage, a few more acts came on and some of the performers were interviewed.

The announcer said it was time for the judges to tally their scores and the program was interrupted for a commercial break.

After a long series of commercials, the program resumed. Morgan held her breath.

"We have a landslide winner. The winner is Miss Terry! Accepting the award for Miss Terry is Mr. Simon from MF, the Music Foundation."

A stout man, with receding blonde hair, entered the stage from a side curtain. He was smartly dressed in a black suit complimented by a white shirt and white bow tie. He thanked the audience and explained: he was authorized by Miss Terry to disclose her real name if she won the talent contest. She was Sally Frey from Coyote Flats. Sally planned to use the prize money to study music at the University of Lethbridge. In addition, throughout the four-year program, Sally would qualify for bursary funding made available by benefactors of MF.

It was the type of feel-good story that can make an audience go wild, and 'wild' they went. The announcer returned to the stage and above the massive applause, yelled, "Congratulations, Sally, from all of us!"

GIRLS WHO DON'T FINISH HIGH SCHOOL

Sally rose early on Sunday morning. Filled with excitement and dread, she hadn't slept well. Last night, before the show aired, Franny had left her to watch Mikey. Now she had to tell her mother the news.

While Franny was still sleeping, Sally got the computer ready. The station that broadcast Talent Scout archived episodes of the show on their website. Sally advanced the video to the announcer introducing her song. Her mother would recognize the show and the announcer. They often watched it together on Saturday evenings and Franny liked to make fun of the contestants.

Sally heard her mother stirring. The sounds were all too familiar:
Grumbling.
The medicine cabinet door opening.
A bottle shaken to dispense pills.
The medicine cabinet door closing.
Water running from a tap.
Quiet.
A toilet flushing.
Water running from a tap.
Footsteps in the hall approaching the living room.
"What are you up to? You have that look on your face."
"Mom, I have something important to show you. Please watch."
Sally started the video.

Franny walked away while saying, "I don't have time to watch. Humph, you'd think people would have better fricking things to do."

"It's not something silly. Come back and just watch, okay?"

Franny stood in front of the computer with her arms folded. She watched, listened and said nothing.

Sally fast-forwarded to the winner. When the program was finished, Franny maintained her folded-arms posture and silence.

Sally waited. She didn't know how to 'read' Franny's reaction.

Or rather, lack of reaction.

Finally, Franny spoke. "So that's what you've been doing sneaking around. Don't think I didn't know you were up to something. So I guess you'll be running off to be a star."

Franny put her hands on her hips and struck a model catwalk pose, "Shall I use our grocery money to buy you some designer sunglasses?"

"No Mom, you didn't listen. It's for music school."

"I told you what happens to girls who don't finish high school."

"I'll finish high school there. I can study music while I get my diploma, and earn university credits at the same time."

"Humph. Well you've got it all figured out. So go ahead. Leave!"

"It's not 'til September." Sally's eyes teared and she pleaded, "I need your permission to go. They won't enroll me if you don't give it to me."

"Humph." Franny sneered, "While you were figuring everything out, did you figure out who'd look after Mikey if you left?"

CHAPTER 32

ICECAP

*Wind, as an energy source, was once considered to be
non-depletable. However, due to global warming, wind
power is decreasing in some regions of the world as average
temperatures rise. — from "As the Wind Blows"*

Iris sat at a table with her head in her hands. She looked up as
Avatar-Morgan appeared in the room.

Several print-outs of what appeared to be rows of
numbers were spread out in front of Iris. She mumbled something.
The only word Morgan understood was, "Elders."

Iris's usual demeanour was composed and confident. The
person who Morgan saw was neither.

Morgan was still trying to understand the scene when Iris
said, "Our icecap has receded at an accelerated pace due to
global warming. We thought we still had several generations
before it would be gone. I performed extrapolations based on
new measurements. According to my calculations, the icecap will
disappear in our lifetime."

Iris spoke as though describing a death sentence. Humans are
influenced by the moods of others and Morgan's mood likewise
became grave.

Morgan recognized the irony instantly. She, Morgan, was feeling
angst and concern for the well-being of Lucid World because it
might be exposed to Nosos World. Her world! Was her world so
frightening, so dreadful? What about her? She had to live the rest
of her life in her world.

Her thoughts of irony morphed into insights. Parts of her

world were unpleasant due to khaos. What about the good parts? Khaos was contagious but khaos could be fought. Through her own experiences she knew this to be so.

Iris changed the subject and delved into the agenda for Morgan's nightly studies. But Iris was distracted with thoughts about the icecap. So was Morgan.

REMINDERS

"Beep-beep-beep," the oven announced.

Morgan entered the kitchen. No one was there. She called, "Mom, the timer went off. Mom, the muffins are ready. Mom, can you hear me?"

Meredith appeared. "Am I the only one with hands? Put an oven mitt on and put the pan on the cooling rack."

Morgan obeyed and in a self-congratulatory tone said, "It's a good thing I heard the beeping or they would have burned."

"Thanks, but not likely. I set the oven to turn off automatically and a reminder alarm on my phone. I was already on my way when you called."

"So then, actually, it's a good thing I heard the beeping so I can take one while they're warm."

Mother and daughter both laughed. Morgan helped herself to a muffin, put it in a napkin and headed down the hall to her bedroom. And then an idea struck her.

RIPPLES

The sun was shining on the mountain and the dome ceiling of the cavern was opened to allow sunlight to shine down inside. The opened transparent ceiling reminded Morgan of an opened sunroof on a car.

Iris had arranged for Morgan to join her in a garden next to a sunlit pool surrounded by purple flowers. Irises! Large speckled fish swam freely among lily pads with pale pink flowers.

They sat on the grass and faced the water. Iris tucked her skirt underneath her legs so the grass wouldn't tickle. Even though

Morgan's avatar couldn't feel a 'tickle', she mimicked Iris's pose.

"That thing we talked about last time. What'll actually happen?" Morgan asked.

"You mean the receding icecap?"

"Yes. What's Lucid World going to do?"

"We don't know."

"Lucid World should join Nosos World. We can fight khaos together," Morgan blurted.

Iris faced Morgan and gently reproved, "Have you not been paying attention, Morgan? If Lucid World joins Nosos, we will all have khaos and no one will be left to fight khaos."

This manner of speaking was not typical for someone from Lucid World and definitely not typical for Iris.

Morgan looked away from Iris. She stared into the water, "I've been paying attention. I know khaos is contagious. People just need reminders. Since I've been coming to Lucid World, I get reminders all the time, and it's made a difference. I have a lot less khaos in my life. Everyone can fight khaos together by reminding each other about it."

Iris reached for a small stone beside the pond and threw it in the water. Tiny ripple patterns disturbed the surface as she said, "I don't think so. What about what happened thousands of years ago before my ancestors hid themselves in Lucid World? If they hadn't left Nosos World, they would have become infected with khaos and there wouldn't have been anyone left to fight khaos, or remind others."

"It's actually a different world now. There are lots of ways people stay in touch with things to remind them. I think your fear of Nosos World is a kind of khaos. It's based on something your ancestors tried and failed thousands of years ago. You have more resources and knowledge than they ever had. You should try to fight khaos again!"

"We've never stopped."

"You fight by looking for a perfect cure for a disease. I think Khyan has the right idea but hasn't gone far enough. You should be with people who have khaos, and show them there is another way. You can protect yourself with reminders. There might be times khaos creeps in and you must fight it within yourself. That's just part of being human. Besides, you already have khaos. To never try something just because someone else failed, is just plain old khaos."

"I don't think you understand, Morgan. Let's talk about something else."

Morgan looked up at the open dome ceiling. She didn't want Iris to read her facial expression that would undoubtedly accompany her thought, 'Does Iris have khaos?'

CHAPTER 33

A LOTUS FLOWER

It's not uncommon for a cat to favour some people over others. Much like people, cats never forget how someone makes them feel. - from "The Lives and Times of Cats"

Morgan didn't hear her parents quarrel often. It seemed they each knew what was, and what wasn't, important to the other; and when to defer and when to take charge. But when it came to visits from Aunt Tamara, established protocols failed. Aunt Tamara was important to both of them, but in conflicting ways.

From arguments Morgan overheard, her mother felt Tamara was critical towards her and domineering towards Daniel. Her father defended Tamara. She had sacrificed so much to be his caregiver when he was a child. Daniel could understand how it might be difficult for her to 'turn it off'. After one such Tamara debate, Morgan waited until her mother was alone and broached the subject. She presumed khaos was involved but couldn't quite connect all the dots.

Meredith stood facing Morgan with her hands on her hips and feet apart. "Now who said I don't like her?"

"Just the things you say about her and how Dad defends her."

Meredith relaxed her posture. "Let's sit down and talk. You're old enough to understand."

They sat at the table in the kitchen and faced one another. For the first time, Morgan felt Meredith was talking with her, as a friend, and not to her, as her mother.

Meredith admitted she found friendship with Tamara to be challenging, and she acknowledged there were reasons for Tamara's behaviour. Tamara lost her mother when she was young. She was still a child herself when she had the responsibility of caring for her younger brother, Daniel, while Morgan's grandfather worked on the farm. Tamara wanted to go to university, but Grandfather couldn't afford to hire anyone to take her place, so she couldn't go.

Meredith summed it up by saying, "I think it left her feeling resentful."

"She could have gone to university later."

"Things don't seem to work that way. It's human nature to feel sorry for ourselves and punish others or try to blame others for our unhappiness."

"So people dislike her because of how she acts. Not being liked makes her act that way all the more."

"It would make sense it would happen that way."

"So let's treat Aunt Tamara differently!"

Meredith defended, "I've tried being a friend to her," and hesitated, "maybe I went about it the wrong way."

"I have an idea."

Morgan went to bed that night feeling excited. Khyan said he had a surprise planned for her next visit. Also, she wanted to talk about Aunt Tamara.

Her avatar materialized in the public square. She lifted her nose. Her nostrils filled with the scent of … flowers? Wait. She could smell? That never happened before.

Khyan smiled warmly at her. "Ahhh, it worked!"

"My avatar can smell! And it's Lotus Day!" Morgan twirled. There were lotus flowers of white, pink, red, and blue everywhere. People carried them and wore garlands. Tables were covered with them. Long leis hung overhead. Pillars and arbours were decorated. It was magnificent!

"Happy Lotus Day, Morgan! Before you leave, I'll introduce you to our avatar technicians who made it possible for you to experience the sense of smell through your avatar."

Khyan watched as Morgan's avatar looked around their surroundings. It seemed she was looking at more than the flowers and festivities. It was as if she was looking for something. Or someone? Her face displayed the same disappointment he saw on Amasis's face last night when they completed the next day's scheduling details. Their fondness for one another was so sweet, but maybe sad too. Without a cure for khaos, realistically, they could never be more than friends.

"Amasis told me about this. I never imagined ..."

Morgan looked down to see what she was wearing. She expected to see the usual casual clothing a Nosos teenager might wear. Instead, she was wearing a dress with a long full skirt, like a princess in a fairy tale. The bodice was periwinkle blue, the skirt was white printed with blue and purple lotus flowers.

"Did Iris design my dress? I love it!"

"No, Amasis did."

Morgan was momentarily lost for words. When she recovered, she said, "It's beautiful and I feel beautiful!"

"As you can see, it's a holiday for everyone here, except us." Khyan winked. "But, I've made arrangements for us to sit," he gestured to a nearby table, "and have our meeting."

They sat at a small low table. Khyan's legs were too long to fit under the small low table so he sat sideways and stuck them out off to the side. Morgan suggested he should have transported himself there as an avatar so his legs could occupy the same space as the table and the lotus flowers.

At first, people came by to express Lotus Day wishes to Morgan, and then Khyan touched the oval device around his neck. A translucent film formed a wall around them. The voices of the crowd were eliminated and well-wishers no longer approached.

In spite of the wall veil, the air was still full of the floral aroma, and the flowers and people were still visible. In that setting, Morgan talked about Aunt Tamara.

Inspired by the surroundings, Khyan suggested Tamara was like a lotus flower. When there is no light, the lotus closes and sinks into the mud. When there is light, the lotus flower emerges out of the mud and bursts into blossom. Tamara is in the dark. Morgan can shine the light.

Lotus metaphors aside, Tamara's behaviour distanced her from others and was a 'flight' reaction to khaos feelings. It discouraged others from forming close relationships, when actually her behaviour was a reaction to unfulfilled needs for love and belonging. It was a cycle, the more she hurt, the more she pushed others away. The more she pushed others away, the more she hurt.

AUNT TAMARA

The next day, Aunt Tamara picked up Morgan in her car and they drove to Lethbridge to shop for a dress for Morgan to wear to the Sugar Makers' Gala.

When Morgan suggested the shopping expedition to Tamara on the phone, Tamara said yes without hesitation.

The actual shopping got off to a slow start. As is often the case when one goes shopping, Morgan had an image of an ideal dress in her mind's-eye. It was the dress Amasis designed for her. There were no dresses in the store even remotely resembling the lotus dress style or colour.

When Morgan described what she had in mind, Tamara took her to fabric stores with the aim of finding cloth and a dress-pattern and having the dress made. This didn't work either as there was no cloth that even remotely resembled that of her lotus dress.

Tamara got Morgan focused on the styles and choices available in the dress shops. Morgan finally chose a dress and Tamara promised to loan her shoes and an evening bag.

When Tamara dropped Morgan off at her home, Morgan invited her to come inside for coffee. Tamara accepted and enthusiastically described details of the shopping expedition to Meredith.

As Tamara was leaving, she turned and smiled at Morgan. The smile wasn't forced. Aunt Tamara probably didn't even know she was smiling.

Later, when Morgan messaged Cara to tell her about the shopping day and send a picture of her new dress, Cara wrote, 'The aunt who looks like her underwear is too tight?'

Morgan wrote back, 'She doesn't look that way when people like her.'

CHAPTER 34

KYLE

Wind direction influences weather. Knowing a particular wind direction helps forecast changes in weather. - from "As the Wind Blows"

Morgan and Meredith sat at their kitchen table, visiting with Katey and her tiny newborn son, Kyle.

"Really? Where are you moving to?" asked Morgan.

Katey answered the question Morgan asked, and the question she didn't ask. "Contrary to rumours, I know who the father is. He's awesome and his name is Austin."

Morgan and Katey laughed. Meredith politely grinned in acknowledgement of the joke.

"He's from Lethbridge, goes to college. My family's moving back there so both our families can help us look after Kyle while Austin and I are in college and until we have enough money."

They planned to live together in Katey's parents' house until Austin graduated and got a job.

"What'll happen if you two don't work out as a couple?" asked Meredith.

"We'll still share custody. Our parents are old friends and we all want to work together as a family."

Meredith thought about some of the cases Karleen told her about, "I hope you care enough for each other to stay together. Joint custody arrangements can be difficult," she cautioned.

"The counsellor made us talk about that. We agreed that if something happens, we'll raise Kyle as parents who are friends.

Not as resentful married people."

Meredith nodded. "That sounds sensible."

Meredith and Katey were talking the way adults talk to one another. This realization struck Morgan and she, too, felt like an adult. She asked Katey what career she had in mind when she attended college.

Katey described programs and opportunities she was considering. Morgan did not yet have any career plans. She had a year of high school left and assumed she didn't have to decide until she graduated. Hearing Katey's detailed plans made her feel immature and unprepared. She wanted to change the subject.

"When I get my driver's licence, can I visit you and Kyle in Lethbridge?"

Katey replied, "Absolutely! Hey, do you want to hold him?"

Morgan answered, "Yes!" and Katey helped Kyle get settled safely into Morgan's arms.

Morgan held Kyle and stared into his eyes. She was mesmerized. Meredith and Katey both imagined Morgan was feeling maternal instincts. Morgan's thoughts were far from maternal. She was thinking about khaos and the little baby she was holding. Did he already have khaos? Might he be saved from khaos? More than ever, she wanted to help liberate the world from khaos.

CHAPTER 35

COUNCIL MEETING

*When using wind power as an energy source, balance must
be maintained between consumption and generation. Wind
forecasting errors can be costly. – from "As the Wind Blows"*

Iris looked around the magnificent marble table. She was
seated alongside the Council of Elders in the same room
Amasis had used to greet Morgan when she first visited
Lucid World.

In their varied colourful robes and headgear, the Elders created
an atmosphere charged with strength and wisdom.

Elder Tabubu, as head of the Council, chaired the meeting. She
signalled to Iris to begin her report.

Iris rose from her chair and spoke without notes.

"During the last three million years there have been four 'Ice
Ages'. After each of these Ice Ages, our planet became warmer and
glaciers retreated. The last Ice Age ended about ten thousand years
ago. Since then, glaciers around the globe have been melting and
shrinking. In recent years, this melting has become more dramatic,
with increasing rates of ice loss since the mid-1980s. The icecap
glacier concealing Lucid World is also shrinking. We can predict its
shrinkage based on its mass and expected temperatures. Previous
calculations suggested we had at least two hundred years before
the reduced size would compromise our camouflage and affect our
supply of drinking water. The rate of shrinkage has sped up on an
escalating scale. Based on my estimates, we have less than twenty
years."

Iris stopped talking. She was finished her report.

Tabubu addressed the group and invited questions for Iris. None were asked, so Tabubu thanked Iris for her report and invited her to stay. Iris sat down.

Tabubu led the discussion. "We need to reconsider our options with a view to the likelihood we have a much shorter time to prepare and to act."

A white-haired Elder addressed the group, "With less time to act, previously considered options may no longer be viable. We need to explore other ways, albeit less ideal."

Tabubu said, "Is there a more workable plan in particular you have in mind?"

"Yes, controlled assimilation. This would involve moving to a remote, but not hidden, area of Nosos World. Interactions with Nosos people would be limited until we discover how to reverse the khaos condition or manage exposure."

One of the younger Elders, a woman with long jet black hair, asked, "How could we ensure restricted exposure be maintained? Governments change. Wars start. Disasters happen. We all know what happened to Island Lucid World when there was a shipwreck nearby."

"Elder Tabubu, may I address the Council?" asked Iris.

"Yes."

Iris rose from her seat. "Respected Elders, I'm involved with the Nosos youth program. Recently, one of them suggested our approach to khaos might be khaos. Initially, I dismissed her ideas as the product of uninformed and incomplete reasoning. Since then, I have reconsidered what she said and I am no longer certain she was entirely wrong."

Tabubu said, "It seems you have another report for us. Please continue."

Iris described Morgan's views on khaos and reminders. She ended by saying, "She was correct when she said illogical fear is a manifestation of khaos. Was she also correct when she said our fear of khaos is illogical because it's based on what happened to our ancestors and it's a different world now?"

Iris hadn't expected anyone to answer; and no one did. There were no questions either.

Tabubu broke the silence. "Those ideas are thought-provoking. Let's reflect on what we've heard today. This meeting is adjourned. We'll reconvene tomorrow."

CHAPTER 36

THE SUGAR MAKERS' GALA

A strong wind that rapidly descends the leeward side of a mountain is often referred to as a 'snow-eater' wind. When this gust arrives, things warm up quickly! - from "As the Wind Blows"

After the town meeting about the sugar factory, plans moved forward. At first, Wilco Sugar had copious criticism of the specialty line. Then, they foresaw innumerable impediments to donating the factory property. They were also unenthusiastic because the co-op would be their competitor. But threatened by negative publicity if they didn't cooperate, and enticed by savings if employees relinquished severance pay, they reluctantly agreed to assist with the plan.

Wilco Sugar volunteered a team of food scientists and product development specialists to refine the process of creating super-sparkly sugar.

The process was patented to give the Coyote Flats Sugar Cooperative exclusive rights to produce super-sparkly sugar. Before that, the matter of compensating Veronica as inventor of super-sparkly sugar had to be addressed.

At first Veronica's parents said there needn't be any consideration paid for the invention. When pressed to reconsider, they agreed a percentage of super-sparkly sugar sales would go toward an education fund for Veronica to pursue her education as a scientist. When funds were no longer required for her education, Veronica would have discretion to direct the education funds to advance higher education; first for her brothers, then for other Coyote Flats students who had meritorious academic achievements.

The next phases required lawyers, engineers and machinists. A community event was needed to raise funds for costs. For many years, Wilco Sugar had sponsored an annual Sugar Makers' Dance. The tradition seemed a perfect opportunity for a fund raising event.

The event, now sponsored by the Coyote Flats Sugar Cooperative, was renamed the Sugar Makers' Gala. To entice people to attend and pay a higher price for tickets, besides the usual annual dinner and dance, the event boasted performances by Sally Frey, winner of the Talent Scout TV show, and the famous Las Vegas singer-performer, Dorian Jones.

Mayor Marco had gone to the same college as Dorian, and they had kept in touch over the years. When Dorian's old friend, Antonio Marco, asked him to perform with Sally at the Sugar Maker's Gala, he didn't hesitate to accept the invitation.

The community hall was not big enough for the expected turnout so the event had to be held at the Coyote Flats High School. The school theatre group transformed the auditorium into a super-sparkly-sugar wonderland.

It was promoted as Coyote Flats' biggest event ever!

The night finally arrived. When Morgan walked into the school auditorium with her parents, the three of them paused at the door to take it all in. The formerly stark functional room was altered beyond recognition.

Shimmering white shapes, giant versions of designs for the new specialty product, hung on ropes of light and twinkled below a canopy of white balloons. The design shapes included: spider webs, tiaras, snowflakes, ghosts and dinosaurs. The canopy filled the auditorium's high ceiling and concealed the auditorium's functional equipment and vents. Tables were set with white linen and adorned with white centerpieces dressed in sparkles. The walls were transformed by up-lighting in shades of blue and turquoise, arranged around the perimeter of the room. The stage was bejewelled with tiny twinkling lights. It was a wonderland!

The decorations reminded Morgan of Lucid World adorned with lotus flowers on Lotus Day. She wished Amasis could see it, and Iris and Khyan, too. She could describe it but words would never capture it. Her peripheral vision caught a fluttering image. She turned to see a white balloon escaping from the ceiling. The balloon's descent was slow, graceful and aimless. Morgan was mesmerized as she watched the balloon settle on a table centerpiece.

BANG! The balloon popped and jolted Morgan out of her trance. The juxtaposition of the gentle descent and the harsh landing turned her thoughts elsewhere. The loud noise was caused by a small sonic boom created when stretched balloon pieces exceeded the speed of sound as they returned to their pre-inflated size. Just like her idea at the town meeting, sometimes small things can produce big results.

There was a loud conversation on the other side of the room. Morgan recognized Mayor Marco's voice. She looked over and saw him standing and talking with a man. For a private conversation, he seemed to talk louder than necessary. It was as if he wanted the entire room to hear. He laughed and said, "Tremendous Dory. You finally got around to visiting me after all these years."

Morgan moved closer and strained her ears to hear the other man say in reply, "Well, Tony, you never invited me before." The two men laughed heartily.

'Ah, that's Dorian Jones,' thought Morgan. She looked around for Sally and spotted her standing with Mrs. Kyatchi, the school career counsellor, who had taken a special interest in Sally. She had applied to the Wilderness Survival Camp group for sponsorship for Sally last summer and she had arranged for Sally to apply to MF for a scholarship.

Morgan approached them. Sally looked gorgeous! She had a stylish haircut and wore makeup courtesy of Mrs. Kyatchi. Morgan thought of Cinderella at the ball and had a weird impulse to check out her glass slippers. They weren't glass, they were strappy gold sandals. They matched her rust and gold dress. The dress brought out the gold flecks in Sally's hazel coloured eyes.

Unlike Cinderella, Sally fidgeted with her fingers, shifted her weight from foot to foot, brushed her hands down her legs to smooth her dress, and bit her lips.

Morgan wanted to help Sally feel relaxed. She thought, 'What would Iris do?'

Once when Morgan was nervous about giving a class speech the next day, Iris asked a few questions about her nervousness and then gave her ideas to think about.

Morgan began. "So are you nervous? If you are, that's actually normal."

"I'm not just nervous, I'm terrified! What if I'm not good enough? What if people wished they didn't have to listen? What if I make a mistake?"

"Lots of people are afraid to perform in public. Being in front of a group of people can bring on feelings of vulnerability. This vulnerability, along with wanting to do a good job, can be scary. It's supposed to become easier the more often you do it. Just think: you've already performed in front of hundreds of thousands of people on Talent Scout and social media. Don't think of your audience as your enemy. Your fear is your enemy. Don't let it beat you. Face and conquer it."

"I don't know how to conquer it. It's just there."

"Don't think about the audience. Instead, find someone in the audience to look at. Keep looking at that person long enough to play a few notes or sing a few words. Maybe you could start out by looking at me or one of my parents. Then, find someone else to look at and do the same thing and so on. That way you won't be looking at the audience as a big scary group. Instead, you'll see them as individual people.

"Besides, nervousness always feels worse than it looks. If you don't let on that you're nervous, nobody else will know. If you act confident, you'll feel confident. If you make a mistake, just keep going. Probably no one will actually notice the mistake and if they do, so what? You're human. Humans make mistakes."

While Morgan and Sally were talking, Mrs. Kyatchi had stepped away. Now, she hurriedly approached and said, "Sally, you need to get on stage. It's time to play."

Panic came over Sally's face. Morgan put her hand on her shoulder and said, "Just remember the things I told you." Sally nodded and gave Morgan a smile expressing both gratitude and doubt. Then, she turned to walk to the stairs leading onto the stage.

Sally did an amazing job! During this segment of the event, Sally was to provide background music, an ambient mood for the cocktail socializing interval. However, when Sally performed, people stopped talking and listened instead.

Morgan stood near the stage and watched the crowd at the gala. Morgan and Sally were among a few teens who attended. Morgan spotted Matt. He was with his cousin Jeff, Katey's older brother. Jeff and Matt were there to help with the sound system.

Morgan tried to catch Matt's eye and give him a 'hello' acknowledgement. He appeared to be mesmerized watching Sally. Morgan thought about the concept of outgrowing baby fat. She'd never thought too much about it before and didn't know whether it was a real thing or not. Matt had either outgrown his baby fat or converted it to muscle. Either way, he didn't look like the chubby sloppy bartender she met at the party.

When Sally's performance was over, and people applauded, Matt stood frozen. He remained frozen and watched Sally's every move as she gathered her guitar and notes. He continued to stare even after people resumed their former interactions and Sally left the stage. Jeff came along and poked him in the ribs. Matt followed Jeff to the equipment booth.

When the cocktail hour was over, everyone was asked to take their seats for dinner. Sally was escorted to sit at a head table beside Dorian Jones.

Morgan had seen Dorian Jones on TV and in movies. His music was not the type Morgan and her friends listened to. They considered him and his songs dated. Her parents said he was a Las Vegas icon. Morgan didn't know about icon stuff. She knew he was famous and his presence was an enticement for people to pay to come to the gala.

To Morgan's eye, Sally appeared relieved to have finished her performance. Then, when Dorian's attentions were turned to her for introductions and small talk, Sally appeared petrified. Dorian smiled warmly at Sally. He appeared to be attentive and mindful to a young girl who was nervous and uncomfortable. It didn't take long until Sally seemed more relaxed in his presence.

Sounds of a loud conversation emitted from just outside the auditorium doors. Everyone turned to look toward the commotion.

Unexpectedly, Franny burst into the large auditorium. People had been holding her back and she broke free from their hold. As a result, she stumbled, making an audacious entrance.

Franny straightened up, shook her head and pulled down on the front and sides of her shirt to smooth it across her belly and hips. These gestures suggested composure and readiness, an illusion which was short-lived. As Franny walked, it was obvious she was intoxicated because her steps were slightly unbalanced.

Franny stopped and looked around the room. When she caught sight of the head table, and Sally seated there, her facial expression changed twice. While scanning the room, Franny's expression was that of a person who lost someone. When she spotted Sally, her expression turned sad and then within seconds became angry.

Their eyes met. Sally's face showed terror.

With arms swinging, Franny stomped towards the head table. As she weaved through banquet tables, she bumped and knocked the backs of any chairs that got in her way.

Franny reached the head table and stood across from where Sally sat. Conversations in the room had hushed when the commotion outside began, so when Franny shouted at Sally, everyone heard everything.

Franny's words to Sally were foul. Only the meaning of words will be repeated, not her actual words.

Franny had to go out (it wasn't clear why) and Sally was needed at home to babysit Mikey. Sally should quit acting like she was something special and stop fooling herself that these people liked her. Everyone was using her and keeping her away from her family and her responsibilities. When the night was over and people didn't need her anymore, she would be alone with only her family to look out for her. Sally was an ungrateful daughter and if she chose these people over her family who had always been there for her, then she didn't deserve her family and maybe they wouldn't be there for her when the others rejected her. Did she forget how people in the town treated her in the past? After tonight, Sally would still be the daughter of a poor mother who the townspeople judged and gossiped about.

After Franny finished shouting at Sally, she turned to leave and started towards the door. Sally got up from her seat, mumbled, "I'm sorry," and followed Franny out of the room.

No one moved or spoke. Mayor Marco rose from his seat and walked up to the stage and the microphone Sally had used earlier. "Ladies and gentlemen, looks like there's been a slight change in our program. We've lost one of our dinner performers. Dory, you're an old pro, think you can handle having the spotlight to yourself?"

Across the room, Dorian nodded his assent. Mayor Marco laughed and said, "Tremendous. I thought so Dory, just like the old days."

To the credit of Mayor Marco, the tension in the room was lifted and most everyone got back into a festive mood.

Morgan was upset and worried about Sally. Also, she felt responsible. What would happen now? Was Franny so angry she'd never let Sally go to school to study music?

Meredith leaned over to Morgan and whispered, "Oh honey, don't worry. Sally'll be fine. Her mother was drunk and over-reacted. I'll ask Mrs. Kyatchi to drop in on them tomorrow. Franny is used to her coming by."

Meredith's words made Morgan feel only slightly better. The magic of the evening was lost for her.

The rest of the night went smoothly and the event was considered a success. Franny's tirade was the fodder for gossip for several days. People wondered why Franny hadn't attended the gala if her daughter was performing.

Franny wasn't at the gala because Sally didn't ask her to come. When Sally told Franny about the gala, Franny made a snide remark about an occasion for big fish in a small pond to show off. Sally interpreted Franny's comments to mean she did not approve of the gala. Sally felt it was pointless to ask Franny to come with her. It would be unwise to flaunt the event, and rile her, in case she might forbid her to go. All the while, Sally was relieved Franny wouldn't be at the gala to get drunk and embarrass her.

When Sally didn't officially ask Franny to come to the gala and seemed to hide her preparations, Franny interpreted this to mean Sally didn't want her there and didn't care if her own mother was part of a big event in her life. Franny felt rejected and dejected, and she got drunk on the night of the gala. In her drunken state, Franny became agitated and went to the gala to admonish Sally.

Khaos, simply khaos ...

CHAPTER 37

AFTER THE GALA

If a structure is not designed to resist high winds, a windstorm can cause it to sway violently from side to side and tear apart. – from "As the Wind Blows"

Morgan was surprised to see her Lucid World friends Amasis, Khyan and Iris, waiting in the treasure map room. Usually only one of them met her when she arrived.

Iris jumped up and rushed towards her, "How'd it go? How'd the decorations look? Tell us about Sally's duet with Dorian Jones. Why was it they couldn't rehearse ahead of time? Oh, I remember, Dorian's plane was scheduled to arrive just before the dinner."

Amasis and Khyan laughed. Iris's barrage of questions didn't give Morgan a chance to speak, let alone answer. Also, this behaviour wasn't usual for Iris. It was obvious she was fond of Morgan.

Then they saw the expression on Morgan's avatar's face. Iris stopped talking, and the guys stopped laughing.

Khyan said, "Let's all take a seat. Morgan has more to talk about than decorations."

When they were settled, Khyan said, "Start at the beginning."

Morgan didn't start at the beginning. She started with the commotion outside of the auditorium and Franny barging into the room.

Iris offered the first reaction. "That's so sad. Mrs. Frey must have been feeling a lot of khaos to behave in such a manner."

Morgan said, "Mrs. Frey! What about Sally? She was embarrassed in front of hundreds of people. Even worse, it's my fault. If I'd left her alone and not …"

Khyan interjected. "Morgan, feelings of embarrassment and guilt are khaos emotions."

Amasis added, "Do you remember our conversation about distortions? It is likely that ..."

Morgan interrupted. "No, no, no! It was awful. Poor Sally. She and her mother are the laughingstock of town. You should have seen the look on Sally's face."

Iris said, "Morgan, sometimes things will go wrong. That's part of life."

Regrets

After Morgan woke the next morning, she laid in bed thinking.

She wanted no more khaos lessons. She wanted to go back to being a normal teenager who did normal things. She had announced to Khyan, Amasis and Iris, "I don't care if I have khaos. I quit!"

When Morgan cried, they consoled her and said they would meet with her in a couple of nights to see if she still felt the same way. If she changed her mind, she could continue with the project. If she didn't, they would say goodbye.

It was Sunday morning, after a late night at the gala, so Morgan's parents didn't press her to get up. She stayed in bed.

She regretted her behaviour in Lucid World. They were her friends. She had cried and acted like a baby. She wished she was there, in Lucid World, so she could apologize and better explain; and thank them for all the things they taught her. She'd have to wait until they contacted her in a couple of nights. When exactly would that be? Would it be tomorrow night or the night after tomorrow night? She wished she'd asked which night it would be. In the meantime, she'd think about everything she wanted to say to them. She was resolved to not continue with the project. She didn't want to part on bad terms and wondered if she might visit occasionally.

It hit her. If she left the program, she wouldn't be able to visit. The Council of Elders would never permit it. She'd never see any of them again.

She'd never see Amasis again. Her mind was flooded with images of him and the things he did when they were together, walking, talking, watching, cooking, and creating. Her heart was heavy. She pictured his dark eyes that had looked so sad when she said she quit.

Her lower lip quivered and tears welled in her eyes. 'Stop it!' The time they spent together probably wasn't even that special. He probably acted that way with everyone. Besides, she had a hunch he and Iris were dating. When she asked Amasis to the school dance, he never answered her question concerning whether he had a girlfriend. Similarly, when she asked Iris if she had a boyfriend, Iris gave a vague answer and changed the subject.

Still, she'd miss all of them. And Luna! Last night, Luna wasn't there. She was probably away nursing her kittens.

Luna gave birth to kittens two weeks earlier. The enclosure where Luna kept her babies was surrounded by dense rock and not in range of any of the devices used to transmit the avatar technology. Since Morgan couldn't visit Luna's new family, Iris took a video to show her. Along with the pictures, Iris conveyed a message from Elder Tabubu: Morgan could name the kittens.

Morgan felt her role of naming was a great honour. She carefully considered various options and used the naming as an opportunity to share something from Nosos World with Lucid World.

Morgan remembered how Khyan described his delight when he experienced the wind for the first time. Living in a windy area, Morgan had grown up taking the wind for granted; and when the wind was blustery, she found it downright annoying. During her time in Lucid World, she learned that a changed attitude creates a changed world. The wind was something she couldn't change. She could, however, change how she perceived it: a natural phenomenon of Nosos World.

Luna had three kittens: two males and one female. Morgan named the female Chinook, a name for the wind which swept the prairies surrounding Coyote Flats. For the males, rather than take inspiration from winds like hurricanes or typhoons, she chose Gust and Puff. Perfect names for adorable kittens.

Two nights ago, Luna brought out one of her kittens to show Morgan. As Luna approached Morgan, holding the scruff of the neck of a miniature Luna between her teeth, Morgan knew this symbolic act meant Luna trusted her and considered her to be family. She recognized Chinook from the video of the kittens. Luna brought her up onto the chair to join Morgan. The kitten's eyes were just recently opened, and she was crying. Luna gave her a couple of swift licks and took her back to the litter.

While thinking about Luna and her family, Morgan felt the saddest emotion she had ever experienced. The realization of her decision sank in.

That evening, after spending the day in her pajamas, Morgan got her act together enough to tie her hair into a sloppy ponytail, and pull on some jeans and a fleece sweater to go for a walk with Cara.

The days were getting longer and the sun setting under high clouds, created the effect of a painted ceiling. The wind was cold but wafted the promise of spring. Morgan, even though dressed warmly, felt a distinct shiver course through her body. She wondered if the shiver was due to the spectacular sunset, the March wind, or the recent events.

Morgan described what happened between Sally and her mom at the gala. Cara had already heard a version of the events from her parents who were there. Cara asked about the rest of the gala: Sally's pre-dinner performance, the decorations, and Dorian Jones. Morgan told her, but without detail or enthusiasm.

Morgan talked about her feelings of guilt for having set up the predicament for Sally. Cara defended Morgan's well-meaning intentions and actions. She admonished her for blaming herself for things she could not foresee or control. Morgan disagreed, saying she should have foreseen the problem with Franny. She knew about Franny's temperament and her objections to Sally performing in public.

They walked to Sally's house. Morgan had not heard from Sally since she followed Franny out of the auditorium. Phoning Sally was out of question due to the risk of making things worse.

Morgan and Cara stood outside the gate. Morgan hoped to get a glimpse of Sally through the window and signal her to come outside. Everything was quiet and the curtains were drawn. A faint light shone from behind one of the curtained windows.

"Which window is Sally's room?" asked Cara.

"I don't know. I've never been inside."

They stood in silence at the gate and waited. They waited for any sound or movement other than creaking tree branches bent by the wind. The wind intensified and Morgan motioned to Cara it was time to go.

DAYS GO BY

Morgan saw Sally at school on Monday morning. They talked between classes. Sally said she didn't get punished. What she described sounded much worse.

That night when Morgan went to bed she expected her Lucid World meeting, assuming they would contact her. First, she would apologize for her khaos behaviour when she last saw them. Then, she would reiterate her intention to quit the program. Next, she wanted to thank them. Finally, during her cleverly worded fond farewell, she would ask if she might be allowed to visit sometime.

She felt a sinking feeling in the bottom of her stomach. Was it the thought of saying goodbye to Amasis? Yes, but no. It was something else. It felt like something in the universe had shifted. It felt like Lucid World had never entered her life and there would be no meeting tonight.

And there wasn't. She woke in the morning without having been contacted.

Two more days passed, and besides dealing with her burden of guilt, Morgan vacillated between feeling relieved and feeling anxious. She felt relieved she didn't have to always be thinking and wondering if her thoughts and actions were due to khaos emotions. She felt anxious because her Lucid World friends hadn't communicated with her since the night she quit and cried.

On the fourth night after her last visit to Lucid World, Morgan laid in bed and thought, 'It'll be tonight. They said a couple of nights and they probably weren't counting the next night and now two other nights have gone by. Since it wasn't last night, it will be tonight for sure.'

Morning came. She hadn't been contacted by her friends.

Days turned into weeks and still no word from Lucid World.

They must have changed their minds about checking back with her to see if her decision had changed. After all, she probably appeared very infected by khaos on that last night.

Morgan hadn't changed her mind. She didn't want to be part of their project, but she didn't want to end things that way.

She wondered if something had happened. Maybe they had been discovered by someone from Nosos and were dealing with the aftermath. No, it seemed more likely they had given up on her and decided she was not worth their bother. She felt morose. Feeling morose because of rejection is a khaos emotion. So what? She didn't have to care about that anymore.

CHAPTER 38

THE ENEMY FORCE IS DISCOVERED

*Who can undo what time hath done? Who can win
back the wind?- verse by Owen Meredith*

Morgan saw Sally at school but not outside of school. Sally had her own problems and knowing the extent of the ramifications of the gala evening made Morgan feel even worse.

Morgan was consumed with regret and anger. She felt regret for how she conducted herself the last time she was in Lucid World. She felt regret for interfering in Sally's life. She felt anger towards her friends in Lucid World who had abandoned her when they should have known she needed them most. She felt anger towards Sally's mother who caused so much khaos in Sally's life; and she felt anger towards herself for causing even more khaos in Sally's life.

Regret and anger morphed into feelings of hopelessness and self-loathing. Morgan got into the habit of going to bed early and staying in bed as long as she could.

Her dreams were intense. Villains provoked her, and she unleashed physical retribution. Unknown assailants stalked and chased her. She rode her bicycle down a steep hill and couldn't reach the brakes.

Threatening dreams triggered a release of adrenalin which caused her to wake mid-dream. Vivid recollection and dream images haunted her the next day.

One night Morgan dreamt about Lucid World. Instead of her avatar arriving in one of the usual meeting places, her actual body arrived in a dimly lit cave. She heard someone crying for help and discovered her avatar lying on the ground. The avatar image faded in and out. She was dying.

Morgan asked, "How can I save you?"

Her avatar answered, "You can save no one until you save yourself."

The next morning, Morgan thought. 'I'm tired of feeling miserable. What point is there to feeling this way?'

Her avatar was right. She had to save herself. She had to save herself from herself and then she could save others. She wanted to be happy, but lately it seemed she was surrounded by unhappy people. Everyone was so glum around her. Was it because her khaos emotions were impacting others?

Illumination! It was all so clear! She was infecting those around her with her khaos. She could change that. Her depressed state was illogical, and to quote an expression Amasis sometimes used, 'khaos, simply khaos'. She would continue trying to reverse khaos even if she had to do it alone.

Why'd she quit? She remembered back to the gala and how terrible she felt after Franny caused the scene and Sally left before her chance to perform with Dorian Jones. She believed it was her fault and misdirected her feelings of guilt by punishing herself.

Why couldn't she see it sooner? It was as if she'd been blinded by something and it prevented her from seeing the khaos.

That's it! That's the force Khyan told her about! When they first met, he told her there was a powerful force in Nosos that would try to sabotage her efforts. He said it would create obstacles and diversions to keep her from her goal. The powerful force! 'Enemy force' was what she called it when Khyan described it and she didn't understand.

She had discovered the enemy force! Now she would conquer it. It all made so much sense. Her subconscious with all of its previous programming of limitations and negativity had sabotaged her.

She was overcome with feelings of strength, love and happiness. Now, more than ever, she wanted to talk to someone from Lucid World.

CHAPTER **39**

AFTER THE EPIPHANY

After Morgan's epiphany, her thoughts of abandonment were replaced by thoughts that something might have prevented Lucid World from contacting her.

When she had asked why Lucid World had chosen participants from only rural areas, she learned that the technology used to communicate with their sleeping brains was sensitive to interference caused by electro-magnetic fields (EMFs); and rural areas have less EMFs than cities. What if something had caused the EMFs in Coyote Flats to increase? To make such a big difference, it would have to be something big like a new power plant. Nothing like that had happened in Coyote Flats. Not even at the factory. The new specialty line was still in the design phase. Nothing had changed in town since her last contact with Lucid World. Not even any new structures, unless maybe a new fence or doghouse.

What if something happened to the transmission equipment installed in Coyote Flats? It was unlikely that Lucid World would use something that could break down, considering they couldn't easily come back to Coyote Flats to repair it. But what about high winds or a hail storm? Maybe they underestimated how intense weather could be in Coyote Flats. If so, maybe she could resolve the problem. But how? She didn't know how the equipment worked, never mind repair it. And she couldn't walk into a repair shop and say, "Hello, do you repair brain wave communication equipment?"

She caught herself. Those were khaos thoughts. It could be

something simple like a loose wire. She didn't know what the equipment looked like. Did it look like a satellite dish, a tower, or something with a long antenna? With Lucid World's advanced technology it might look like something she couldn't even imagine.

Not only did she not know what it looked like, she didn't know where it was located. On one of her first visits to Lucid World, Amasis said the equipment was installed near her home. How near?

She scoured the yard and checked the exterior of her house. She saw nothing that suggested anything out of the ordinary. What about the roof? No, that didn't seem a likely location because snow often covered the roof.

An optimum location for such equipment would be protected from the elements, such as snow, but not so sheltered that the signal would be obstructed. Also, it would need to be hidden or inconspicuous, and located where no one would move or change things. A protected and elevated location would be ideal.

It hit her: the church steeple! The church was several blocks from her house, driving or walking, but it was close as the crow flies. The steeple didn't have a clock or a bell, but there had to be room up there because there were venting louvers in the sides. How would someone get up there? The choir loft was the highest point in the church and a likely location for access.

The next day, after school, Morgan made her way to the church.

As usual, the front door was open. She walked into the foyer. The stairs to the choir loft were off to the side. Before heading to them, she peeked into the main church. No one was there; all was quiet.

Cautiously and slowly, she climbed the stairs listening for voices or sounds of movement from the loft. Other than the soft creaks her feet made on certain of the steps, it was silent.

When she got to the top of the stairs, she surveyed the room. No one was there. She had a story ready if someone was. She would say she had been there on Sunday and left her sweater behind.

So where was the access to the steeple? She assumed it was probably somewhere in the ceiling, like a door to an attic. She looked over the entire ceiling. There were lights and ceiling fans but no sign of a door. She walked to the rail at the edge of the loft and looked out at the ceiling that covered the rest of the church. There were more lights and ceiling fans but no sign of a way to get to the steeple. Access would have to be somewhere near her present location because the steeple was at the front of the church and directly above the choir loft.

Maybe there was a side door to gain access. She looked around again. There was a door. She put her hand on the knob and turned it.

"What are you doing?"

Morgan jumped and wheeled around. It was Enid Meany. She had her hands on her hips and her lips were more pursed than usual.

"Actually, I'm looking for my sweater?"

"Well you won't find it in the janitor's closet. There's a lost-and-found box in the coat room."

"Oh, so that's what this is. I thought maybe it was the door to the other room."

"What other room?"

"You know, the one in the steeple."

"There's no room up there. The steeple is just a decoration."

"What about the window louvers? Aren't those for air and light?"

"Those are imitation louvers; they're part of the design. I must say, you are a very strange girl. Oh, don't look so surprised. Did you think I'd forgotten what you said to Winnie and me that day when I dropped my bag?"

Morgan's face turned red; she mumbled an apology, and left.

EARTHQUAKE REPORTS

After that, whenever Morgan went somewhere in or around Coyote Flats, she was on the lookout for potential locations for the communication equipment. Other than becoming much more knowledgeable about lighting and heating apparatuses, her efforts were unrewarded.

Morgan considered other possible reasons Lucid World had not reached out to her. If only she could communicate with other khaos project participants, she could learn if it was just her who hadn't been contacted. She only ever met one other participant, Elvis. But Amasis moved him so fast she never had time to ask his last name or tell her hers, or find out where in Hawaii he was from.

She looked for people named Elvis in Hawaii. She found a lot of information about Elvis Presley, who had done movies and performances in Hawaii. On social media, there were guys named Elvis from Hawaii who were close in age, but none of them resembled the Elvis she met. She remembered his appearance well. He was cute, handsome and charismatic, all rolled up in one.

Hidden away within a mountain cavern, under an icecap, could all be so precarious. Many things could go wrong. Lucid World had brilliant scientists and inventors. But as people have witnessed time after time throughout the ages, humans are no match for the powerful forces of nature.

The news carried numerous reports of recent earthquake activity. Morgan gasped at the thought.

Morgan never knew the location of Lucid World. She deduced it was likely in Northern Africa, the Middle East, or Asia, somewhere near where the earliest advanced civilizations started.

She thought about the rose finch birds she and Amasis watched. He identified their species as Carpodacus rubicilla. She researched the natural habitat of the species and found Afghanistan, Georgia, Kazakhstan, Mongolia, Pakistan, Russia, and more. Too many places!

What about the treasure map? She called it that because the images it depicted reminded her of what was often ascribed to maps used by pirates. It was created by the founders and recorded the journey they took to get to their mountain home. It showed forests, rivers, mountains and the direction of the sun rising and setting. She had often gazed at the map and could recall all of its details. Perhaps she could match it to topographic maps in areas where the rose finch lived.

She spent hours. The sequence of hills, forest, river, forest, mountains, lake, river, and mountains, was not unique. Her attempt at matching topography failed.

Next, Morgan researched earthquake reports. She didn't only focus on those considered severe, because a mountain cavern could implode from less than what might be considered a catastrophic earthquake.

There were several earthquake reports and some of them from areas of seemingly probable locations for Lucid World. She felt powerless. It was only a hunch, but what if she was right? They could be trapped or injured or worse. So much time had already passed since she had expected to hear from them.

She pictured Amasis pinned down because the suspended marble table had fallen on his legs. While he pressed the oval device around his neck, he called Morgan's name. She shuddered.

What could she do? If she told anyone about her fears, they would think she was telling a fantastic story and would never believe her. She had no proof and the whole thing, starting with the existence of Lucid World, really was incredible. Even if she could get someone to believe her about Lucid World, a destructive earthquake was only a theory. Further, if her earthquake theory was correct, where would they look? There could be hundreds or thousands of mountains in areas impacted by an earthquake.

When Morgan resolved to continue in her efforts to reverse khaos, she considered how she might do so without the guidance and reminders from Lucid World. She thought teachings from the Dalai Lama would be useful and she had already read some of his teachings. He was quoted as saying, 'If there is a solution to a problem, there is no need to worry; and if there is no solution, there is no need to worry.' Morgan remembered Amasis quoting it to her.

So which was it in this situation? Stop worrying and figure out a solution; or stop worrying and accept she couldn't change things? She just didn't know.

She thought about Djer's search for Kasta. Djer never found Kasta; Kasta found him. The image of the treasure map again came to mind. She imagined Kasta crossing mountain ranges and rivers to get to his friend.

DJER

It was hot that day. Djer quenched his thirst with much beer and wine at the new moon festival. He went to bed early with a heavy head.

During the warm season he often slept outside on the roof with his family. Not tonight. With the merriment from the festivities, it was too noisy outside.

Several hours after Djer retired for the evening, shouts woke him. There was a commotion outside. He listened. It wasn't the sounds of merriment. It sounded like shouts from guards who were stationed at the high wall which enclosed the garden of flowers and fruit trees surrounding his home.

He sat up in bed. Before his eyes could adjust and focus in the dark, he heard the sound of his name. Not just the sound of his name, the sound of a voice he had not heard for many years, but had never forgotten.

Chapter 40

Meanwhile Back in Lucid World

*Cats function on the principle that it does no harm to ask
for what they want.* - from "The Lives and Times of Cats"

The two friends were in a corner of a large room in a habitable 'safe area' building. The building had been used as a factory where clothing and shoes were made. It was now a place for them, and others, to spend their days. Much of Lucid World was uninhabitable.

"What's that sound?" asked Iris.

"It's just the sound of small rocks falling. I heard it, too. I don't think there's cause for alarm," said Amasis. "Or did you mean the sound of trickling water?"

"No. Not those noises. Shhh listen. It sounds like a cat crying," explained Iris.

Several days ago, the residents of Lucid World were awakened early in the morning, by the distant sound of a wailing rumble accompanied by the dizzying sensation of a vibrating mountain. It was followed by loud moaning sounds of faults straining and popping deep below.

As they lay in their beds holding their breaths, it was quiet for a moment. But before anyone could exhale, thunderous cracking sounds of hundreds of thousands of tons of rock rumbling, grinding and groaning surrounded them. Slamming smashing sounds came from directly above. When the mountain finished its fierce temper tantrum, small rocks rained on the upper structures.

Then there was a long quiet. People lay in their beds surprised to be alive. Dust stung their throats and nostrils.

When the dust settled well enough to see, inhabitants of Lucid World gathered in the large community square. 980 people lived in Lucid World. A count was performed. 980 were accounted for. 978 were present in the mountain and two, a father and son, were away in Nosos World.

Rubble and debris had fallen from the cave walls and ceiling, but no one had perished and injuries were minor; likely because the collapse happened early in the morning while most were still in their homes.

Debris and dust was not the only aftermath of what must have been an earthquake. Overhead structures, which previously served functions such as controlling light and air, now had a new function: keeping a fallen mountain crest off what was left of Lucid World.

There was no way to leave the mountain cavern. The overhead structures did not cover the passageways. The passages were blocked with colossal boulders and sheets of rock.

Structural engineers and geologists believed collapse within the cavern was imminent. It was just a matter of when it would happen. It could be minutes, days, weeks or months. They determined which section of the cavern was least likely to collapse. Buildings in this section used the exterior cavern wall as part of their structure. The cavern wall was solid to the outside of the mountain and would be less likely to collapse than buildings in the interior of the cavern, which consisted of clay.

Food and supplies were gathered and everyone moved to the safe area.

Over the next two days, Lucid World experienced mild aftershocks. These aftershocks caused some of the overhead structures, weighed down by stone, to collapse onto several sections of the cavern. Fortunately, it happened away from the safe area, in locations predicted to be most unstable. There was a lot of dust and noise but no one was harmed.

Engineers and geologists deemed if equipment, chemicals, or any force was used to remove debris it could cause implosion of the entire mountain. The residents of Lucid World were trapped.

Radio, wifi, satellite, cellular … none of it worked. Transmitters and receivers capable of contacting Nosos World had been strategically located near the outside passages to minimize interference and were now destroyed by shifting and falling rock.

Fortunately, air still flowed from outside. Also, fuel and power reserves were abundant enough to provide light and most creature comforts. But the main supply of emergency food was kept in storage rooms near the passageways. These storage rooms had been blocked or destroyed. With strict rationing, the food and drinkable water would barely last a week.

Their only hope was for those who were away in Nosos to return home, and rescue them, in time. In the interim, they could only wait.

Iris and Amasis were accustomed to being together while working on the Nosos youth project. Now, relegated to the safe area, they continued to spend their days together. Khyan was not with them. He was with his father. They were the father-son team whose return was anxiously expected.

During their time together, Iris and Amasis often discussed successes, failures, ideas and stories related to their project.

Morgan's name came up often. Like the other Nosos youth, she would wonder why they hadn't contacted her. In light of Morgan's state of mind when they last saw her, they suspected she might feel rejected. How was she coping? Was she able to see she had misdirected her feelings and had experienced illogical emotions of khaos? They missed her sense of humour and sense of adventure.

While reminiscing, Amasis told Iris about the time Morgan invited him to her school dance and how disappointed she was when he told her it would be impossible.

Iris teased him. "Morgan never invited me to a school dance. But then, who could blame her for falling for your good looks and charming personality?"

"Khaos made her think she needed someone to accompany her to the dance. I was the one who met with her when she talked about it. Had it been you, I'm sure she would have asked you."

His voice carried a serious quality. This made Iris wonder if perhaps she was on to something and there was a romantic attraction between Amasis and Morgan. "Hmm," she said, "I've seen Morgan act very differently when you're in the room. Her avatar eyes are just fixated on you."

Amasis gave up trying to be serious. He laughed and said, "I agree that her avatar makes some interesting faces."

Amasis was telling the story of Morgan's dislike of garguey, without having tasted it, when Iris interrupted to ask about the noise.

"I'm sure it sounds like a cat meowing. It gets louder and then softer. Shhh I hear it again."

After a minute of silence Iris said, "Now I don't hear it. Maybe it was responding to your voice when you told the story about Morgan."

Iris had no sooner uttered Morgan's name when "Meow!" was heard by them both.

It sounded like it came from inside of the wall, but the wall was thick dense rock and earth. How could that be?

Ancestors who settled Lucid World, found the mountain by way of ancient maps and legends. So they had to consider the possibility of people tracking and finding them using similar means. As a precaution, before they built the infrastructure inside the cavern, they used ultrasonic waves to locate near-adjacent caves. They tunnelled passageways to them, and concealed the entrances, so they could take cover in the event of an invasion. After many years, when the threat of invasion was unlikely, some caves were turned into storage rooms and others were forgotten or built over.

So it was possible there was a cat inside the wall.

The two friends looked for any sign of a door in the wall, but found nothing. Since the entrances to the small caves were meant to be hidden, the cut of such a door would be imperceptible. Also, it may be behind a facade, tapestry or shelf.

If they couldn't access the cat from where they were, maybe they could find where the cat got in and rescue it from there.

Although communications with the outside world were impossible due to the damage, communications within Lucid World were fully functional. A mass message was sent requesting anyone who lost a cat during the earthquake to contact them.

It didn't take long before a message came back from Elder Tabubu: Luna and her three kittens were missing.

"If it's Luna behind the wall," said Amasis, "that would explain why we heard a louder meow when we mentioned Morgan's name."

Iris nodded and said, "Luna is fond of Morgan." She laughed and added, "Especially after we created the interactive virtual-robot cat brush."

The storage alcove where Luna kept her litter, was recessed into the external cavern wall. During aftershocks, the building around it crumbled. The friends deduced there was likely a passageway large enough for a cat, and Luna had taken her babies into it. But now they couldn't get to it because the collapsed building was in an unsafe area.

"So if we're right, and Luna and her kittens are trapped behind the wall, how can we hear her through a stone wall?" asked Iris.

"Just thinking about that," replied Amasis. "The secret caves were for hiding if there was an invasion, so they would have needed a supply of air."

The duo inferred that holes would have been bored at the entrances and it was through these holes that Luna's meows emitted. The holes weren't visible because the rock was porous and irregular. But it meant there was a door nearby and, if they could find the door, they could get to her.

The sound of water dripping meant Luna might have access to water. The babies would have Luna's milk. How long could Luna go without food?

They couldn't blast or drill because of the cavern's instability. The wall was likely too thick for a laser-cutting torch and they'd lose too much time trying. They needed to find the hidden door and open it.

CHAPTER 41

FRANNY AND SALLY

Winds on Mars travel faster than winds on Earth.
Combined with the lower atmospheric pressure of Mars,
the motion of sand particles causes Martian rock to erode
differently than Earth rock. – from "As the Wind Blows"

Back at the Frey house, a lot has happened. Let's start with when Sally and Franny left the gala. They walked home in silence. Franny marched ahead with her head held high; Sally with her head hung low.

When they arrived home they found Mikey sitting on the floor crying. Franny yelled, "I told you I'd be right fricking back! You can blame your sister for being left alone."

Franny stormed to her bedroom, slammed the door and didn't resurface. Not even the next morning.

Mrs. Kyatchi came to check on them. She found Sally and Mikey breakfasting on dry cereal without milk. Sally was drinking coffee; Mikey was drinking water. Mrs. Kyatchi asked if they had any milk or juice and when they said they had none, she got in her car, drove away, and returned with a bag of groceries.

Franny still hadn't come out of the bedroom. Alarmed, Mrs. Kyatchi was reluctant to leave. Sally assured her everything was fine and if they needed anything they would call.

Franny did eventually come out. Her mood was quiet and aloof.

During the days that followed, Franny's depressed mood continued and she drank more than usual. More often than not, she was 'passed out' on the sofa. She only ever left the house to buy cigarettes or alcohol. She got Sally to run all of the errands and do the shopping. Had Sally been old enough to buy cigarettes and alcohol, Franny would have never left the house.

Sally had never seen her mother binge so hard before. When Franny bumped into things or fell, Sally feared she might really hurt herself. Also, Sally was concerned while she was at school, and Franny was drunk, Mikey was essentially unsupervised. He was just three years old and needed help with most things.

Sally wanted to tell Mrs. Kyatchi about the situation, and ask for help. But she feared Mrs. Kyatchi would be required by law to get outsiders involved. Outsiders wouldn't understand how things worked in their family and might take Mikey and her away from Franny. In spite of everything, Sally loved her mother.

Sally had become her mother's mother. Franny relied on Sally to take care of the entire household, and everyone in it, including Franny.

When Sally desperately needed nurturing, she had to be the nurturer. There was no one to turn to for guidance or support, or to unburden her distress. Sally tried to talk to Morgan about the situation shortly after the gala. But Morgan was racked with guilt in spite of Sally's insistence it wasn't Morgan's fault and she did not blame her. Sally ended up consoling Morgan.

The only person Sally could think of to talk to was Cara. She had not become as close to Cara as she had with Morgan; but she felt she could consider Cara a friend.

Sally tried to find an opportunity to confide in Cara but every time she saw her, she was with Morgan or girls from the basketball team. She couldn't phone Cara after school because Franny was always home and would be sure to be listening.

One day, Sally's worst fears came to fruition. While at school, a police officer came to the classroom to fetch her. They drove to the hospital. Franny was in a hospital bed with a cast on her arm and a bandage on her head. She didn't speak and appeared heavily sedated.

A fair-complexioned woman who Sally didn't know was with Mikey at Franny's bedside.

The woman was from a child protection government agency. She introduced herself as Mrs. Destiani.

Franny had fallen and hit her head on the sharp corner of a table. She had a head injury and a broken arm. A neighbour phoned the police after hearing Mikey crying long and loud.

Mrs. Destiani asked if Sally and Mikey had any family who they could contact. Sally didn't think so. She didn't know who her father was or who Mikey's father was, and Franny never told her about her grandparents or if she had any aunts or uncles. Whenever Sally asked about family, Franny said, "They're all dead." Sally wasn't sure if this was true because Franny wouldn't tell her how or when they all died.

Mrs. Destiani grabbed her phone from her coat pocket and excused herself to make some calls. She was gone a long time. Sally and Mikey sat by Franny's bed watching her breathe. Franny's eyes were closed and she seemed unaware of their presence.

When Mrs. Destiani returned, she had a strange look on her face. She appeared both pleased and troubled. "I have news. I found your grandparents. They only live about an hour's drive from here. They're truly anxious to see your mother and to meet you. They'll stay with you while your mother is in the hospital, and ..."

Sally was shocked, surprised, stunned. Her emotions ran the whole gamut. Questions flooded her mind. The foremost question related to the unfinished sentence: and ... what?

Mrs. Destiani took Sally and Mikey to their home and promised to return later that day with their grandparents.

WHATEVER IT TAKES

When Mrs. Destiani got to her office, she closed the door, sat at her desk, and picked up the phone.

"Hi Mere, it's me, Karleen. It's good you called me when you noticed Mrs. Frey's name in the hospital admission records."

"How is she? What about Sally and her little brother?" asked Meredith.

"Mrs. Frey took quite a fall. She has injuries that will keep her in the hospital for a while. I've made arrangements for someone to look after Sally and Mikey."

"How long will she be in the hospital? Sally's old enough to look after Mikey for a couple of days."

"Indeed. The situation is more serious than just a couple of days in the hospital. I can't go into any other details although I doubt I have to. You likely suspected things were bad when you called me to get involved."

"Oh my! Morgan will be devastated when she finds out how bad things are. She feels responsible for what happened at the gala and now she'll blame herself for this, too."

"Franny Frey's condition isn't anyone else's fault. What happened would probably happen, sooner or later anyway. It's good it happened this way; and neither Franny or her children, or anyone else for that matter, were seriously injured. Be sure to explain that to Morgan."

"I will and I'll suggest Morgan go to Sally's place. I mentioned it before but she said Sally wasn't allowed to have friends over. With Franny in the hospital, that shouldn't be a problem. I'm sure Sally will be happy for the support."

After the conversation ended, Karleen Destiani didn't move. She sat at her desk, hand still resting on the phone, in a forward leaning position, as if frozen. When she finally moved, she sat erect and took a deep breath. As she exhaled she uttered the words, "Indeed. Whatever it takes."

CHAPTER 42

MISSING CHILDREN

They called her name. She meowed. With successive calls, her meow grew louder. It stood to reason that Luna was on the other side of a door in the wall, but they couldn't isolate where that might be.

Sound waves are created from vibrations. Vibrations coming from behind the door would travel to adjacent walls. They needed instrumentation to locate the point of origin. The instruments required for geological ultrasonic testing through rock were stored in one of the collapsed areas. Even if the equipment could be located, the process would take too long with all the setup, calibration and calculations required.

"It would've been easiest for our ancestors to bore air holes where the barrier is thinnest, so there should be a higher concentration of air holes on the actual door," said Iris.

"Yes!" exclaimed Amasis. "That's it! Air holes will show us where the door is. Air currents will show us where the air holes are. And smoke will ..."

Iris joined in and they said in unison, "...show us where the air currents are."

They removed everything from the walls, brightened the lights and closed off the room.

Soon they were at their stations wearing masks to breathe, and watching for smoke patterns.

The smoke rose from a fire lit in a container in the center of the room. Initially, it hovered like a big cloud. However, before long, there was movement and the smoke drifted towards the wall. It appeared to crawl along the wall and not favour any particular spot. Then, as the amount of smoke built up, it became denser in a particular section.

They extinguished the fire and lit a candle. Iris held the candle and systematically moved it across the wall location favoured by the smoke. There was an area about three feet across and four feet up from the floor where the candle flickered more than elsewhere on the wall.

She knocked lightly on the focal wall section and called, "Luna, are you there girl?"

"Meow meow meow," replied Luna in a rapid succession.

Because any vibration could trigger more rock collapse, their only option was to scrape away at the rock, find an outline of the door, and apply leverage to pry at it.

They found and raided a maintenance room where various tools were kept.

They laboured for hours, scraping at the rock. From time to time, Luna cried out to them. When they didn't hear her, they assumed she was tending to her kittens or too tired to talk.

When the targeted surface was smooth, a fine line was perceptible. They chipped on both sides of the line, low to the ground, and created a hole large enough to insert a wedge.

Amasis plied the wedge carefully, back and forth. A 'crack' sound emitted and a thick corner chunk broke free. It created an opening large enough for a cat!

"Looks like your muscle building exercises paid off," teased Iris.

Amasis laughed and flexed his muscles.

A silver black spotted cat poked her head through the opening and shyly exited the wall. Iris lifted her and commented she was thin and weak.

They offered her food and water. She ate ravenously. Because she had not eaten for five days, they thought it wise to give her only small amounts at intervals.

"Where are your kittens, Luna? Bring us your babies, Luna," prompted Amasis.

Luna gave no heed to Amasis's request. Had the kittens survived?

Luna might be more likely to go back for her babies if no one was there to distract her or feed her, so they left her alone in the room and shut the door.

Amasis and Iris stayed on the other side of the door. They discussed whether they should contact Elder Tabubu. They held off until they knew the fate of Luna's kittens. When they went back into the room, Luna was gone.

When Luna reappeared, she dragged a miniature version of herself by the scruff of the neck, using her mouth. The kitten cried inaudibly.

The kitten had been in darkness for five days. Its eyes had only just opened days before it was moved inside the wall, so its eyes were sensitive to the light. They dimmed the lights and made a bed for Luna and her kitten to lie on. Luna licked the kitten's soft fur.

When the kitten tried to suckle, Luna swatted it and got up to look for more food. They dispensed another small portion of food and again left the room.

When they returned, Luna was laying on the blanket nursing two kittens.

"Only two," said Iris. "Where's your other baby, Luna?"

Luna got up and went to Iris. Iris sat on the floor and held Luna in her lap. She fed Luna another portion of food and took Luna back to the small opening in the wall. "Go get your baby." Luna backed away from the hole. Iris tried to push her into the hole. Luna resisted.

"Which one is missing?" asked Amasis.

"The girl, Chinook, is missing. The two that are here are the boys, Gust and Puff."

Again they left the room and stood a distance from the door which they guaged would be outside Luna's hearing range.

While waiting for time to lapse, Iris thought about Sally and Franny. Morgan had tried so hard to help Sally. Chinook and Sally both needed their mothers. Iris hoped Morgan could help Franny and Sally find their way.

Amasis's thoughts went to Morgan. She would be so disappointed and upset if they couldn't save Chinook. The thought of giving her such news filled him with sadness. But wait, would he even ever see her again? He experienced a different kind of sadness, unlike any he had ever felt before.

When the two friends returned, they were disappointed to see Luna still on the blanket and still with only two kittens. Luna leapt up to ask for more food.

"After what she's been through, I'm not surprised she's more motivated by food than by maternal instincts," offered Iris. "It's amazing she didn't abandon all of the kittens when she became hungry. Luna's a good mother."

"Hey look, Gust left the blanket and he's exploring," said Amasis. "What if Chinook went to explore while Luna was at the passageway meowing to us?"

"If Chinook wasn't where Luna left her, she probably was left behind. If Luna can't find Chinook, maybe we can get Chinook to find her."

The cat rescuers recorded sounds of Luna's meow, purr and heartbeat. Using a long semi-flexible wire, they reached an amplifier into the passageway opening.

They waited. They increased the volume. Nothing happened.

"Maybe Luna deliberately left her behind. A cat will abandon a weak kitten so it can nurse the healthier ones," suggested Amasis.

"I told Elder Tabubu. She's thrilled that Luna and two of her kittens were found and is on her way."

Amasis proposed they leave the speaker setup running overnight, even though it probably wouldn't do any good. Kittens can't go long without their mothers and it had already been several hours.

"Take it out," Iris instructed.

Amasis looked surprised and confused.

"I'm not giving up. I have another idea. Chinook's eyes have been open for a couple of weeks but it's dark in the cavern so she needs to rely on her other senses such as sound and ..."

"Smell!" Amasis finished Iris's sentence.

They gathered bits of Luna's saliva, fur, dander, and breast milk to apply to swatches of gauze attached to the same wire hosting the amplifier. Luna wasn't too happy about the prodding and poking. She seemed to forgive and forget once it was done.

The amplifier was replaced with a microphone. A small fan, at the wall opening, blew Luna's scent into the cave.

Luna was the first to hear it. As she moved towards the opening in the wall, her ears rotated like satellite dishes. Coming through the microphone receiver was a barely audible tiny meow.

Luna entered the opening in the wall. She returned within seconds holding a grey kitten by the scruff of the neck.

"It's not one of Luna's kittens, it's a grey kitten!" exclaimed Amasis.

Laughing, Iris said, "It's not grey; it's just dusty and dirty."

Luna dropped Chinook onto the ground and licked her in a rough manner. Chinook squealed and complained. Luna admonished accordingly.

Elder Tabubu arrived just in time to witness the marvelous sight of a complaining kitten being cleaned and disciplined by her mother.

CHAPTER 43

GRANDPARENTS

The Earth's rotation causes winds to be deflected to the right in the Northern Hemisphere, and to the left in the Southern Hemisphere. - from "As the Wind Blows"

Two cars pulled up in front of the Frey house. Karleen Destiani stepped out of one. A man and a woman stepped out of the other. The man, trim bodied, with a full head of black and grey hair strode confidently. The woman, slightly plump, held on to the sides of her styled short reddish-blond hair, to keep the wind from dishevelling it. Both were dressed in clothes more appropriate for a wedding or a funeral than visiting someone's home in Coyote Flats.

When they arrived at the door they rang the doorbell. Based on the disrepair of the exterior of the house, they guessed it might be broken so they also knocked.

Morgan was there with Sally and Mikey. As Meredith suggested, Morgan stopped by after school. Before the cars arrived, the girls were watching out of the window.

Not wanting to appear too anxious, when Sally saw Mrs. Destiani's car come into view, she motioned they should move away from the window.

Sally didn't answer the door until she heard the knocks. She opened the door to three people standing on the doorstep. The woman, who Sally supposed was her grandmother, rushed forward without an invitation to 'come in'. She grabbed Sally, held her tight, and cried. "Oh my darling, my darling, my darling ..." The man followed his wife and stood beside her.

Karleen saw Morgan standing off to the side. She slipped past Sally and her grandparents to join Morgan and whispered, "I'll give you a ride home."

The woman continued to hug and rock Sally as if she would never let her go until the man put his hand on the woman's back and said, "Margaret, let's introduce ourselves to our grandchildren." Margaret released her grip, wiped the tears from her face with the back of her wrist and nodded assent.

Sally walked over to Mikey and lifted him into her arms. The man addressed Sally and Mikey.

"Sally and Mikey, I'm pleased to meet you. My name is Joseph. You can call me Grandpa Joe. This is your grandmother, Margaret. You can call her Grandma Marg."

Margaret cried again. Karleen approached Joseph and handed him her card saying, "Call if you need anything. I'll see you tomorrow."

After Karleen and Morgan left, Joe suggested the newly acquainted grandparents and grandchildren make a pot of coffee and sit around the kitchen table to talk.

When they were settled, Sally asked, "Why didn't my mom tell me about you?"

Margaret had quit crying and was now composed. "Probably because it would bring back painful memories. We only just found out about you sweetheart."

"Why? What memories? What happened?" asked Sally.

Joe and Margaret exchanged a look and Joe said, "Sally's old enough to understand." Margaret nodded and he added, "We brought toys for Mikey. He can play with them while we talk."

After Mikey was settled on the floor with his new toys, Margaret began. "When your mother was a teenager, she got involved with some older wilder friends. To say those friends were a bad influence would be an understatement." She looked at Joe but didn't wait for his reaction before she continued, "They were heavy partiers and chased after men who played in bands."

Joe said, "We tried to stop her from seeing them but she did it anyway. So we grounded her from leaving the house, except for school. But she skipped school."

Margaret sighed, "We didn't know what to do. We were afraid

if we did more, we'd lose her, and if we didn't, we'd lose her. One night, she snuck out of the house while we were sleeping and she took her sister, Nancy, with her."

Margaret dropped her chin and shook her head, "We didn't even know they were gone until morning, when our neighbour, who was a policeman, came to our house. Car accident ..." Margaret's voice trembled. Joe moved his chair closer to hers and put his hand on her hand. "Nancy died."

Margaret took a deep breath and continued. "They were riding in a car. The driver was drunk. He lost control, went off the road and hit a tree. Frances and the driver were wearing seatbelts. They had only minor injuries."

Margaret inhaled through her nose and exhaled through her mouth as she patted at her chest. "Nancy was in the back seat without a seat belt." She waved off Joe's attempt to interject. "She died on the way to the hospital."

Joe squeezed Margaret's hand and picked up where she left off. Frances was in the hospital for two days. On the day she was supposed to come home, they went to pick her up but she was gone. They looked for her. None of her friends, old or new, knew where she was. They hired an investigator who reported that Frances was living in a nearby town.

Joe had been talking at an even controlled pace but now his speech sped up, "We went there to tell her we loved her and to come home." Joe stopped abruptly and sadly shook his head, "We never got the chance. She opened the door, took one look at us, and slammed the door in our faces."

The expression on Joe's face was as if someone had just slammed a door in his face right there and then. "When we got home, there was a phone message. Said she was moving and if we tried to find her again, she'd move again. Her last words were, 'Both of your daughters are dead'."

Margaret put her head on Joe's shoulder and sobbed quietly. He stroked her hair and said, "After that we left her alone. A day hasn't gone by that we haven't hoped she'd come home."

Margaret sat up straight, "Now she's a grown woman with two beautiful children. Just look at you." She reached over and touched Sally's hair to move it away from Sally's eyes.

Sally had questions but she could see her grandparents were emotionally exhausted.

Joe changed the subject, and the mood, by asking about the guitar propped in the corner of the room. Sally told her grandparents about the TV show contest and her plans to study music. The news lifted their spirits.

Next, Sally told them about the gala and meeting Dorian Jones. Then she stopped and cried. "That's when it got terrible for Mom. It's my fault."

Mikey got up from the floor where he had been playing and waddled over to Sally. He put his arms around her waist and said, "Don't cry Sally. Do you want to play with my toys?" Sally hugged him back and lifted him onto her lap.

Margaret and Joe reassured Sally that it wasn't her fault. She did nothing wrong.

That night, Joe and Margaret slept in Franny's bedroom. It sounded to Sally they slept well based on the two distinct snore sounds she heard through the walls.

Sally, in contrast, hardly slept that night. She had a lot to think about.

She used to dream and imagine what it might be like to have grandparents. She sometimes heard classmates talking about their grandparents. Also, there were lots of TV shows and movies showing children and loving grandparents. Sally never believed it was something she and Mikey could have.

Her grandparents seemed to be kind and loving. But she didn't feel right liking them. She felt she was betraying her mother.

In the morning, Joe went to the store for groceries and Margaret made a 'feast' for breakfast. Sally didn't want to let on they didn't normally eat that way so she politely said, "That was good, thanks," and left it at that. Mikey kept reaching across the table and asking, "What's this? What's this?"

After breakfast, Joe phoned Karleen Destiani and made plans to meet her at the hospital. He told Sally he didn't know what to expect when he and Margaret reunited with Franny, so he thought it best if they went alone. He made the appointment for later in the day, when school was finished, so Sally could watch Mikey while they were away.

At school, Sally told Morgan that her grandparents were taking over and cutting her out of important matters concerning her mother. Morgan had an idea.

LIBRARY CART

Sally phoned her grandparents from school. She told them she had an afterschool project she had forgotten about, and her friend Cara would come over after school to look after Mikey.

When classes ended, Morgan and Sally headed to the hospital. In Coyote Flats, most places are within walking distance. They ran rather than walked. They needed to get there before Margaret and Joe.

Hospital staff was accustomed to seeing Morgan because Meredith sometimes volunteered her daughter to help with small tasks like delivering flowers or distributing books and magazines to patients. When Sally and Morgan arrived at the hospital, they casually sauntered past the reception desk with a 'hello' from Morgan.

Meredith looked up from her desk as Morgan and Sally entered her office. "Hi girls. Morgan, I wasn't expecting you. Is everything okay?"

"Sally's here to visit her mother. I walked with her from school, so I thought I might help out while I'm here by going around to the rooms with the library cart."

Meredith eyed Morgan suspiciously. Then remembering it was she who suggested Morgan check-in with Sally the day before, she trusted Morgan and whatever she was up to.

The girls went to the library and put an assortment of books on a cart. They pushed the cart to the hospital ward where Franny's room was located.

"Is your mom in a single or double room?" asked Morgan.

"Double room. Her bed is closest to the window."

They rolled the cart to the room entrance and peeked in the door. The privacy curtain hid Franny's bed. The roommate patient was sleeping.

Next, they went to the sun room at the end of the hall. The

room's expansive windows looked out over the parking lot. When they saw Joe and Margaret's car pull into the parking lot, they pushed the cart back toward Franny's room and abandoned it in an inconspicuous location in the hallway.

They crept into Franny's room, past the sleeping patient, and hid in the bathroom, which was out of view from Franny's side of the curtain. They left the light turned off and door opened slightly. Through the slit in the door, they had a direct view of the curtain and the foot of Franny's bed.

Three of them, Joe, Margaret and Karleen, walked into the hospital room. Karleen pulled the curtain back slightly to make room for them to stand around the bed.

When Franny saw her visitors, she turned her head to face away from them and towards the window.

Karleen walked around the bed to the side Franny faced and said, "Mrs. Frey, your parents are here. You're a grown woman and indeed you have the right to choose to have them in your life or not. But before you decide, there's something you should think about. The authorities intend to remove your children from your home unless you can prove you can look after them."

In the bathroom, Sally 'gasped'. Morgan put her arm around her.

Karleen continued. "To do that, you have to go into an addiction treatment program. If you agree, you have two choices for the custody of your children. They can be placed in a foster home or you can let your parents back into your life."

In a low raspy voice, Franny said. "If I had a smoke, I could fricking think." Her hands shook.

Karleen replied, "Indeed. I'll see about getting you a nicotine patch to help with your craving for tobacco, and something to help your alcohol withdrawal, too."

Karleen left the room. No one spoke. The only sound was the sound of Franny breathing.

After several minutes, Margaret walked around to the side of the bed, grabbed Franny's hand and held it between her own two hands. Margaret said in a whispery voice, "Oh my darling, we have missed you so much. Please let us help you get better."

Franny jerked her hand away, sat up and yelled, "They're my

children! I won't let anyone take them away from me. I'm going home."

Sally let out another gasp. In the dim light Morgan saw Sally put her hand over her mouth.

Franny tried to get out of bed to leave. She didn't have enough strength and got tangled in the tubes and wires around her face and arms.

Joe came around the bed and gently guided her back to a reclining position. Franny's only protest was heavy breathing. She was too weak to do more.

Joe said to Margaret, "Let's just sit beside the bed with her. We don't need to talk and no decisions need to be made right now."

Eventually, Franny's breathing softened and she fell asleep.

Margaret whispered to Joe, "I need to use the washroom." She got up from her chair and walked towards the bathroom.

Sally's hand gripped at Morgan's arm. Her nails dug into Morgan's flesh. It hurt. Morgan's heart pounded; she could feel it in her ears.

Margaret stopped, turned and walked back to Joe. She whispered, "I don't think I'm supposed to use this one. I saw a visitor washroom where we got off the elevator. I'll be right back."

Sally's grip relaxed. Morgan hoped the patient in the other bed wouldn't wake up and need to use the bathroom.

Margaret returned. Moments later, Karleen returned with a nurse. A nicotine patch was applied to Franny's shoulder and a syringe with fluid was injected into Franny's arm.

The nurse suggested tomorrow would be a better day and they should come back then.

The visitors left the room. The girls made their escape.

SUGAR COATING

When Sally got home, she found her grandparents in the kitchen. Margaret was at the counter making dinner; Joe was at the table reading to Mikey.

Sally asked how her mother was and when she might come home. Her grandparents gave vague answers only. Sally didn't get the sense that their ambiguity was for Mikey's benefit. They really weren't going to tell her.

Margaret asked Sally to help with dinner. While stirring a pot on the stove, Margaret said, "That Cara girl, my goodness she was tall, anyways, wasn't that nice for her to sit with Mikey while we were at the hospital? I offered to pay her but she wouldn't take it."

Marg's comments about Cara coming to sit with Mikey were the prelude to an interrogation. Sally was not used to this. Franny's manner was blunt and direct. Franny did not 'sugar coat' what she wanted to say or ask.

What kind of project was Sally working on after school? Did she know about it before today or did she forget?

Sally was in the middle of washing vegetables, as her grandmother had asked, so couldn't escape. It didn't matter. Morgan had prepared Sally for the possibility of questions. So the answers were easy.

Margaret and Joe hadn't been truthful with Sally when she asked about her mother. So Sally considered it tit-for-tat.

If she hadn't been hiding in the hospital room with Morgan, she'd be completely in the dark.

FIGHT OR FLIGHT

Sally and Morgan talked on the phone that night.

Sally brought up the social worker's comment 'alcohol withdrawal'. Sally always assumed Franny wanted to get drunk. Why hadn't she realized it was an addiction and encouraged her to get help? She felt she'd let her mom down.

Morgan suggested it was more complicated than that. "Your mom couldn't face her feelings after her sister died, so she ran away. Humans are wired for a fight-or-flight reaction. But no one can physically run away from what's inside. So she's using alcohol to escape — it's actually a 'flight' response."

"Maybe that makes sense."

"You couldn't have helped her because you didn't know about her sister or the accident."

"Okay so now I do, and maybe she needs less flight and more fight."

"Umm, not sure that's actually the right approach."

Always Telling Me What To Do

On the following day Joe, Margaret, Sally and Mikey went to the hospital together. Franny was sitting upright. Mikey ran up to the bed and climbed in. Joe moved to stop him and he started to cry.

Franny opened her arms towards Mikey and said, "It's all right baby. Climb up on this side."

Sally helped Mikey scramble onto the bed. Mikey snuggled into Franny while Sally stood there feeling uneasy.

"Humph. You just gonna stand there? A hello and a hug might be nice." said Franny.

Sally leaned over and put her arms around Franny's shoulders and said, "How're you feeling?"

"Not great," snarled Franny. "I have a cast on my arm," Franny raised her arm as high as the sling would permit. "Tubes, needles, stupid nurses," she rolled her eyes, "and lousy hospital food." She stuck out her tongue.

As if she had just remembered something important she said, "Oh, and get this! Last night they woke me up from a sound sleep to give me a fricking sleeping pill." She shook her head, "Typical."

Margaret moved forward to speak. Joe gleaned her intentions. He extended his arm to block her advance and shook his head.

Sally pulled a chair closer to the bed, sat down and said, "Mom, they told me about your sister and the accident. They, we, love you."

Joe looked at Margaret and nodded. Margaret said from across the room, "Frances, honey, we know you miss your sister. We loved your sister and we love you. We're so sorry. We did our best to keep you both safe. If there was anything we could do to change things, we would."

"What!? You think I blame you? You've never understood me. Not even when it came to Nancy's death." Franny shook her head while saying, "Typical."

Margaret cocked her head like a confused bird, so Franny

added, "It was my fault Nancy died! Why would I blame you?"

"Isn't that the reason you ran away? We grounded you. That's why you and Nancy snuck away while we were sleeping. If we hadn't forbidden you to leave the house ..." Margaret was crying uncontrollably. Joe put his arm around her and hung his head sadly.

Perturbed, Franny said, "I was the one who made Nancy ride in the car. She didn't want to, she wanted to go home. I told her to quit being such a baby and have some fun."

Franny's facial features were tight and rigid. She glared defiantly at Margaret and Joe.

Shocked, Margaret stopped sobbing and asked, "Then why'd you run away?"

Franny snapped, "I told you! It was my fault. I killed Nancy. I know it, you know it. Don't pretend you don't. Now get the frick outta here and leave me alone!"

Mikey had long since left Franny's arms to play with some equipment clips hanging from the bed-frame. Franny's hands trembled and she grabbed at the bed sheets and held them tightly to her chest.

Sally ran to get help. She returned with a nurse who asked the visitors to leave and let Franny rest.

Sally kissed her mother on the cheek. "Should we come back tomorrow?"

Franny shrugged.

The family filed out of the hospital room in a quiet procession.

CHAPTER 44

A STRANGE-LOOKING HELICOPTER

Wind plays an important role in piloting a helicopter. A headwind flows opposite to the path of the helicopter and slows it down. A tailwind pushes the helicopter in the same direction and increases its speed. – from "As the Wind Blows"

Khyan had leapt at the opportunity to co-pilot the helicopter with his father. His father's usual co-pilot couldn't accompany him, and Khyan was far enough along in his pilot training to fill in.

Now they were listening to air traffic control transmissions from airports in the vicinity. There was banter about an unidentified aircraft.

It was their helicopter! Something was wrong. They should have been invisible to anyone monitoring the skies.

Lucid World's satellite was supposed to emit a signal to cloak the helicopter. Khyan's father deduced the satellite must have malfunctioned; or communications from Lucid World were not transmitting to the satellite. He reached over to the control panel and opened a channel to call Lucid World. No one answered.

The father and son had left Lucid World a week earlier, to obtain supplies from Nosos World. The last time they communicated with Lucid World had been six days ago.

It was not unusual to complete a project in Nosos World with infrequent communications to Lucid World. It was protocol to avoid unnecessary contact due to the possibility of transmissions being intercepted, and misinterpreted, by surveillance operatives in Nosos World.

Khyan's father knew what they had to do, and he and Khyan had been busy doing it. They again tried to contact Lucid World. Still nothing.

Khyan piloted the craft while his father plotted a route to a remote location, far from air traffic control towers and radar, so they could land undetected and decide what to do.

They landed in a clearing where it was unlikely anyone would see them. There, they attempted to communicate with Lucid World using various means and devices: radio, satellite, wifi and cellular. No response. It was baffling: with all the different technologies and devices that could communicate with Lucid World, why couldn't they reach them?

Khyan searched the computer for news. Regional news for the Nosos civilization nearest to Lucid World reported an earthquake in the area. It was 5.7 on the Richter scale with the epicenter located not too far from where Lucid World was hidden.

The realization sank in. Either their external communication had been damaged or they weren't able to communicate.

They plotted a course to Lucid World that they believed would ensure minimal exposure to detection. Flying without cloaking concealment was against protocol. But their better judgement told them they should get back as soon as possible, so they deemed the risk necessary.

The helicopter could fly at extremely high speeds. Khyan's father piloted it at maximum speed to get to Lucid World while there were still hours of daylight remaining.

Several hours later, the icecap crowning Lucid World was in view. The icecap appeared smaller in size, compared to when they left, and it no longer concealed portals on the mountain top. The large openings, designed to provide fresh air and refracted sunlight, were supposed to be camouflaged. The icecap enhancement projection equipment was not functioning. They saw nothing else different or unusual on the mountain.

They landed next to the helicopter hangar in a large hollow on the side of the mountain. Usually, someone from the ground met the pilots and helped move the aircraft into the hangar. No one came to meet them.

They traveled to the nearest entrance to Lucid World. Entrances were tunnels leading to stairs, or elevators which descended to the bottom of the cavernous space that was Lucid World. A short way down the passage they were encumbered by loose stones on the path. They travelled further and were stopped by a wall of boulders and large rock shards.

Father and son split up and tried all the entrances. Each entrance presented similar obstacles; some closer to the opening, and some further down the passageway.

They met back at the hangar and fetched an all-terrain vehicle to climb the mountain, and inspect the air and sunlight portals.

Beneath the portals, there should have been a transparent dome protecting Lucid World from the elements. Through it they should have been able to see down into Lucid World. Instead, all that could be seen was rock and debris.

They needed to find out if anyone was still in there and if they were alive. Khyan's father looked for a place where he might shout down below.

Ever since they'd been unable to communicate, Khyan's thoughts often turned to his family and friends. If only he could get a message to someone, to learn of their condition and ask how to help. He thought that internal communications might still be functioning. If so, he would be in range, since his present location did not have solid rock between it and Lucid World.

Using his oval neck device, Khyan attempted to contact Iris. He was unsuccessful so he moved to another location above the dome and tried again. After a few tries and changing his location each time, Iris answered and asked excitedly, "Khyan, are you here at the mountain?"

"We're on the top on the mountain trying to look down on what used to be the see-through dome. Are you trapped?" Khyan hesitated, "Are any dead or injured?"

"None are dead and surprisingly, there are no major injuries. That may change though."

"How can we get to you?"

"Any vibration or shifting of the mountain could cause further collapse or implosion; so boring through walls or removing debris in the tunnels is inadvisable. I think we have to proceed using a Jenga[5] type approach."

"Are you referring to the game?"

"Yes. You know, the game objective is to pull out blocks in a tower without interfering with adjacent blocks and causing the tower to tumble. In our case, it wouldn't be blocks, it would be rocks; and it wouldn't be a tower, it would be the dome. We need to remove debris from above with minimal disturbance of surrounding rocks."

CHAPTER **45**

TODAY'S CHALLENGES

Cats generally make good mothers to their kittens. However, a mother
cat suffering from illness or poor nutrition may not care for her kittens,
leading her to reject them. – from "The Lives and Times of Cats"

K arleen met with Joe and Margaret at the hospital. She suggested they come without Sally or Mikey. They conferred in the lobby, then proceeded to Franny's room and assembled around her bed.

Joe spoke. "The doctor said you're ready to be discharged." Franny didn't let him finish.

"It's about time! Someone, help me get unstuck from all of this equipment and stuff. Where are my clothes?"

Joe said, "Not so fast, Frances. The government will take your children from your home as soon as you go back there, unless you go into a supervised addiction program."

Franny flopped back onto her pillow. "Typical. It's the same as before, isn't it? The two of you," she sighed, "always telling me what to do." She rolled onto her stomach.

They attempted to get Franny to face them, or to say something. Joe and Margaret looked at Karleen with alarm.

Karleen said, "I have an idea. Let's leave her for now, I'll call you later."

Karleen was a resourceful woman and able to 'pull a few strings'. Franny was kept in the hospital, for psychiatric therapy.

Franny cooperated and stayed in the hospital. She considered it to be the least offensive alternative in the short term.

During Franny's extended hospital stay she had numerous sessions with therapists. Her cooperation with the prolonged hospital stay did not extend to the therapy sessions. She was non-responsive during private sessions and hostile during sessions with her parents.

Sally and Mikey were again excluded. Sally received only abbreviated versions of what was going on at the hospital. She interpreted her grandparents' vagueness to mean her mother had not yet agreed to undergo treatment for her addiction. Sally knew everyone meant well but she resented being kept away and uninformed. After all, she knew her mother better than anyone.

Cut off from important matters involving her mom, Sally confided her frustrations and fears to Morgan. Morgan gave Sally platitudes of hope and reassurance. But later that day when alone with her thoughts, Morgan realized she had let Sally down. There had to be more she could do than repeat tired phrases to Sally.

Morgan thought about khaos answers buried in the subconscious. When someone sincerely wants an answer, they'll find it. It may come in a dream or a book.

After school, Morgan went back to the hospital. Her first stop was the gift shop to buy flowers.

Carrying the flowers, Morgan strode up to the reception desk, "I have a flower delivery for Mrs. Frey. I think she's been moved to a private room, which room is it?"

Morgan's next stop was the library where she filled the cart with various random books and one particular book she'd seen there before. The book was titled, Today's Challenges Bring Tomorrow's Rewards. She thought the title alone might resonate for Mrs. Frey. She left the flowers on the table in the library. They had fulfilled their purpose.

Morgan rolled the book cart to the nursing station on Franny's floor. She greeted the attending nurse and said, "Mrs. Frey asked for this book. I think she's sleeping and I don't want to wake her. Could you please put it in her room later?"

The nurse replied, "I'm sure she's awake, I was just in there. If the door's open, just go in."

This wasn't what Morgan planned. To avoid suspicion she had to follow the nurse's suggestion. Besides, she had never formally met

Franny Frey. She doubted Franny knew who she was.

Morgan rolled the book cart to Franny's room and said cheerfully as she entered, "Library books. You can choose what you like or I can leave a few books behind."

Franny was propped up in bed, staring out the window. She turned her head and scowled, saying, "I don't want books. Go bother someone else."

Morgan laughed nervously and replied, "Hahaha. All right, no problem. I'll just leave a book here and you can read it, or not, whatever you like."

Morgan pretended to randomly grab a book and set Today's Challenges on Franny's bedside table.

"I know you! You're that girl who put all of those fricking ideas in Sally's head. What's the matter with you? You so bored with your own life you need to interfere in other peoples' lives? Think you're better than Sally and you know what's good for her? We were happy before you came along and poisoned her. And look at what happened. Sally hates me. I'm in the hospital. Now the government is trying to separate us. It's your fault. I hope you're happy."

Morgan's eyes filled with tears. As she was just about to turn and flee, she had an a-ha moment. She was being bullied. No wonder Sally had so much difficulty repelling the abuses of bullies. Sally's mother was a bully.

Bullies are insecure and try to make others feel bad to raise their self-esteem. If bullies don't get reinforcement for their behaviour, the bullying is negated. Reacting to a bully only encourages them.

Morgan composed herself. "Mrs. Frey, I'm sorry for the troubles. Sally loves you and she's worried for you. I'm her friend. I hope we'll be friends for a long time, but when we get older our lives might go in different directions. You're her mother. You're her family and you're the one she needs. You'll always be her mother. That'll never change."

Karleen was standing in the hall, just outside the doorway. She had been on her way to see Franny but when she heard voices, she waited outside, not wanting to interrupt. When she recognized Morgan's voice, she listened to the conversation. After Morgan's last words, it seemed an opportune time to enter the room.

Franny looked relieved when she saw Karleen but said, "Oh

great, another Meddling Millie. If my life is so interesting, why don't you two get together and start a reality TV show."

"Mrs. Frey, I heard what Morgan said to you. She's right. We're all truly sorry for your troubles. You still need to be a mother to your kids."

"My 'troubles' are of no business to either of you. Besides, what would you know about it?"

Karleen answered. "I've had my share; and I know how painful parts of life can be. Our lives are made up of many different pieces. It's all of them, and what we do with them, that truly makes us who we are. If you are going to keep your family together, you have to fit the pieces of your life together. No one can do it for you. You have to be the one to do it. You either make an effort to pull your life together, or you'll lose your children."

Karleen tilted her head towards the door, to motion to Morgan, and they walked out together.

NANCY

When in the hall, Karleen said, "Let's go sit in the visitors' lounge and talk."

Morgan and Karleen settled into a corner of a room filled with an eclectic assortment of sofas, chairs and small tables.

Karleen began, "You're a good friend to Sally. She needs your help, and I have an idea."

"The last time I tried to help her, I ..." Morgan caught herself. No more self-pity for her. "What can I do?"

"First, I want to tell you about something that happened seventeen years ago."

Morgan nodded. "Okay."

No one else was in the room but Karleen kept her voice low anyway. "In the neighbourhood where I grew up, my best friend Nancy lived next door. She had an older sister named Frances.

"Frances was stylish and beautiful. We worshiped her and followed her around, even when she told us to 'get lost'.

"The sisters shared a bedroom and my window faced theirs. One night, I heard arguing outside. I looked and saw Frances walking away and her sister, my best friend, running after her.

"That was the last time I saw Nancy. She was killed in a car crash."

Karleen's voice went soft and lumpy.

"Then Frances ran away from home. So I lost them both."

Karleen grabbed a tissue from a box on the table beside her chair and blew her nose. "Not long after, my father's work transferred him, so our family moved to Lethbridge. I never saw or heard from any of Nancy's family again until recently."

When Morgan heard the name 'Nancy' she connected the dots. "Nancy. Is that who Sally's grandparents told her about?"

"I didn't realize it at first. When I searched for family who might help Mrs. Frey and her children, I discovered Franny Frey was Frances. I didn't recognize her at first; but when I knew who she was I could see the resemblance."

Morgan furrowed her brow and squinted, "So didn't anyone recognize you? Not Sally's mom or grandparents?"

"Nope," said Karleen as she moved her head side-to-side. "When I lived next door I was twelve years old, wore braces and had a messy pony tail. As you can see, I don't look like that now. Also, I use my ex-husband's last name."

"So did you tell them who you are?"

"Not yet. I need to keep it that way for a little while longer. The universe brought Frances back into my life so I could help her, and now I need your help."

Boo Hoo

The next day, when school was over, Sally rode her bicycle to the hospital. She knew her grandparents wouldn't be there because her grandmother would be home making dinner.

She arrived at the hospital, and followed Morgan's directions to make her way to her mother's private room. She was careful to not risk detection. Based on reports from her grandparents, she feared she might be turned away if she checked in at the reception desk or the nursing station.

Sally was on a mission. Her mother was not responding to the therapy. She needed motivation.

Last night Morgan visited Sally and they talked in private, away from Sally's ubiquitous grandparents. When Morgan told Sally she needed to get more involved, Sally protested. She wasn't allowed to see her mother because her well-meaning grandparents had cut her out, probably to protect her. Morgan gave Sally the courage to take matters into her own hands.

Sally walked into her mother's room. She was lying on her back, staring at the ceiling.

Sally cleared her throat, put an index finger vertically in front of her lips to indicate 'shush', and whispered, "I don't think I'm supposed to be here. Maybe keep your voice down."

Franny's eyes widened and her lips emitted a small conspiratorial smile. She whispered back, "I told them I wanted to see you and Mikey. They said I had to get better first. Look at me. I'm fine!"

The last two words were louder than a whisper and Sally reminded her to keep her voice down.

Franny obeyed, "When I get out of here it'll be just you, Mikey and me again."

Franny's pace of speech sped up and sounded feverish. "No one's taking you from me. We'll move away. I've done it before. I'll do it again. No one's gonna tell me what to do. Not before! Not now! Never!"

"Mom, no, you're not fine. None of us are fine. We have a problem. Moving won't solve it."

"You're siding with them. They've turned you against me."

"No! I'm on your side. You're sick. You have an addiction and it almost killed you. We can't live this way."

"Look here little-Missy, I don't like your tone. And stop exaggerating. I've always been clumsy. I fell."

"Mom, you were drunk!"

"I've been depressed lately and so what if I had a few drinks? That's not why I fell. I tripped on one of Mikey's toys."

"Mom, no. It's been way more than a few drinks ever since ..."

"Whose fault is that? My daughter is ashamed of me. She doesn't even want to fricking be seen with me in public."

"You could have come to the gala if you wanted. You acted like you thought it was stupid, so I thought you didn't want to go."

"Admit it. You didn't want me there. You're embarrassed that I'm your mother."

Their voices were no longer whispers. Sally closed the door to the hospital room. Maybe the staff would assume the closed door meant a private procedure or a therapy session was underway.

"I was never embarrassed of you, at least not until that night. You saw to it. You made sure you embarrassed me in front of the entire town."

"There you go, acting all superior. Do you think you're better than me? Besides, who cares what other people think?"

"Mom, you should care. The government thinks you can't look after Mikey and me."

"I can look after you ungrateful brats just fine. If you want to live somewhere else, go! I won't stop you."

"You haven't been looking after us. I have." Sally began to cry.

"Oh boo hoo. You think I'm such a bad mother? Go live with your grandparents. But just so you know, they will control you. Good luck with that!" Franny turned over in bed so her back faced Sally.

Sally walked to the door but stopped before opening it. She had failed.

She turned, walked back to the bed and addressed her mother's back. She spoke loudly and sternly.

"I've spent time with them, yah they're controlling. I get it. You say you don't want to be controlled, but you are, by your addiction. You can let your addiction continue to control you and things will get worse, or we can take control together. I can't do it for you. I can do it with you. We can do it together. Either we get control or we get separated."

Sally didn't wait for a response or lack of a response. She walked to the door, opened it and left the hospital room.

When she got into the hallway, she burst out crying and ran to the stair well. She opened the door, ran up a few steps and sat down. The heavy door closed behind her with a loud solid thunk.

Moments later, as she sobbed heavily, the door opened. She looked down and saw Matt standing there. She knew him from school. Morgan had told her about his role at the party and the tiff they had during the assignment. Morgan had also told her he was actually an okay guy after all.

Sally turned her head downward, and to the side, to hide her wet red face and said, "I'm sorry. Do you need to use the stairs? I'll get out of the way." Sally slid to the side of the step with her face still pointing down and to the side.

"Nah, I saw you come out of the room and start crying. Are you okay?"

Matt sat beside her, handed her a tissue and asked a few more questions. They established that no one had died or was dying. That broke the ice and made Sally smile.

Matt said he was there because his mother was recovering after surgery. His parents had recently divorced and he needed to be there for her. His mom and dad used to fight and argue, so home life was maybe a little better than it used to be. Sally confided to him about her home life and the frustrations she felt.

Sally teared up again and Matt put his arm around her. He said, "I've learned that it's the biggest loves that cause us the biggest hurts. And it never hurts less when we take it out on ourselves or others."

CHAPTER 46

ISOLATED PEOPLE

The wind chime is a musical instrument through which the wind acts as both player and composer! – from "As the Wind Blows"

Morgan and her brothers were getting ready for school. Meredith was in the kitchen putting breakfast items on the table while watching the morning news.

"Come watch. HURRY!" called Meredith from the kitchen.

The screen showed a woman reporter standing in front of the United Nations Headquarters in New York City. In the background, flags of member countries fluttered in the breeze.

Morgan, Dylan and Ryan hurried to the kitchen and stood beside Meredith.

The reporter said, "United Nations representatives held a press conference just a few hours ago. They disclosed news of an emergency meeting related to the rescue of an unknown tribe of people who were discovered after a recent earthquake destroyed their home.

"The UN refers to them as isolated people, a term describing people who, by choice, live without significant contact with other civilizations of the world.

"Unlike other groups of isolated people, they are technologically advanced and multi-lingual. They've requested an international press conference to introduce themselves to connected civilizations of the world and ask for help in finding a new home."

Morgan jumped up and down. "I was right! It was an earthquake! Oh my god, oh my god. I hope they're okay! No wonder!"

Meredith scowled. "What? Shhh," and demonstratively waived her hand to signal Morgan to stop talking so she could listen.

The reporter said, "The news conference is set for 8:00 PM, Eastern Standard Time. This will be a historic moment you won't want to miss. We'll be covering the event live."

Meredith turned to Morgan. "Now what were you saying and jumping around about?"

Realization registered. They would not believe her. She didn't care. She had to say it anyway. She'd kept things to herself for too long.

"I know the people the reporter is talking about. At least, I'm pretty sure I do. Some of them are my friends. I've been worried about them ever since they quit meeting with me at night."

Morgan stopped talking when she saw the expression of alarm come over Meredith's face. She looked at Dylan and Ryan, and their expressions mirrored their mother's.

"Honey, that's just not possible." Meredith reached her hand and placed it on Morgan's forehead. "You don't seem warm, how do you feel? Are you dizzy or faint?"

"I'm not sick," Morgan sighed. "I knew no one would believe me. Maybe I can talk to them after the press conference and then you'll believe me."

"Now Morgan, what you are saying isn't possible. You probably had a dream about something and it seemed so real it feels like it happened."

There was no point to trying to explain. Morgan shrugged and said, "I guess so," and sulked away.

She heard her mother on the phone with her father. She must have phoned him at work. He'd gone in early, as most days recently, while they re-fitted the factory to accommodate the new speciality line.

"Yes, I heard the news. I'm not surprised everyone's talking about it. That's not the reason I called. I'm worried about Morgan. She seems delusional, doesn't have a fever, she's very confused and thinks the lost civilization people are her friends. What if it's a neurological problem? I'll make an appointment with the doctor."

GOVERNMENT MAN

Despite Meredith's protests, Morgan insisted she felt fine and left for school. She and Cara had arranged to meet at the corner to walk to school together.

Morgan almost forgot to stop at the corner. As she waited for Cara, questions ran through her mind. Were the isolated people from Lucid World? Was everyone okay? Would she get to see them? Where would they live? What about khaos? Would they catch it?

Cara arrived at the corner and they started walking. Cara apologized, "Oh I hope I didn't keep you waiting too long. I got behind, watching that news about the advanced tribe of people who were discovered. Did you see it?"

"I think I actually know some of those people."

"Um, you know news reporters?"

"I know some of the advanced tribe of people."

"Oh come on. How could you? The news said they've just been discovered and are in New York City."

"I know them from before they were discovered."

"Yeah? I don't get it. That doesn't make any sense. Are you all right?"

Cara stopped walking. Morgan stopped too.

"You're as bad as my mother!"

The girls walked the rest of the way to school in silence. Morgan's peripheral vision caught Cara furtively observing her.

Morgan and Cara had the same classes that morning. They took their usual seats, Morgan sitting directly in front of Cara.

Distracted, Morgan sat through the lessons. She tried to pay attention but couldn't.

"Morgan! This is the third time I've called your name. The Principal wants you in her office. Take your books and things with you." The teacher's eyes were fixed on Morgan and her hands were on her hips. "It's just as well. Your head is somewhere in the clouds today."

Morgan stood and gathered her belongings. She turned and made eye contact with Cara, half expecting Cara to get up and come with her. She'd been called to the principal's office before and it usually related to something she and Cara had done together.

Cara shrugged her shoulders.

Morgan shuffled off to the principal's office. What was she in trouble for? Was it because she hadn't been paying attention in class?

The Principal was pacing outside her office. When she saw Morgan, she hastened towards her.

"Morgan, a man came to my office and showed me government ID from a department I've never heard of. He said your parents are on their way and you have to go to a meeting. Do you know what this is about?"

"Ahhh, I dunno."

"Well, go get your coat and meet me at the door. He's outside waiting in a car. I'll walk with you to make sure your parents are there, and to find out what's going on."

Morgan dashed to her locker, put her books away, and took out her jacket and bag. Her heart pounded! This unexpected summons must have something to do with Lucid World, but what? Had her friends survived the earthquake? Were they safe? What kind of meeting? Were her parents going to the meeting with her?

Morgan hurried to the door. The Principal was standing there looking through the glass out to the street. Morgan joined her.

Through the glass of the door they could see a long sleek black limousine parked out in front of the school. Was that the car!? Morgan and the Principal were both too surprised to comment.

As they approached the impressive vehicle, a man stepped out of the front passenger side of the car, walked to the back of the limousine and opened the door. He had closely cropped ginger hair, broad shoulders and thick arms. His eyes were covered by dark sunglasses. He wore a leather jacket and cowboy boots.

The Principal moved in front of Morgan and approached the open door first. "Daniel? Meredith?" she enquired as she bent down to look into the car.

Morgan heard her father's voice. "Hello, Thelma. Well, I imagine you must wonder what's going on. It's all so exciting but unfortunately, we've been sworn to secrecy by the gentleman standing beside you."

The government man frowned and crossed his arms.

Daniel continued, "I can tell you this much: be sure to watch the UN press conference."

Principal Thelma straightened up slowly. She made a gesture with her shoulders and head to say, "I don't know what to say." She stepped aside and the man holding the door motioned to Morgan to get inside.

Just before Morgan bent down to get into the limo, she saw Enid Meany and Winifred Bittar standing across the street watching them with their arms crossed and mouths wide open.

Morgan had never been inside a limousine. It was like a living room lined with comfortable sofas.

The door-holding government man said, "Miss, please take a seat. We have a plane to catch."

Meredith and Daniel sat together holding hands. Morgan sat facing them. The man closed the door and walked to the front of the car to join the driver in the front seat.

As they drove away, Morgan saw that Mrs. Meany and Mrs. Bittar had crossed the street to join the principal. Principal Thelma was talking and waving her arms around. Enid's arms were tightly crossed against across her chest and Winifred had both hands on her hips.

A PLANE TO CATCH

Morgan's family often spoke quickly, interrupting one another when excited about a topic of conversation. Inside the limo, Daniel, Meredith and Morgan talked at the same time, and somehow comprehended what the others said!

Morgan asked: How did they end up in the limousine at her school? What meeting? A plane to catch: to where? Was this about her friends in Lucid World? Did they know if her friends were okay? What about Dylan and Ryan, where were they?

Daniel and Meredith asked: When she said Lucid World did she mean the isolated people who were discovered? How'd she meet them? How'd they communicate? Where did they live?

We know Morgan's answers. Meredith and Daniel told her what they knew.

Each of them was visited at work by the 'government man' and told that Morgan was connected to the recently discovered isolated people. He provided only vague answers to their questions and said Morgan probably knew more than he. The only thing he knew for sure was that he was to fetch Morgan and her parents and bring them to New York City for the press conference. So they went home, packed bags and arranged for Aunt Tamara to stay with Dylan and Ryan while they were away.

As they drove, Morgan's phone chirped with messages. A worried Cara had gone by the principal's office to see if she was still there. She overheard teachers talking about Morgan being picked up in a limo for a meeting related to the morning's news report.

The limousine stopped at the Lethbridge airport. Through the car windows, Morgan and her parents saw news reporters and cameras. Apparently, news of a private Gulfstream super-jet, parked on the tarmac of the small airport, had reached the media.

The government man got out of the car, flashed his ID badge and barked orders. When the reporters stepped aside, he opened the back door of the limousine and escorted the Kiths to the side of the terminal building.

They walked through a gate and onto the runway. There it was! A beautiful, white, sleek jet—waiting just for them!

CHAPTER 47

KARLEEN RESIGNS

To winnow grain means to throw it up in the air so the wind can blow the husks and dirt away. – from "As the Wind Blows"

Karleen sat at her desk and opened her laptop. She typed, 'Letter of Resignation' and stopped. She had put off writing this letter. But after receiving a call from the accounting department asking about unauthorized expenditures for counselling services for a Coyote Flats family, she could delay no longer.

She hated politics and budgeting games, and she refused to play them this time. If she hadn't, Frances may not have made it to the next step. But the situation was more involved than not following department protocols. Because she couldn't chance being taken off the case, she didn't disclose her conflict of interest when she learned of her connection.

None of it truly mattered anymore, did it? After all, she was writing her letter of resignation.

It wasn't uncommon for people in her line of work to get emotionally involved in a case and use bad judgement. That wasn't the reason she was quitting.

She leaned back in her chair and closed her eyes while she pictured the sign on the door. It would read, 'The Nancy Foundation for Family Healing'. The foundation's mandate would be to help single parents with addiction problems. Meredith would help her with government grants and fundraising; and she already had a commitment for a substantial private donation to start the foundation, from the drunk driver in the accident that killed Nancy.

She thought back to the first day at her new school after her family moved to Lethbridge. She was terrified and wished Nancy was there with her. And then she was, in the strangest of ways.

The girl who sat next to her in class turned out to be the sister of the driver. Like Nancy's family, hers, too, had deep wounds from the tragedy. The coincidence and their mutual need for support and healing developed into a friendship. They kept in touch over the years. She recently told Karleen that her brother came into some money from a successful business venture, and he said there was only one thing he wanted to buy: a time machine to go back and undo the terrible thing that happened.

When Karleen called him and told him she found Frances, he asked if there was anything he could do. She told him her plans for the foundation to help people like Frances. He offered to contribute financially and to help with the business aspects of running it.

"Wow, that sounds amazing," he said, "but have you thought about yourself? Foundations take time and money to get started and often, during the start-up phase, there isn't enough for salaries. How'll you live?"

Indeed. She needed money to live and fortunately, she had it. She had just paid off the mortgage she carried alone after she and Scott divorced, and had a little money leftover in the bank.

She ran her fingers through her blonde hair and shook her head in disbelief. Her parents told her that her unusual name was because she was the namesake of an old friend of her father. This summer she learned Karl was more than just her father's friend. Her father and Karl trained for the RCMP together and Karl saved her father's life when he almost drowned in a boating accident on a fishing trip.

Not long after Karleen was born, the two men had a falling out when Karl applied for an RCMP posting Karleen's father wanted and both were too stubborn to let it go. This summer she received a letter from a lawyer's office informing her Karl had passed away and left a bequest for her in his will. When she asked her father why Karl would do such a thing, he suggested it was Karl's way of reconciling with him from the grave.

Reconciling? She thought about the word her father chose. What did that mean to him? Did it mean forgiveness? If so, giving it or asking for it?

It was sad. Not for the reason most people feel sad when someone dies. She wouldn't miss Karl. She never knew him. It was sad that her father and Karl had held onto their anger and resentment. Not only did this rob them of their friendship, it would have robbed them of some part of themselves. Something Morgan said when they talked that day at the hospital came to mind. It's not logical for a person to forgive only when the other person deserves it. A person should forgive because they, themselves, deserve it.

Karleen turned her mind back to the task at hand. The last few months had brought many changes in her life. Besides coming into a small inheritance, she met Meredith, reconnected with Frances and now was about to embark on a brave new career adventure. She had put off resigning because she was unsure if she was brave enough.

She thought about all of the people she wanted to help. Would they all be as stubborn as Frances?

Frances had finally agreed to go to rehab, and gave temporary custody of her children to her parents. Karleen nodded her head in satisfaction. Her hunch had been right. Frances had been punishing her parents and herself all of these years. She needed to see her behaviour for what it was. The act of punishing didn't give her control, it robbed her of control. No one could tell her that, except Sally. The Sally she met in the hospital room that first day was meek and afraid. Sally found courage and strength, faced with adversity and with a little help from Morgan.

'When Frances is released,' Karleen thought, 'I think she'll be open to letting her parents back into her life. I hope so.' Frances still had a difficult road ahead of her. She would need all the help she could get. Karleen laughed as she recalled Frances's words to her when she learned Karleen's identity. It was 'truly funny' and very much like the Frances she once knew.

Frances's words to Karleen were, "I thought there was something annoyingly familiar about you. Thanks for still following me around after all of these years."

Karleen wiped a tear from her eye and began typing.

CHAPTER **48**

SMARTIES AND POPCORN

M argaret and Joe stayed at Franny's house while she was away at rehab. Margaret made projects of cleaning, organizing and shopping for household items. Joe busied himself with repairing, painting and yard work. Sally appreciated the many improvements, but was nervous about what her mother's reaction would be when she came home.

On the day of the UN news report, Sally arrived home from school and excitedly described the events at school that day: Morgan was picked up in a limousine, there was a mysterious government man, and the principal told everyone to watch the press conference. Joe suggested they should all watch together. Sally asked if Matt could come over and watch with them. Her cheeks blushed a little, right after she asked.

Margaret went to the store and took Mikey with her. Just as Margaret was setting her groceries onto the cash register conveyer belt, Mikey grabbed a package of candies included in Margaret's grocery items.

"No Mikey. Those are for later. We're going to mix them up with our popcorn and share with Sally and her boyfriend, and Grandpa Joe. I think you'll like it. Smarties and popcorn is Grandma Marg's favourite TV snack."

Susan Costadinawich was in line at the cash register, in front of Margaret and Mikey. She had just finished paying for her groceries. She turned around and stared directly at Margaret. "I've only ever known one person who liked smarties and popcorn mixed together. It couldn't be. Margie? Good heavens, after all these years!"

Margaret's jaw dropped and for a moment she held her hand up to cover her gaping mouth. "Suzie! Oh my God! It's been so long. Let me pay for these and then let's go over there and talk." Margaret pointed to a corner of the store.

With groceries paid for and the three of them standing in the corner, Margaret began. "Do you live here? I thought I heard Alymer took a job at the Taberville Sugar Factory."

"Yes and then some years ago he was transferred to Coyote Flats. I've been here ever since."

"How is he? Did you have children?"

Susan shook her head sadly. "He passed away ten years ago. No, we never had children."

Susan's eyes teared up. Margaret hugged her.

The language of true friends is not really a language at all. It's a chemical reaction. Once the synthesis has occurred, it can't be undone by time or distance. If Suzie and Margie didn't know this before, they knew it now.

Margaret sketched out the circumstances surrounding why she and Joe were in Coyote Flats: the reunion with Frances and discovering they had two grandchildren.

Mikey was standing, well behaved, and holding his Grandma's hand. Margaret's and Susan's attentions moved to him.

Margaret was just about to introduce her grandson when Susan said, "I know this little boy." Susan had often thought about Mikey after the 'close call' at the garage.

Susan's brows raised and eyes widened. "He's Franny Frey's son. Franny is Frances? I can't believe I didn't recognize her."

"Yup, she's our Frances. She's had a hard life."

"We're staying at her place and I need to get back. Come with me? We can talk there and I know Joseph would love to see you."

Susan's head nodded and her face beamed.

CHAPTER 49

THE WORLDS MEET

*Cats are territorial and introductions to new cats
require diplomacy and patience. An improper or hurried
introduction can cause cats to become bitter enemies.
Conversely, with a proper introduction, cats can become
lifelong friends.* – from "The Lives and Times of Cats"

Tabubu stood on a podium in front of cameras and microphones. She looked small but confident. She wore a bright orange and blue robe contrasted with a bright green hair scarf.

"Future friends and neighbours, my name is Kiya Tabubu. On behalf of my people, I come to you with our introduction, gratitude, and a request.

"I speak for my people, and myself, when I say our emotions are overflowing with appreciation, excitement and anticipation. Let me begin by first offering you an explanation. Then I will attempt to answer the many questions you surely have."

Kiya Tabubu shared highlights of their history. Then she described the khaos condition.

"We have learned many things about this khaos change. But we have not yet learned how to reverse it."

Next, Kiya provided details of the earthquake, their entrapment and their rescue. Then she stopped, smiled and said, "Humans have a bountiful ability to love and help one another. There are many examples of this in your world, especially when others are less fortunate or helpless, such as we were.

"When our rescuers returned to the outside world, your world, and let it be known people were trapped, we received the love and help to which I refer."

She thanked all who assisted in freeing them from entrapment. It was not an easy undertaking. The amount of collapsed rock, the remoteness of the location, and the harshness of the terrain made their rescue dangerous and difficult.

"Losing our former home brings me to the request I mentioned earlier. We wish to rejoin your world and work together to eliminate khaos. We need a home in a moderately remote place. We're not asking to go back to our former isolated existence. Rather, we want to interact with the rest of the world in a manner that will not distract us from our work."

Kiya then offered to share Lucid World's superior technology and vast library of knowledge and world history; with the understanding that anything that could harm others, such as designing new weaponry, would not be shared.

"I must tell you, at one time, not too long ago, we would have requested a home distant from established civilization, and so remote that we would have no interaction with the outside world and no exposure to khaos. It was recently brought to our attention, by a young woman from your world, that isolation to avoid exposure to khaos is a form of khaos. Illogical fear is a manifestation of khaos. Our fears relating to exposure are illogical fears because they are based on what happened to our ancestors; and in her words, it is a different world now. We can make choices to minimize one's exposure and reactions to khaos. Khaos may be contagious, but khaos can be repelled, as long as we continue to remind ourselves and others not to give way to khaos-based emotions."

Kiya looked to the side, in the direction Morgan was seated, made eye contact with her, smiled and nodded. When Kiya turned her attentions back to the audience, Morgan looked at her mother to see her reaction. There it was, all in one expression: loving pride, acknowledgement, wisdom, and a wee bit of 'I'm still your mother'.

Kiya was still speaking, "We have identified a few locations we think would be suitable. I have appointments with representatives from the respective countries to enter discussions concerning establishing a new home.

"We feel great joy as we rejoin the world and embark on what we hope will be our joint mission to eliminate khaos from the lives of the people throughout the world."

Kiya smiled naturally and warmly.

A sea of reporters stood below the podium platform. They raised hands and microphones and there was a flood of questions.

During the speech and question period, Morgan and her parents were seated with Amasis, Iris, and Khyan. Morgan thought back to what happened when she and her parents arrived in New York.

New York City

The private jet landed in New York City. From the window, Morgan saw Khyan, Amasis, and Iris standing on the tarmac waiting for them.

As Morgan walked down the steps from the jet, her friends ran towards her. When her feet touched the tarmac, she was hugged in succession by all three of them. Feeling their solid warm bodies was so comforting and wonderful that Morgan cried tears of joy. Iris and Amasis did too. Khyan kept his eyes dry but his face was filled with exhilaration.

When Amasis hugged her, she didn't feel the surreal thrilling sensation she experienced when she dreamed he came to rescue her after the Barfie Doll incident. Instead, she felt safe and where she belonged.

Iris spoke first. "Morgan, we missed you. We desperately wanted to communicate with you to let you know what happened. Until today, we couldn't."

Amasis spoke next. "I missed your sense of humour. The time would have gone by much faster while we were waiting to be rescued."

Khyan smiled brightly at Morgan and said, "I'm so proud of you, Morgan. You're responsible for many of the changes in the way our people will interact with the rest of the world."

Morgan had not yet spoken. The first words she could form and utter were, "Me? How'd I do that?"

Khyan replied, "We'll tell you all about that later. How've you been? Are you happy to see us?"

"I'm sooo happy to see you! I was worried something had happened." Morgan quickly added, "It wasn't illogical worry."

All four of them laughed. Morgan continued. "At first I felt sad and upset. Then," Morgan looked at Khyan specifically and said, "I discovered the enemy force!"

Khyan looked puzzled. "What did you discover?"

Morgan replied, "You know, the force you told me about. The force that tries to stop people from achieving their goals. I have so many things to tell you."

Khyan laughed and said, "Enemy force. I forgot that's how you referred to it. After the gala, when I observed your reaction to the incident with Sally and Franny, I wanted to explain to you how the force and khaos emotions cause behaviours that are bound to produce failure and unhappiness. I never got the chance. It sounds like you not only discovered the enemy force, you conquered it."

"Luna and her babies ... are they all right?" asked Morgan.

Iris and Amasis exchanged conspiratorial grins. Seeing this, Morgan asked, "What? What happened?"

Iris answered. "Luna and her three kittens are fine. They're safely lodged with Elder Tabubu. We have quite a story to tell you though."

Daniel and Meredith were standing off to the side waiting for Morgan and her friends to finish their reunion greetings. Daniel said shyly, "Uh Small Fry, I'm sorry to interrupt. Your mother and I want to meet your friends."

"Sorry, Mom and Dad," apologized Morgan.

After the introductions, her parents seemed uncomfortable and it was Amasis who helped carry the conversation. Morgan thought it was unusual for her parents to appear shy and lost for words. When she thought about it further, she realized her parents were still assimilating everything that happened that day.

The government man approached and said, "The press conference is beginning soon. We'd better get to the UN Building now!"

Morgan asked, "The others, like me, who visited Lucid World. Are they here too?"

Khyan answered, "Due to distances and limited airport access near their respective communities, they won't arrive until tomorrow. We hope you and your parents can stay until then so you can meet them."

Morgan looked pleadingly at her parents. Daniel, seeming to have recovered from the day's surprises, winked and said, "Well, I'm sure that can be arranged."

CHAPTER **50**

THE LUCID FIVE AND ONE

Eight teens sat around a large oval table. Their physical appearance and clothing varied. The table was carved from volcanic rock, native to Easter Island. Khyan, one of the eight, addressed the small group.

"Today marks one year since Lucid World reunited with Nosos World. Thank you everyone for joining us, in the flesh, for this commemorative celebration."

Khyan paused and looked around the table and acknowledged everyone with his eyes. Before he could continue speaking, a young man with black wavy hair, wearing a floral print aloha-shirt, interjected, "If it's a celebration, it probably means food. When there's food, I'll gladly make a trip in the flesh."

Everyone laughed. Khyan replied. "Elvis, yes there will be food and lots of it."

Elvis, from the Island of Hawaii, laughed good-heartedly.

Easter Island, part of the South American country of Chile and one of the most remote islands in the world, was the new home to the people of Mountain Lucid World.

Much of Easter Island is uninhabited. This, in combination with its remoteness, was why it was one location the Council of Elders identified as a suitable potential new home. After Lucid World approached them, the government of Chile invited the people of Lucid World to make Chile their new home. The local government and people of Easter Island welcomed them. They sectioned off part of the island so Lucid World could carry on with their research and studies without interruption or excessive exposure to khaos.

It didn't take long for the new Easter Island residents to get settled and reconstruct the transmission avatar technology. Soon they could continue to meet with Morgan and the four others who had been part of the khaos reversal project.

All five of the Nosos World youth were international celebrities for several weeks after Tabubu's press conference. The press called them the 'Lucid Five'. Tabubu hadn't disclosed their identities. But the media didn't take long to locate and identify the five.

The Lucid Five were Morgan from Canada, Elvis from the United States, Marisa from Peru, Emma from Costa Rica and Jonas from Greenland. Since all five lived in remote communities, the travel inconvenience soon caused the press and paparazzi to lose interest and leave. The Lucid Five and their families were able to resume fairly normal lives.

Mountain Lucid World had been located in the Caucasus Mountains, a mountain system in Eurasia. The five were initially chosen so their home time zones were several hours different from the time zone in Mountain Lucid World. This facilitated communications during Nosos World sleeping hours and Lucid World waking hours.

Easter Island's time zone was the same, or only a few hours different, from the time zones of the homes of the Lucid Five. As secrecy was no longer required, meetings now took place in the afternoons when Morgan and the others got home from school. Sometimes the Lucid Five avatar visits overlapped, and the five got to know one another and became friends.

Easter Island's remoteness and distance from the home communities of Morgan and the others meant this was the first time the five had physically travelled to Easter Island.

In rejoinder to the conversation regarding celebration food, Amasis said, "Morgan, I hope you'll try the garguey."

Everyone laughed again. Morgan replied, "I'll try the garguey if you blindfold me. It really looks disgusting."

After everyone finished laughing, Khyan continued, "This has been an extraordinary year. Many of our plans to enlighten people about khaos and to remind them to think and act without khaos have been implemented. I'm pleased to report many more projects are underway. Tomorrow, we'll have a brainstorming session to consider new ideas for communicating reminders. That's tomorrow. Today, we'll celebrate and eat!"

Iris spoke. "Khyan, can we tell them the big news now?" Iris was beaming.

"Absolutely," said Khyan. "Would you like to tell them?"

"I'd love to," said Iris and she addressed the Lucid Five.

"We've upgraded our transmission-avatar meeting technology and can now invite more youth to work with us. Soon, several hundred teenagers will visit us daily. So we've expanded our Lucid World team. They're trained, briefed and ready to begin!

"Morgan, I can tell from your expression you're wondering how this will affect you. That's the best part! We're counting on the five of you to help us and mentor the newcomers."

Iris explained logistics and answered questions. Everyone was enthused. One question that arose concerned language.

Amasis explained, "The newcomers are from many different countries and speak different languages. Our translation technology is highly intelligent and has been used in Lucid World for many years. We've reprogrammed the avatar-transmission systems to stream through the translation equipment."

Morgan asked, "Are we still going to call this place Lucid World? It doesn't seem right anymore, now that Lucid World and Nosos World are one. I mean, I think we should drop the word 'World'. But the name 'Lucid' by itself doesn't sound right."

Khyan answered this time. "I agree. The Elders do too; they've been thinking about it."

He then adjourned the meeting and invited them to follow him to the celebration party.

Several hundred people were at the celebration, enjoying the music, entertainment, dancing and food, in a room adorned with bright tiles and tapestries. Many people wore bright clothing. With everyone dancing and moving about, the scene resembled a kaleidoscope of changing colours.

Morgan, Emma, and Marisa sat together. A family native to Easter Island overheard them talking and discovered Emma and Marisa spoke Spanish. They introduced themselves and engaged the girls in conversation. The islanders explained differences in the Spanish dialect and then began teaching words in the language native to the island, Rapi Nui. Morgan politely left the group and sought Amasis.

She had an idea for a name to replace 'Lucid World' and she wanted to get feedback from Amasis. Also, she wanted an excuse to spend time with him.

Before Morgan could locate Amasis, she was approached by Elvis. "Let's go for a walk. It's a full moon and the reflection on the water is amazing."

Morgan considered her options. She could seek Amasis who was probably preoccupied with tasks, hang around and attempt conversation using her broken-Spanish, or go for a walk with Elvis who was always funny and witty.

Morgan and Elvis walked outside and onto the windswept grass hill. They headed toward the ocean. The grass looked white in the moonlight and the ocean surface appeared to have a shimmery path leading from the shoreline all the way to the moon in the sky. In the distance, they could see moonlit statues of the moai: the monolithic human figures carved out of rock by the Rapa Nui, people indigenous to Easter Island.

Morgan remarked, "We studied these statues in school. I can't believe I'm actually here seeing them. This is something we can't experience on virtual visits."

Elvis made a move to reach for Morgan's hand. She anticipated his intentions and blurted, "I just remembered something I have to do. Sorry, I need to go back."

Elvis nodded and walked back to the party with her. Morgan wasn't very talkative, so Elvis carried the conversation with small talk about the plans to expand the Nosos youth program.

Back at the party, Morgan saw a platform where a band of musicians were setting up to play. She raised herself on to it and stood at the edge. Her eyes hunted the room. There were so many people! When she spotted Marisa and Emma, she hopped back onto the floor and made her way over to them. She had to zigzag through hundreds of people to reach them. The band played and it was loud.

"Have you seen Amasis?" she shouted. Marisa and Emma both shook their heads, no.

Now what? The celebration buzzed with energy, but she just wasn't into it. She went through the crowd to the door, and headed back down the path to the ocean.

In the distance, she saw a familiar masculine shape standing on the shore, looking out over the water. She approached quietly from behind and stood beside him.

She reached her hand out to his. He looked at her, smiled, and then took her hand and squeezed it.

Holding hands, Morgan and Amasis stood looking out towards the shimmering moon path on the ocean.

Neither spoke. Morgan shivered a little in the breeze, and Amasis put his arm around her. The breeze picked up and gave a message to birds sitting on a nearby cropping of rocks. The birds took flight and headed out to sea. The bird's journey was recorded by the moonlight as a silhouette in the sky.

Morgan whispered, "The name fits. We are one world. This moonlit path can traverse the entire planet. We are 'one'. In Latin, the word is 'una'. Lucid World, here on Easter Island, should be called Una."

GOODNIGHT

"After you and your avatar left today, Khyan gave me some exciting news! Morgan, he will fly me to Coyote Flats next week!"

Ever since the anniversary celebration, Morgan and Amasis had a nightly ritual of talking via video chat before bed.

They routinely saw one another during Morgan's avatar afternoon sessions on Easter Island, but that was to take part in the Nosos youth program. Easter Island's time zone was only two hours ahead. To have private moments and conversation, they talked each night before bed.

"That is exciting! I can actually finally introduce you to my friends. Hey, guess what?"

Amasis laughed, shook his head, and said lovingly, "I'm sure I can't."

"Cara, Veronica, and I applied to go to the same university."

"Have you decided what you want to study?"

"Yes, I think so. Neuroscience. I want to study the brain and research ways to reduce khaos."

In Morgan's excitement, she didn't give Amasis a chance to react to her news. She jumped right into talking about the people he'd meet when he visited and what was going on in their lives.

With financial help from the Music Foundation, Sally was studying music at the University of Lethbridge. "She loves it! Also, I think it's been good for her mother to become less dependent on her. Sally needs to have a life of her own."

Sally's mother moved to Taberville to be closer to her parents and was going to college to train for a job to support Mikey and herself. "Sally says: so far so good."

The old woman who used to be Morgan's neighbour, Susan Costadinawich, moved back to Taberville. She often looked after Mikey while Franny went to school.

Morgan's mother left her job at the hospital. She worked with Karleen at The Nancy Foundation for Family Healing. "I'll ask Mom to give you a tour of the foundation. She's really proud of it."

Morgan's father and her brothers, Dylan and Ryan, started a Coyote Flats baseball team. The new sugar factory co-op sponsored them. "Hey, can you play baseball?" asked Morgan.

"I've never tried, but I'd like to. What's the name of their team?"

"Super-Sugars. Hey, did the Council decide on a name? Did they like the name Una?"

"They liked it, but there was just one problem. Every time they said 'Una', Luna came running and expected to be fed."

"Hahaha. On that note, goooodniiight. Love ya."

~ The Beginning ~

NOTES

The story told by Amasis, of garguey "creatures" living in a river, was inspired by Richard Bach's book, *Illusions*.

1.   Nicholas McKay is credited with inventing the lint roller in the mid-1950s. It was patented as the "Lint Pic-Up" and McKay's invention was sold through the company he started, Helmac Products.

2.   Friedrich Gustav Emil Martin Niemöller(1892 – 1984) was a German anti-Nazi theologian and Lutheran pastor.

3.   Aesop was a legendary Greek teller of fables. The general consensus is he was born around 620 B.C. as a slave. Legend has it that he was given his freedom as reward for his wit and his tales. Aesop's Fables refers to a collection of fables credited to him. They have been passed down through the centuries at first by word of mouth and then in written form. A favourite is the fable of The Miller, His Son, and Their Ass.

4.   Dalai Lama (Tenzin Gyatso) (1935 -) The fourteenth and current Dalai Lama is often referred to as simply The Dalai Lama. He was born to a farming family in Tibet. He is a charismatic figure and public speaker. His efforts in the cause of peace and a free Tibet have made him an international celebrity. He was the first Dalai Lama to travel to the West. In 1989 he was awarded the Nobel Peace Prize.

5.   Jenga is a game of skill created by Leslie Scott, and currently marketed by Parker Brothers, a division of Hasbro. Players take turns to remove a block from a tower and balance it on top, creating a taller and increasingly unstable structure as the game progresses.

ACKNOWLEDGMENTS

I would like to express my gratitude to the people who helped and inspired me in the creation of *Lucid World*.

My husband, Tony Fierro, believed in me, in the story and the book. My writing consultants, Carol Sill and Donaleen Saul, always told me what I needed to hear and not what I wanted to hear. Carol was also my skilled and talented editor, who guided me throughout the story's development and transformation. She was always patient, flexible and a pleasure to work with. Diane Feught created a beautiful and captivating book cover design. My beta readers offered encouragement, inspiration and valuable feedback. A special mention goes to Karleen, Donnie, Paula, Kirsten, Martha, Joy, and Shelley, for the gift of their time, reading the story and providing me with honest and thorough feedback.

I am grateful to everyone who encouraged me during the development of this story.

This book is dedicated to my father, Edward Wojtowicz. He was a loving and compassionate man who became gravely ill and passed away during the time I was writing *Lucid World*. Now forever free of khaos, he has the peace of Shambhala.

Made in the USA
Columbia, SC
27 October 2017